The Heights of Abraham

un Roman en Anglais (mostly)

Elizabeth Mostyn

THE PHENOMENOLOGICAL DETECTIVE

ISBN 978-1-7394052-1-2

Cover design & typesetting by Raspberry Creative Type

1

23 février 2018

"Oh my God!" says Patrice, in a low tone so not to make his son jump as, mirrors checked and signal made, he begins to turn into an alley off the main road – too narrow for the Peugeot. The boy is almost eighteen now and has passed his theory tests easily. The French system requires one year's accompanied driving of three thousand kilometres, with repeated testing to check the candidate has completed the requirements.

Patrice, who passed the Police Advanced Driving examination many years ago, is the person lucky enough to be designated for the driving practice – in a third-hand, ex-*Police Judiciaire* vehicle obtained for the purpose. His police rank allows him a driver and he does not keep a car of his own in Paris. Although Colette is also a designated accompanying driver for Jean-Pascal, there is no question of using her beloved Citroën DS21 for practising anything. The 1978 "Goddess" remains in her comfortable garage in Versailles.

If they scrape the car along the sides of the alleyway, Amélie will enjoy making great fun of her brother. She long

ago declared herself sceptical of his genius at the driving –
elle réussira[1] when it comes to her turn.

Patrice is usually content with allowing Jean-Pascal to
drive him. It is relatively restful, and he must hardly ever
shout "Watch out!" or "That was close!". His son drives
neither too fast nor too slowly, takes no risks, and reads
the road well. He will be an exemplary driver. Unhappily
for Jean-Pascal, Patrice has made the mistake of explaining
this to Amélie, which caused a serial inferno of trouble.
The daughter is trying various geriatric nicknames for her
brother: *vieil homme, barbe grise, infirme*. She has not yet
fastened on the insult that perfectly satisfies her.

On this cold, bright, winter morning, Patrice folds his
arms tightly over his chest and breathes in – as if either of
those things will slim the bulk of the car to suitable
proportions for the space available – and slowly closes his
eyes.

There is no grinding noise, no shuddering feeling of
metal bodywork against masonry. When he opens his eyes,
they are through, in open streets. *D'accord*, the boy judges
space better than his old *papa*.

***

At work, Patrice is faintly annoyed that his day has been
disturbed – he has several crimes to investigate, and a team
to manage. Unhappily, the team is depleted due to
Commissaire Adjunct Dominique LaSalle being on leave of
absence, working with drug addicts in the *banlieues
défavourisées*.[2]

Into the usual infestation of crime, Guillaume Delahaye,
the divisional commissioner – that is, his *patron* – has

---

1   she will ace it
2   social housing on the outskirts of Paris

dropped an order for Patrice to attend an urgent meeting. This is bound to be organisational and, probably, *merde,* and Patrice is not anxious to be there. He wanders off from the temporary *salle squad* on the ground floor and takes the lift to what the junior officers call the *suite penthouse.* They also insist that there are *lapines*[3] there, although there are not.

There is no one at the secretary's desk outside, and Patrice wanders into the large, glassy, main office of the *divisionnel.* It is a beautiful room, divided by furniture and nice rugs into several areas. The *divisionnel's* desk faces the window with a terrific view over Paris, but there are any number of sofas and chairs in conversational groups, where one can sit and relax and drink coffee from Monsieur Delahaye's personal high-end coffee maker. Seeing no one there, Patrice wonders which furniture should have the benefit of his *derriére* as he waits.

Before he has decided between the cherry red of the closest group, and the midnight blue of the one nearest the windows, Monsieur Delahaye appears (from his private lavatory) and greets him affably.

"*Bonjour,*" he says cheerily. "*Ça va?*"

"*Ça va?*" *says Patrice.* "I am fine!"

"*Bon!*" says Delahaye. "I have something serious to discuss with you." He invites Patrice to sit, and they migrate to the midnight sofa and two matching chairs, on a nice Turkish rug in crimson and midnight blue. Patrice longs for the coffee the commissioner does not offer.

"I attended the new year conference of principal police commissioners last month," he says, "and, now that I have studied the final report and been in conference with the *Ministère de l'Intérieur*" – he gestures towards his desk – "I

---

3   bunny girls!

have made a decision based on the way the crime statistics appear to be moving."

Bon Jésus, thinks Patrice, steeling himself for a new idea *aliéné*.[4]

"I have decided," says *le patron*, giving himself a well-earned pat on the back, "that we shall form a new detail, a *Détail des Crimes Complexes*, which will have experts on all aspects, working together!" He pauses, looking celebratory, and then begins to explain that criminals are getting much more sophisticated, and many crimes have multiple aspects. They need different types of expertise.

"These days," he says, with a confidential air, "we have few burglaries or robberies simple, few incidents of violence which are just that. Many crimes involve drugs, or people trafficking, on top of their usual theft and violence. And then there is the cybercrime. Totally beyond many of us!"

Patrice wonders whether the commissioner thinks he doesn't know this.

"There are organised crimes, the Mafia, and other things: hate crimes, race crimes, domestic violence, so many … but our special divisions don't much talk to each other. So, we miss things!" He folds his hands over his not inconsiderable paunch, in satisfaction. He has just dealt with all the crimes of Paris in a few sentences.

Then he tells Patrice that it is up to him to read the report, to decide what officers, with what specialities, he needs, and to recruit them. After all, the *divisionnel* has done the hard work for him.

***

The detectives of Patrice's team, of the *Police Judiciaire*, were shunted before Christmas to the largest interview room

---

4   insane, mad

at *le Trente-Six*, the main *PJ* headquarters in Paris, so that their usual *salle squad* can be painted. *Inspecteur* Fleur Olivier has been up to the fourth floor this morning to assess progress, but there is none. And no one there, either. She has been moaning about this ever since she got back to her desk. There are distinct disadvantages to the ground floor offices.

"*D'accord*," says Patrice, "we have some crimes to lay out. As well as Monsieur Delahaye's latest idea to work on."

He nods to Fleur and the detective opens her notebook, flipping to the relevant page.

"We have several cases which are not yet finished, although I am going to court tomorrow, on the shooting in Passy. You'll remember that Monsieur Zabi decided to prosecute after *Docteur* Rousseau was clear that it could not have been accidental? The *juge d'instruction* expects a guilty plea, and then it will be over as far as we are concerned."

"*Mais*," says Patrice, "I am not so sure. We can wait and see whether it will come back to us. What else, Fleur?"

The senior *inspecteur* says that there are a couple of new fraud cases which will need a lot of work. Complicated. Patrice sees that she would like a cigarette but is not allowed to smoke indoors any more. She sniffs instead, and picks up a cup of cold coffee.

"The other cases, not finished, are the cold case of the little boy who was snatched from his mother's car two years ago. His name is Nikolas Pellisier, and he lived in the nineteenth *arrondissement*. His father is, maybe, still a *sous-chef* at Allons Grande, the restaurant in Neuilly; his mother is a homemaker. You recall that the case has been cold for more than a year. But something of the child's turned up last week – a woollen glove, with his name stitched in – from a litter bin close to the Tour Eiffel?

"*Alors*, I think the other case is yours, René?"

René Mercard, who is, currently, the junior member of the team, is not listening and must be poked in order to comment on his open case of thirteen separate car thefts, which now appear to be not separate at all. He has an excuse, today; he has been on his feet all night.

"*Oui, patron?*" he says. "*Désolé*, I have not been to bed yet ..."

"I need an outline of where you are with the Archange case," says Patrice. "How many car thefts are we looking at currently?"

"Twelve," says René. "*Non, désolé, patron,* thirteen.*"

"And what are we thinking?" asks Patrice, who knows his officer's difficulties from personal experience.

"A ring, I suppose," says René. "It cannot be amateurs; they are all expensive, horrendously expensive, cars. You cannot sell them on in a bar, not even the Bar de l'Archange. The connection is organised crime, maybe even Mafia. The one which disappeared yesterday was a Bugatti Veyron. Nice car!"

"And they are all Ferrari or Bentley or Rolls-Royce," Fleur contributes, "the odd E-Type Jaguar, a special one, even unique! It's big money, *patron* ..."

"*Alors*, stolen to order. But order of whom?"

"I think it's very big," says René, "and we may need some input from Organised Crime and/or Intelligence."

"Intelligence?" Fleur almost screams. "*Dieu!* Please not ..."

"I know," says Patrice calmly. "They can be difficult. But they have information we do not. If we decide to do that, we shall have to make sure we can keep them under control or just give them a small portion of the case. They never acknowledge that it is complicated at our level as well as at theirs. What do you think, both of you? Shall I call Monsieur Benay? I could ask him for just one agent ..."

"*D'accord*," says René, who is inexperienced enough to think the Intelligence Service can be controlled.

"*C'est nul,*[5]" says Fleur, who isn't.

"What else?" asks Patrice, who has been drawing penguins on his notebook and now makes a note to call *Commissaire* Emmanuel Benay later.

He clears his throat and regards Fleur and René, who are both now listening intently.

"Monsieur Delahaye has a new idea." Both *PJ*s groan. "At last someone has realised that specialist departments do not talk to one another and therefore miss things. His idea, though, is not that communication is improved, but that a new Detail is invented."

"A new Detail?" asks Fleur, been there before.

"*D'accord*, a Complex Crimes Detail. It is to have representatives of specialities, like drugs, vice, homicide, violent crimes, technology, forensics, organised crime."

"But we are to have charge?" asks René. "Of the whole thing?"

"That won't work," says Fleur. "Never has, never will!"

"Nonetheless," says Patrice, "I am to decide what I want, identify suitable personnel, and recruit them by the end of the month."

They have got no further when there is a telephone call, answered promptly by Mercard:

"*Allô? Police Judiciaire, Détail des Crimes Complexes!*" The other two stiffen in surprise at his establishing the new department so peremptorily. René tells them, when it is finished, that a police detective from Romania wishes to come and talk to them.

---

5   that sucks!

***

Although Dominique LaSalle, also known as Pucelle, is currently on leave from the *Police Judiciaire,* she is still pursuing an issue which came up at the end of her captivity in the *banlieues défavourisées.*

She is determined to search for, and find, L'Éléphant, who had cared for her during the time she had been held. The Elephant had departed, with her dead son, Paon, the Peacock, in her arms, and although Pucelle had tried, a little, to find her, she had failed miserably in the time since the Russian's murder.

She is single-handedly canvassing the *banlieues,* asking people who will have known the Elephant, at least by sight, because she never spoke. She is so large she would be hard to miss. This is the second difficulty which has presented itself to Pucelle since leaving, even temporarily, the police. She no longer has the resources of a policeperson.

The first difficulty, of course, has been that she no longer has an income.

Today, she hopes to address that problem. She has an interview with a small charity which supports immigrants, in the Rue Provence. This will be the first interview she has attended since she joined the PJ. She expects it to be somewhat bizarre.

The Rue Provence is quiet on this Friday morning in February, and Pucelle easily finds the dusty second-floor office of Immigrant Health & Support, with its manager, Madame Frieda Hanzel, who is clearly an immigrant herself. She does, however, speak good French, and Pucelle is determined to make this interview count for two of her goals simultaneously: get a job, and advance her search for the Elephant.

The white woman, who is wearing a beige trouser suit of nineteen eighties provenance, with a grey shirt, and a plastic hairslide holding her dirty-blonde hair out of her eyes, welcomes the extremely tall applicant by saying she is delighted that Pucelle has arrived. Pucelle wonders whether others don't turn up, and is immediately answered by:

"Not so many actually get here! They are put off by the address and the state of the place. I don't care because they are not the sort of people I look for ..."

Pucelle can think of little to say and introduces herself by, simply, her name:

"*Je m'appelle* Dominique LaSalle," she says.

"Good to meet you, Dominique," says Frieda. "I was hoping you would come. You said, when we were talking on the telephone, that you speak Russian. That would be fantastic for us!"

"I have a little Swahili as well," says Pucelle. "And please, call me Pucelle. No one calls me Dominique – so I probably won't answer to it!"

"Why are you called Pucelle?" asks Frieda.

"I am taking a break from my commission as a police officer," says the Black

woman. "It was my police colleagues who nicknamed me, years ago, when I first arrived from Orléans. Jeanne d'Arc, *n'est-ce pas?*"

"Ah. I see. Do you think that you having been, or still being, a policeperson will affect your work in supporting immigrants? I must admit I am a little worried about it ..."

"It will have an effect," says Pucelle honestly. "It must do so. But I think I have enough maturity to manage it. I am not young, as you can see ..."

"*D'accord*, and a little toughness will be a good thing," says the woman. "Many of the applicants we get – not that we get all that many – are sympathetic, but too much so to do the work. Do you see what I mean?"

"I do," says Pucelle. "But I must tell you that before I joined the *Police Judiciaire*, I spent many years in a convent."

Frieda looks shocked for a moment, before saying that nuns are fierce enough to well do the work she requires.

2

Colette Lanier is arguing, by telephone, with her daughter, Amélie, almost *16 ans,* who would very much like to stay out with her friends until *23 heures.* Colette does not wish her to do so.

"*Non,* you cannot," she says. "You know what your curfew is, Amélie. You must be home by *22 heures*!" She hears muttering from the girl but cannot tell what she is saying. It cannot be anything good. She wonders what has changed so much. Amélie is a good girl but has always been given to subversion and has suddenly started being even more difficult.

Her elder child, Jean-Pascal, , never argued, just stopped talking to them completely. Colette is not yet sure which she prefers. Patrice says it doesn't matter; they will do what they will do.

"I can be there for 22.10," says Amélie, testing the limits.

"You heard what I said. There is no room for negotiation. Be here or be grounded!"

Colette hears the telephone hang up. She turns to Sartre and tells him his sister is being *difficile* again. The Bedlington looks up at her with a whimsical expression on his little woolly face, before running off and bringing back his favourite toy, squeaking it to encourage her. He is sure that throwing it for him to chase will make her feel better.

***

"*Alors,*" says Patrice, "it is a multiple homicide case then, with four victims. And, let me see if I have got this right, the Romanian police want to recruit from another force to investigate it for them?"

The Romanian detective is tall and dark, with a strong Latin look. He could as well be Italian or Spanish or even an especially dark Frenchman from the south. He is not any of these; he is from Alba Iulia in Transylvania. He stares at each of the French detectives as if daring them to start with the Dracula jokes.

"Transylvania is just a particularly lovely part of my very beautiful country," he says in defence, "which has been much in dispute with Hungary, and other places, over the years. There is nothing horrific about it, except for the Vampire Tours dreamed up by the tourist offices! Vlad Dracula hardly lived in Transylvania; he was the prince of Wallachia – which is a different place."

"I am sure," says Patrice, conscious of having got away with something. "Now, tell us why you cannot use your own homicide detectives."

"I have brought this," says Officer Melichian, "a document published at our centenary which details the attitude of the present Romanian Police Service. I'd like you to have it because it explains what has happened since the Second World War in terms of how things are now. I hope that it will make you realise that we are a loyal and ethically sound organisation."

"I am sure you are," says Patrice, though he is not at all sure. He takes the leaflet, with a large amount of text, and reads the first few paragraphs:

"For the Romanian police, the communist era was only a pause period in its status as a democratic fundamental institution of the group of states of the world for which respect for human rights is just as important as fighting crime.

"We say this because more than a hundred years ago, before the historical act of the Great Union of the Romanian People around the Carpathian arch, Romania's Royal Police Force was a founding member of the International Criminal Police Commission, founded in 1914 at the Monaco Congress.

"The Commission was then constituted as an institution for the common fight against national crime, with obvious international trends, becoming the core of the future Interpol. In less than a century, the institution of police turned from a body anchored in oriental mediaeval time, and defender of an outdated tendency, into an essential institution of a modern European according to recent ages.

"Even in the post WWII period, until fully being accepted into the selected club of the European Union Member States at the same time with embracing the typology of the integration of modem procedures of the sister states' police, the Romanian police has managed to maintain a high level of professional performance; few of the similar institutions had such a high rate of solved cases."

"D'accord," says Patrice, wonderingly. "That helps a certain amount, I imagine." He is concerned, naturally, that the last paragraph he read skipped lightly over the reign of Ceauşescu and the *Securitate*, which is, surely, not to be dismissed so easily. "*Alors*, in view of that, why can you not use your own officers?"

"Because, I am ashamed to say, we still have two things in the more rural parts of Romania which handicap our investigation of this case. The first is that superstition, in small places, is still very prevalent – and there are things about these murders which encourage that. I have had quite senior police agents who have refused to enter the houses where the murders happened. It is incredible in these modern times!" He looks shamefaced, sorrowful.

"The second thing is that the investigation of anything is still impaired by mistrust of our police. This is left over from the communist era, of course, although things are totally different now. You have just read that! What you must understand is that Romania is a big country, with a long and distinguished history – but the ravages of the communists went deep, and some people, in the more primitive parts, are still afraid. Especially the older people ..."

"*D'accord*," says Patrice. "And so you need investigators from outside."

"My minister of the interior has spoken to Interpol and apparently they recommended your team. He says that Interpol know and trust your integrity. They would use you if they needed someone to investigate with absolute integrity. They appear to love you so much!"

Officer Silviu Melichian settles back in his chair with a sunny beam on his face. He probably has the feeling of having dumped his problem on the clever French *nemernici*.[6]

____

6   bastards – in Romanian

And is waiting to see what they do with it!

***

Monsieur Melichian is staying in one of the impersonal hotels recently constructed in Paris for tourists. He will wait there as Patrice's team discusses his problem, decides whether it can help, and gets the necessary permissions if needed.

Patrice will have to decide whether one or several of them should travel to Romania, or whether they can do some of the work from *le Trente-Six* – if, indeed, they want to do it at all.

"What is the weather like in Romania in March?" asks Fleur, shivering slightly in anticipation of the answer.

"Wet," says Faye Benoît, their civilian clerk, who is just coming through the door. "We went on holiday there last year, in June, and it had been raining since the previous November!" She places a pile of new case files and the morning's mail on the desk by the door.

"*Merci,* Faye," says Patrice. "Are we becoming meteorologists?"

"I wouldn't mind going to Romania," says René. "I have never been to Eastern Europe, although my mother is from Hungary."

"*Ne perds pas la tête!*[7]" says Patrice. "I haven't decided, yet, whether we are going."

René looks both shamefaced and truculent, turning slightly away, pretending to examine a serious stain on his desk. Fleur asks if they are sufficiently accustomed to working with foreign police forces.

"I think so," says Patrice. "And some *PJ* officers have worked in conjunction with Romanians before – there is an accord in place where we assist one another. I'm sure

---

7   Don't lose your head!

Monsieur Delahaye can update us on it, if we need it."

"I'm not sure we should do it. Don't we have enough here?" asks Fleur.

Patrice is quiet for a minute as he contemplates what she says, carefully adjusting the order of the things they have on their current list.

"I don't suppose you'll need anyone to take notes while you are in Romania?" says Faye, still here, even though she does not usually wait to be dismissed.

Patrice looks faintly cross. He has not decided yet. He confines himself to a stony stare at the young woman. She is only around *25 ans* and is from Normandy; although dismissing her as provincial is sophisticated *merde* – he is from the country himself.

"What have we?" he asks the team, just two apart from himself. Have to get on with that while Pucelle is away on her strange mission to the *banlieues*.

"Police in Transylvania have four murders, in three different places, within the large and rural district. It has, impossibly, the hallmarks of the beginning of an outbreak of vampirism, which is a real thing, not just an ancient myth. Local officers are hesitant, or worse, to go anywhere near it."

"*Merci*, Fleur," says Patrice. "Anyone else?"

"*Quoi?*" says René, almost asleep again. "*Moi?*"

"Go home!" says Patrice loudly. "Don't return until you can keep awake for more than three minutes."

René staggers up from his chair, picks up his backpack and says, "*Au revoir*," as he goes through the door. At least he doesn't have to negotiate the *ascenseur ancienne* before he can get to street level.

Patrice looks around and catches the eye of Faye, and asks her, politely, if she would like to do some work more like a detective?

"*Oui, patron!*" she exclaims. "I have always wanted to do that!"

***

Although Patrice is wavering about a decision whether to undertake this Romanian case, partly because of the unsolved cases the team already has, plus the small pile of new possibilities just dumped on the desk by Faye, he is soon drawn into the situation by a telephone call from Lyon. From Interpol.

"We should be extremely pleased if you would assist with this," says *Polisens Chef*[8] Mats Larsen, seconded to Interpol from the Royal Swedish Police Force. "This thing looks nasty, and could turn worse unless the investigating officers are very careful. And I understand, from your *patron*, that you are about to try out a new pattern for dealing with complex cases?"

"Ah," says Patrice, "so this is an experiment, *n'est-ce pas*? Or are you trying to make us fail?"

"Not at all!" says the Swede. "I am sure you can cope."

It is obvious to Patrice that the Swedish *flic* knows exactly how to press the right buttons. No way Patrice can let Interpol get away with that!

***

By the time Patrice arrives home at Île-Saint-Louis, he is confident that he and his team will be travelling to Romania at the request of the Transylvanian police. He himself is supressing a whole string of Dracula jokes, not very good ones, including a racist one about Italians.

Colette has been home but gone out again to walk Sartre.

---

8   superintendent – in Swedish

18

Jean-Pascal is in and studying in his bedroom whilst continuing to text his friends with the other hand. There is no sign that Amélie has been here, although it is *19 heures*. He goes to the kitchen, to see what there is to eat, and finds a note taped to the work surface, informing him that Colette and Sartre are bringing Indian food. *Que c'est délicieux!*

He has poured himself some orange juice and taken some to Jean-Pascal, just as Colette and the Bedlington arrive home, the rich scent of curry draping them like a thick blanket. As, between them, they serve the meal onto heated plates, Patrice asks where is the daughter, and Colette replies that she has a pass until *22 heures* – she will likely have eaten with her friends.

"I did not get her any food," says her mother. "If she can't be bothered to join us, she can go without!"

Patrice cringes. Another round in the endless, though recent, wrangling between mother and daughter. He can do without it.

As they enjoy chicken pasanda and naan bread with garlic and coriander, a mountain of fluffy rice, along with the German lager from the fridge, Patrice begins to tell his wife about Monsieur Delahaye's "new" idea.

"And which specialities do you think you want?" asks Colette. "And will you include someone from Intelligence? You'll have to, *quoi*? But controlling them will be *difficile* ..."

"I haven't thought too much about it yet," says Patrice, "but I know that I need a tech specialist or two immediately. We are extremely behind in that."

"I know," says Colette. "Even my system *ancien* at Versailles is better than yours!"

"It isn't just the system," says Patrice. "It's someone who knows what it will do and what it will not. I realise that what we see on television isn't real, but I cringe every time I hear a TV detective tell a techie to find where a cell phone was at *13 heures* on Friday and gets the answer in ten seconds! One day, perhaps ...”

“*Alors*, what’s the plan, then?”

“The *PJ* actually has a technical department in Paris, did you know? They keep it hidden, obviously. But I may go there tomorrow and refuse to leave until they second someone, preferably brilliant!”

“I can’t help thinking,” says Colette, “that maybe you should have done that before ... you’re such a *Luddiste*![9]”

They are drinking their coffee when Amélie arrives, to much enthusiasm on the part of Sartre. It is one minute past her curfew. She gruffly says goodnight and goes straight to her bedroom, slamming the door.

Bon Dieu!

They pretend that she did not stamp through like a rhinoceros, and return to coffee and conversation.

“What do you know about Dracula?” asks Patrice.

“Doesn’t exist,” says Colette. “Although ...”

“Although?”

“There have been outbreaks of vampirism at times, throughout the world.”

“Have there? I thought it was just a novel!”

“No, dear old Bram Stoker might have based it on some things about the hero, Vlad Ţepeş, who fought the Ottoman Empire in what is now Romania. Vlad the Impaler, you know. He was extremely bloodthirsty, impaling people, but he wasn’t a vampire!”

“So, just old myths and legends then?”

“*Absolument*. Why are you asking?”

Patrice tells her it is a case. The team has been invited to go to Romania to investigate four homicides.

“*Bon*,” she says. “Can I come with you?”

---

9   Luddite

3

Benjamin d'Aroque is a blond, curly-haired, twenty-year-old *brigadier*,[10] of medium height, and sculptured muscle developed by passionate attendance at his gym. He has been sent to the old *PJ* large interview room to meet Monsieur Lanier, who needs staff.

M Delahaye is behind this, mainly because no other senior officer in the *PJ* can think what to do with the young man. Delahaye is aware that Patrice has already tamed at least one officer who was thought "*difficile*" – René Mercard. He can have another. Sorted.

Benjamin arrives in a spring snowstorm of unusual ferocity, and Fleur Olivier, who sometimes adopts the mien of a *vieille femme devineresse*, says it is a bad omen. René laughs before saying he thought the team was supposed to say what it wants itself?

"We've hardly started the list yet," he says, and Patrice says it's bound to happen, there are always officers who are hard to place. René, who has been one, shuts up.

"Monsieur d'Aroque," says *le patron*, "where was your last posting?"

"I have been at Seine-St-Denis, and then was sent to *l'aéroport* Roissy Charles de Gaulle for a while. But there is not much work for me there, so Monsieur Delahaye thought you might be able to use me?"

The three detectives stare at the young man, trying to work out what the difficulties around his deployment might be. Doubtless they will find out in time. Patrice, who is dedicated to saying nothing if not able to say something nice, says:

---

10   corporal

"What a fortunate person you are, the *divisionnel* taking such a personal interest in your career!" Thinking, something bad; must be.

***

"One person we shall definitely need," says Patrice, "is a sensible forensic psychologist. I don't mean someone who will tell us that the serial killer is a man, aged between 25 *et 38 ans*, highly intelligent, who has a history of being abused by his parents and is obsessed with reading Japanese comic books."

"You don't want a profiler?" says Fleur. "I am so glad. I get really upset when one is mentioned."

"*D'accord*. From where will we get one?" asks Patrice. "Maybe *Docteur* Rousseau will know someone?"

"It seems to me," says Fleur, "that one of the universities may have better results. Several of them have big psychology departments, and it's a very popular subject – with all the crime-scene-type television programmes …"

"The *patron* said that he doesn't want someone like that, though," contributes René. "Not someone who is in love with easy conclusions and that kind of fantasy stuff – and totally sure they are correct at all times."

"*Non*," says *le patron*. "I want someone who is prepared to be part of the team, not a star in her own right. Someone who has heard that the FBI-type profiling system was withdrawn in America in 2014, because it was not reliable and had little, if any, scientific underpinning. Someone, I should prefer, who is interested in language analysis and direct communication."

"*Bonne chance avec ça!*" says Fleur.

***

"Alors," says Amélie, "I was a minute late. So what?" She does not extrude bubblegum, as American teenagers do; she does not roll her eyes, like the English. She stands there, defying her mother with every bit of body and mind, rebelliousness in every atom.

"And next time you will be two minutes late, or five, or ten. You are provoking me Amélie! You should not do that."

"Does it matter?" says the girl. "Why is it so important? Who cares if I come home, like a good little girl, at exactly ten o'clock? Who will die if I am late?"

Colette does not immediately know what to say to that. Of course, the child is right; no one will die, no one will be hurt (except Colette's pride). Really, she knows, in the great scheme of things it does not matter. The importance of it is in discipline. It's a big lesson about that, and about reliability; about character and accountability. She ponders how to convey this to her daughter without sounding like a reactionary idiot.

"If you cannot be trusted in little things, little, tiny things, how will anyone know you can be trusted in great big things?"

"There is nothing so big," says Amélie. "When there is, it will be different!"

Colette watches her, speechless, as she slams the outer door, whispering, so her mother cannot hear. Did she really say *"Dégage-toi*[11]*"*?

***

"What do you think, Fleur?" asks Patrice. "We cannot take the whole team, even though thin, to Romania. We only have two weeks anyway before we must be ready to begin

---

11   Piss off!

23

Monsieur Delahaye's new project. What can we do in two weeks?"

"If we have all the paperwork and reports of what has already been done, perhaps we can interview, or reinterview, those witnesses we feel are likely to have something extra to say – and so speed it up considerably."

Fleur does not like the sound of the Romanian Project in any way whatever, although she cannot, immediately, think of any way of avoiding it without losing face in front of the combined police forces of Europe. There is no way that two weeks is going to be enough either.

Unless there is such a thing as an open-and-shut case (in which she does not believe), it is unheard of to process and solve a homicide case in two weeks. She adds, to herself, that this is especially impossible in a foreign country, whose workings they do not know and whose culture they do not understand.

She knows that she does not have to say all this out loud; the *patron* already knows what she thinks. They have worked together for a long time. She lets out a long "humph" sound and he transfers his gaze to René, who is nearly jumping up and down with excitement at the prospect of going to Romania.

"*Patron*," he says, "we can work fast when we must, *n'est-ce pas*? And you say that deadlines concentrate the mind wonderfully! If we have a definite end point, we may be inspired to get everything done in due time."

Fleur looks at the younger man with some affection; he is still so green – although he has learned some things, he does need to slow down. He has a point, though.

"If you go to Romania, René," Fleur asks, "on this rather strange case, how are you going to solve the car-theft ring thing? Or can you do that by tomorrow morning?"

René's face drops, excitement draining away through his

tooled-leather boots. Fleur and Patrice both see that he is too occupied with the thought that some of the team will be going to Romania and he will not. It is *nul*.

"What do you think, Monsieur d'Aroque?" Patrice asks the young man, whose voice has not been heard in the single day he has worked for the team. Benjamin's face turns a shade of pink, and his lips work to try to say something. At least, thinks Fleur, he isn't quite so arrogant as René was straight from the police academy. He thought he knew everything and that the team had nothing to teach him. He found out he was wrong at *09 heures* on his first day.

Eventually, Benjamin finds his voice. The fact that the *patron* waits for his reply is only the first weird thing he will have to get used to.

"Not sure," he says quietly, so not to disturb anyone, "that this is a real case, *patron,* and that anyone should go for it. Could it be a political trap?"

"And if it were?" asks Patrice.

"I-I-I don't know," says the young man. "Just wondering who has what to gain from humiliating the Paris *PJ* ..." His voice is hesitant and unsure. Patrice will file his comment for future thought, although the new man does not know yet.

"*Alors.* As Benjamin says, it is possible that there are other agendas here than simply solving the murders. But we cannot take that into consideration at this moment. It would be best to avoid Romanian politics and just do our job. But I suspect there will be political implications somewhere, and we cannot know that in advance," says Patrice.

"What do we know? We know that there have been four murders, with the identical method. Although, we have not yet looked at post-mortem reports – so we have not yet established that that is truly the case. We do know that the area police, responsible for these rather isolated villages, are reluctant to investigate, even though they have been rigorously disciplined by the officer, Monsieur Melichian, who came to visit us. We know that these homicides have not been committed by vampires. We do not believe in vampires."

"They do need an outside team to investigate," says Fleur reluctantly. "If there is as much superstition as Melichian says, the fear is likely to ratchet up as they get into it. These tiny villages, they are so incestuous and inward-looking. We are not without some of that in France ... the village is a crucible, where strange things get trapped and need to happen, and people's relationships matter a great deal. You don't know whose cousin you are talking to and what is their history, whose bastard child is whose ... it is excessively complicated!"

"Maybe that's the key to it," says René. "If you stay a long time, as long as it would normally take, you will get mired in amongst all the weirdness and go native! Maybe having a strict deadline would work in your favour." He is working himself up again, although still certain that Patrice will not be taking him. He'll be left in Paris chasing around after stolen cars. *Il veut vomir.*[12]

Patrice looks at each of his three officers, with a side glance at civilian Faye Benoît, who is sitting quietly at a desk but listening to what may become a job opportunity. It is time for Patrice's decision.

"This is a peculiar case," he says, "but it is a serious case, in which human beings have died. The Romanian police has a problem with which they have asked for help. I do not know exactly why they have asked for us. We shall doubtless find out eventually.

____

12   He wants to vomit

"The essential features, at first look, appear to be that there is much fear attached to a case of this kind, as well as a great deal of superstition. Not to say many opportunities for using things which are not true to muddy the waters.

"We shall take the case for a maximum of two weeks, before we begin to form our new Complex Cases Detail. I shall lead the Romania team myself, with René Mercard as second-in-command. Benjamin d'Aroque and Faye Benoît will come along. Fleur Olivier will stay here and liaise with the computer technical expert – whom we have not found yet – and René's car-theft ring will wait until his return.

"I am assuming the three of you have valid passports, because we may need them as Romania is not in the Schengen agreement, and Faye, please find out this morning whether we need visas. Mention that the Romanian police have asked for our help.

"Benjamin, please telephone the technical department and get them to send over a few computer people for us to interview. René, ring around the universities and see if you can get a hold on whether any of them might have a forensic psychologist who could join us for a time in the next few weeks. Everyone, do it now, please!"

***

"What do you mean you're taking just René, Faye and the new guy with you to Romania?" asks Colette. It isn't acid in her tone, but it is something a touch corrosive. Patrice realises immediately that he has made a mistake.

"It isn't a holiday," he says. "And it's limited to a total of two weeks. There will be no time for fun, or sightseeing."

"And?" She looks at him as if he has done something bad, which she can do sometimes. He tells her that she would have been welcome to come with them, but no one will have any time to spend with her; their schedule will be tight.

"If there was any way we could slip in a little holiday, I would do it."

"Would you? You wouldn't keep me out so you can just go with your team?"

"*Je te ferais ça?*[13]" he says.

"Doesn't matter," she says. "I can look after myself. And I can assist with any research you need to do, in between seeing the sights. By myself!" There is a trace of a pout for a split second, before her face clears and she smiles at him. "I'll not come if you don't want me," she says in a voice full of sweet reason. "But I could easily keep out of your way – just fly along with you and stay in a hotel. I expect you will all be staying in someone's police house, *n'est-ce pas?*"

"I don't know yet," he says. "I'm not trying to exclude you, *chérie*. I know your penchant for travel ..."

"I've never been to Romania," she says. "It is supposed to be stunningly beautiful. And it's in the EU now, so easy, isn't it? I would like to go, I have to admit. And Jean-Pascal will be fine on his own. I am not sure about Amélie, though. We have been having a tussle recently about her curfew ..."

"She's growing up," says Patrice. "She's just pushing to see how far she can go. How bad is it?"

"Not very bad. Yet. It will certainly get worse before better."

Patrice suddenly has an idea. He examines it, quickly, from as many points of view as he can see straight away, turns it around and lets it show itself to him.

"What about," he says, "Amélie coming along too? Then you will have someone to do the sights with you. It will be very educational for her."

____

13 Would I do that to you?

"What do you think I should do so that I can put the car-theft thing on the back of the cooker?" asks René, when he and Fleur find themselves alone in the *salle squad*.

"How far, exactly, are you?" asks the older detective, wrinkling her eyes. She is quite happy not to be going to Romania; she doesn't want husband Edgar's head boiling. And she would much enjoy a short period of quiet at work.

"Not very far, really," says René. "They just seem to be disappearing into nothing. I get a report from the officer who has interviewed each owner. And they're all furious because of losing their incredibly beautiful car, which was also so incredibly expensive. But they primarily want a crime number so they can claim on their insurance.

"I thought maybe it was an insurance scam at first, but that does not seem likely now. Few of the insurance companies have paid up. None of the owners has any previous record, not even speeding, which is unusual with premium cars."

"That is unusual," comments Fleur. "That might be something you can take further when you return, *quoi*?"

"*Peut-être*," says René. "I think they are being stolen to order – they'd be impossible to fence in any normal way. But there is no trace of the cars being shipped, so where are they going? I'm asking myself who would want such expensive cars, and have decided it is most likely to be Arabs. The Middle East is a hot destination for luxury cars. But why have them stolen when you have all the money in the world to buy what you want? Doesn't make sense!"

"*Tiens*," exclaims Fleur. "Maybe it's the Russians? Or Chinese? Albanians, *peut-être*? By the way, what was it the *patron* told you to do 'immediately' before he went out?"

"*Merde, j'ai oublié!*[14]" says René. "I am expected to find a forensic psychologist for the new team. Better get on with that." He pulls his telephone log out of the desk drawer and turns to the numbers of all the universities in Paris.

4

The administration department has recommended six technical experts to be interviewed by Patrice's team, and Benjamin has already seen two of them himself. He did not take to either. He knows one of the others, who was at the police academy with him; Benjamin thinks he's an idiot.

He is not at all sure whether he should have spoken to the other two on his own; he hardly knows the team himself – he'll be seen as taking too much on himself again, *n'est-ce pas?* This is what he does, takes too much on himself. Perhaps their shortage of time will work in his favour, and the willingness to take responsibility, of which he has a great deal.

"There are still three people to see," says Benjamin to Fleur, who has just returned from lunch. They are alone in the *salle squad* (*temporaire*) and she has been moaning, yet again, about the hardly started state of their usual premises.

"Do you think it will be all right for me to have spoken to two of them already? I wasn't sure ..."

"It'll save time," says the much older, much more tired detective. "We always like to do that. Why have you only seen two out of the six? And there are only three still to see?"

---

14 Damn, I forgot!

"The odd one out is Thierry Lucroy, and I know him already. We were at the Academy together. We didn't get on. Is that a reason for not seeing him? That I don't want to work with him?"

"Why don't you?" asks Fleur.

"Because he's a bully," says Benjamin. "He always had a few similar people around him, and they played stupid jokes on the others, especially the women cadets. I didn't like that, and unless he's changed a great deal he would be very difficult to work with. I also don't think he's very bright. A bit late on the bookwork always – although that may have been just bad discipline ..."

Fleur wrinkles her nose even more than usual and says that she doesn't like the sound of Thierry.

"We have enough to deal with," she says, "without courting trouble from the beginning. Although, I have to say that anyone who doesn't fit will be quickly reassigned. Monsieur Lanier is no *jeu d'enfant*![15] Do you want him to see this officer? And the other two? Or do you trust your judgement?"

He looks at her, full of anguish; he wants to trust his own judgement and be seen to trust it. But he is new, straight out of his shell. Is going his own way disrespectful? He is torn between the two imperatives. Fleur looks at the newbie with compassion and slides him gently off the hook.

"*T'inquiète*.[16] It will be fine. The line lies between saving time and not cutting corners. You'll learn where it is. It will get easier. Just tell *le patron* what you have done clearly and don't try to make it sound better than it is. Never lie to him. He won't have it. And he always knows anyway!"

---

15   pushover

16   Don't worry (Verlan – via *Ne t'inquiète pas*). Verlan is the ever-changing language used by young people, and often criminals, between themselves, so others don't follow what they're saying.

"I am thinking that, maybe, some others should see the three who are left," says Benjamin. "Do you think it should be several people. or all the team?"

"*Non*," says Fleur. "Being interviewed by more than three people is intimidating. Personally, I think two is usually sufficient. With us, anyway, it is always difficult to get everyone together – unless for a team meeting scheduled well in advance.

"I am here this afternoon, and *le patron* will be, in about fifteen minutes, when he has finished taking his son out for driving practice. I think that will do. Telephone the three right now and get them to come in this afternoon. One per half hour, fifteen minutes between them. The *patron* will let you do most of the questions, with himself and me just butting in when we want to know something. I'd be surprised if we don't all come to the same conclusion immediately. We usually do. We did when you were presented to us!"

"Oh!"

***

Patrice has come home for lunch because Amélie is there and he wishes to speak to her. Colette has ruled out directly suggesting her daughter keep her company on a trip to Romania, predicting that the girl will say there is no chance she'd go with that *salope*.

Patrice, who is shocked at the idea their daughter would dream of referring to her mother as a bitch, offers to help by bringing it up when he and Amélie are alone. He will be extremely careful with her.

"You don't usually come home for lunch," says the girl as he looks in the refrigerator for something to eat. Surrounded by Sartre.

"*Non,* I do not usually have enough time," he says. "But today, I want to talk to you about something. And I have promised to take Jean-Pascal out in the car before I return to work." He removes butter and pâté from the fridge, and half a baguette from the cupboard, and breaks off a piece of the bread for the Bedlington, who would have chosen the pâté for himself. "Have you eaten?"

"*Oui,*" she says. "I had a little salad, with some chicken curry from last night. There is none left …"

"I realised that you have a study day, so I thought maybe you would like a break and a chat with your old *papa*!"

"*Oui,*" she says, "that's always good. And Sartre and I are going for a long walk when I have finished my reading."

"What are you reading?" he asks, hoping for philosophy, but she says it's English, it's Dickens's *Bleak House*. He approves, although not universally adoring Monsieur Dickens, only *Bleak House*, *Pickwick*, and the *Two Cities* one. He says that he is happy to discuss the book any time. She seems pleased.

She makes coffee for both, and they take it, with Patrice's sandwich, into the *salon*.

"What was it you wanted me for?" asks Amélie, being so pleasant that her father loses his small anxiety.

"*D'accord,* I have been asked," he says, "by the Romanian police, via Interpol, to investigate a group of homicides in Transylvania, which they feel they are too compromised to work on."

"Ooh!" says Amélie excitedly. "Dracula and that! Are the murders by draining the blood from the victims?"

"I am not allowed to tell you that," says her father. "You may now make a vampire joke if you can think of one. But make it a good one, and preferably not racist."

Amélie looks at him with disappointment; she cannot quickly think of anything which does not feature "out for the Count" or "stake-frites", although she is confident that she will find something later, possibly in the middle of the night.

"*D'accord*," says the detective. "Your *maman* would like to come to Romania because she has never been there and it is very beautiful, with mediaeval buildings and much scenery. But I can only be there for two weeks, and I shall be very busy indeed. I shall have no time for sightseeing with her. I thought you might like to come along, then you can accompany Colette sightseeing – even looking for Dracula if you like!"

Amélie gives him a look of distaste. She would really like to go to Romania – missing school would be excellent – but *avec sa mère*? *Non!*

Patrice, not normally slow on the uptake, cringes at his mistake. Amélie is not to be trifled with. Several changes of mood pass over what to him is still her childlike face in a split second. All her various agendas are displayed. He wonders where she will come down. He waits for an answer.

"*D'accord, Papa*," she says, "I'll be glad to accompany *maman*."

What just happened? Patrice asks himself. What is she up to? Anything? Nothing?

***

"*Patron*, there's a woman out there in a wheelchair!" says René as if the sky were falling. Patrice stares at him, wondering what on earth that is supposed to mean.

"And?" They have plenty of disabled people in and out of the building; it is accessible. Perhaps fewer criminals and more witnesses. Uh.

"*Non, patron*," the younger detective says, "she's not a witness. She's a *flic*! She says she's come about the techie job. From Admin." Patrice gives him an "I'll deal with you later" look and rapidly goes to open the door.

There is indeed a woman in a wheelchair sitting on the other side. She is in her mid-twenties and has exquisite copper-coloured hair, in a highly fashionable style sculpted on top of her head. Her skin is almost translucently fair, and she has freckles across her *retroussé*[17] nose. She is lightly but expertly made-up, with her dark brown eyes emphasised with taupe shadow and medium mascara.

Patrice takes in, because that is what he does, a light citrus perfume. He can see the newcomer is dressed in a cream silk knitted sweater and rust-coloured full skirt, patterned with leaves. There are tiny gold dots in her earlobes. All this takes a very short time; Patrice is accustomed to summing up new people in fractions of seconds. He greets her and introduces himself.

"*Bonjour,* monsieur! *Je m'appelle* Clémence Godard. I have been sent by Administration to see if you can use my talents in technical services."

The other two possible people have already been seen and found wanting.

He tells her she is welcome and stands back so she can wheel herself into the *salle squad*. She runs silently over to the closest desk, as if expecting him to take a seat at it. Which, bewitched, he does.

René is sitting at his own desk, pretending to study car-theft reports and keeping out of the way. Fleur, enchanted by Patrice's enchantment, isn't bothering to pretend to be working; she is waiting in her own place to see what happens next. Patrice offers the woman coffee and asks Benjamin to go get it for the whole team, from the café on the corner. Other interviewees have not been so fortunate and have

---

17   turned up

had to make do with the *approvisionnement dégoûtant des détectives*.[18]

"Madame, or is it Mademoiselle, Godard," says Patrice, "have you your resumé to show us?" She has, in triplicate. Patrice passes a copy each to Fleur and René, taking the opportunity to introduce them as Madame Olivier and Monsieur Mercard. He also adds that he has sent Monsieur d'Aroque for the coffee. Mme Benoît is out of the office this afternoon. René abandons his pretend work to read the impressive curriculum vitae.

"I see you studied mathematics and computing at university," says Patrice, "and your marks appear to have been good enough to undertake further qualifications. Was there a specific reason why you decided to apply instead to the police academy?"

"*Oui*," says Clémence. "All my life I have wanted to be a policeperson. I have dreamed of it. I had to fight for it." She does not volunteer to tell them why, and Patrice will not ask until they are alone. He is concerned about his officers' privacy, but he needs to ask some straight questions about this young woman; although he will never be brusque.

"Why do you want to be a policeperson?" asks Fleur, causing Clémence to turn the chair slightly to the right to face the female detective.

"I believe it has the right balance of intellectual stimulation and helping people that appeals to me. I have been in the offices of administration, helping with the setting up of new computing services, since I graduated from the Academy. Now I want to do something else; I want to be a real police officer, a detective, investigating crimes and helping people. That is what I've always wanted!"

She ends with a slightly shrill tone. She is more nervous

---

18   the detectives' disgusting supply

than she appears. Patrice says nothing for a little while, just turning over the pages of her documents and musing. Eventually he asks how she feels about imprisoning people, perhaps for the rest of their lives.

"I do not," she says, "think of imprisonment completely as punishment. I am not persuaded criminals are able to pay for what they have done, although it is a cliché everyone uses. For violent crimes and such, there is, in my opinion, no such thing as justice. If a person died, no one could make it right – which is the meaning of 'justice'. The murderer cannot, ever, make it right. Better, I think, to try everything in the name of rehabilitation. To make the criminal a credit to the society."

"What if," says René, suddenly recovering his voice, "the criminal is a serial killer or someone who has committed an especially abominable homicide, or more than one? Is it possible to rehabilitate him?"

"It might well not be possible," says Clémence. "But punishing her is not likely to make her able to fit into society. I think it may be necessary to never let her go free. To protect the public."

"And how do you think she," asks René, switching carefully to the feminine pronoun, "should be treated for the rest of her life?"

"As well as possible," says Clémence. "She has lost her freedom because of what she did. Is that not enough?" There is silence in the *salle squad* as Benjamin returns with the coffees and distributes them around the room. He has bought one for Faye, who is not there.

"What do you think about capital punishment?" asks Fleur, who is a well-known supporter of the lethal slice.

"I deplore it!" says the young woman. "I could not be a policeperson if we still used *la guillotine!*"

Fleur sniffs. This is a familiar argument.

"Well, you are all right then," says Benjamin, who has not heard any of the conversation. "The last criminal was guillotined in 1977, and capital punishment was outlawed in 1981."

***

Pucelle, who not only got herself a job but also seeded an extension to her enquiry about the whereabouts of the Elephant, is working back in the *banlieues* on her first day of employment. Frieda has sent her on an easy job, just to have a look around, an orientation with the area – which may have seen a few changes since she was last there. There are few changes to see; it is a little dirtier, just, as she makes her way towards the apartment building where she was kept captive. There is little chance that Elephant will come back there, and she doesn't need to see the *appartement* to remember what it was like.

There are no residents, even in the few intact apartments on the same floor as the place she was kept. She had thought to ask them if they had seen the Elephant. Still limping a little, she walks down the stairway which she negotiated on her bottom when she was leaving. Her leg aches in remembrance. It is no less filthy than it was that day. There are people living on the floor below. She knocks on the first door.

5

Clémence Godard has wheeled herself into Patrice's private office, one of several off the squad room (temporary), steeling herself for the inevitable question: "What's wrong with you, then?" Everyone asks it, but she still has no standard reply. Replies have been through many versions, none completely satisfactory.

Should she say that we all have disabilities, some are just more visible than others? Is that patronising? Sanctimonious? Should she try to persuade that asking what's wrong is pejorative and demeaning to people who count themselves as disabled, or even "differently abled"? – not that she embraces the latter, because it is not true for her. Or does she want to get the job?

The *patron* seems friendly and polite, well politically correct. It is possible that he is an exception to the usual baseline of poking fun at people with disabilities. Or he's faking; also possible.

What would she do if he ignored the fact that she uses a wheelchair? If he just treats her like someone who can walk into the office? She'd have to point it out to him, she thinks. There are things she can't do.

"Mademoiselle Godard," he says, his grey eyes regarding her across the desk, "I must ask you some questions. I should like you to know, first, that I do not discriminate against anyone, no matter what their abilities, colour, race, creed, nationality, sex, gender, sexual preferences ... Did I get everyone? I often find that a simple negative doesn't catch it all."

"*Non*," she answers, "I think you may have got everybody. For the moment anyway."

"The only things I wish to know are those which may affect the way you do your job, and most of them I would ask any applicant. Those are things like, do you have the emotional resilience to do the work? Do you have the physical stamina to work long hours and, sometimes, chase after suspects? I already, I think, have your answer to the second question, although I do not know about the first."

"*Oui*," says Clémence, "I am emotionally resilient, because of how I was brought up and educated. I am a naturally calm person and have a solid self-image. I'm confident and cope well socially. The other answer, of course, is that I can't chase criminals, except if they are also in wheelchairs.

"I can push myself after them quickly – I have good upper-body strength, on account of using the wheelchair all my life. But there is no way you can call me physically fit. That would be *absurde*! You can ask whether I am fit within the limitations of my disability, though ..."

"And are you?"

"I am. I have a physiotherapist who visits me every Sunday morning, and who works with me to maximise what I have available. As I was born with spina bifida, there is a tendency for atrophy of lower limbs – so I make sure I have the physical therapy I need."

"I do not know a lot about spina bifida," admits Patrice, "although they prescribe folic acid to expectant mothers, don't they, to close the spinal canal in the foetus?"

"They do," she says. "And it helps, too. But not for me, obviously. My disability is produced by my spinal canal not closing, and producing a myelomeningocele between two vertebrae. They operated in utero and managed to close it, but the nerve damage is not repairable.

"So, I don't have use of my legs, and have no feeling from about halfway down my abdomen."

"I see," says Patrice. "The only other thing I need to know is about your intellectual capacity. I was under the impression that most people with spina bifida have some degree of learning difficulty. Obviously, with your qualifications, you do not. I just need to know whether you know of any decline in that kind of function which might impact your work? I dislike asking this, but I don't know if it happens. And I need to know."

"I don't know of anything like that at present," she says, "but I can't predict the future. I will undertake to let you know if I spot anything. Just like any other officer. It depends, a lot, on who you talk to about how many people with SB have learning difficulties – I don't think they know!"

"*Alors*. Thank you very much for all that. And welcome to the Complex Crimes Detail."

***

"Romania does seem to be a beautiful country," says Colette after work is over. "Did you happen to have an opportunity to talk to Amélie about, maybe, coming with me?"

"I did," says Patrice. "Not a problem. She's delighted. She said so."

"*Tu rigole, c'est ça?*[19]" Colette is astounded.

"No, I'm not. We discussed it and she said she was glad to come."

"Do you think she's up to something?" asks her mother, cautiously.

"Like what?"

"Oh, I don't know. Just something. She'll probably sell me to a passing bandit – do they have them there? *T'inquiète*, it'll be all right, *n'est-ce pas*? Where are you going?" she asks. "To what airport will you, we, fly? And what then?"

Patrice tells her their date of travel, already arranged with Monsieur Melichian, and that they are flying to Cluj Napoca, in Transylvania, will be collected by a Romanian police detail, and driven to the small town of Pâclişa, where they will stay in a small hotel. They will be loaned a police car for their various journeys to three villages, which seem to have no names yet and are a few miles away, where the murders took place.

---

19   You're kidding, right?

"Ooh," says Colette, "that sounds very exciting. Secret, even. Are you to go in disguise?"

Patrice pretends to be disdainful of that and says that of course they are not! He says that they will have to be ready to go, though, there will be no waiting around – and the travel date is the day after tomorrow. He will have no more time to take Jean-Pascal out for the driving.

"*D'accord*," says Colette. "But you may have to tell Amélie what clothes she will need. She will take the wrong thing just to make a fool of me!"

"If we both tell her that it is still winter in Romania, that will probably do it ..."

Colette is not so sure.

***

"*Ce sera super!*[20]" says Fleur. "That we have an excuse to make them fix the *ascenseur* properly. Because when we move back to the fourth floor, you will need reliable transport!"

Clémence Godard had not expected this when chatting with Madame Olivier at the *Trente-Six*. Few people, and fewer police officers, see the wheelchair as a positive asset. She smiles a little and waits for the superior officer to determine the topic of conversation.

"Tell me all about you," she decides. "I know everyone says that, but it's most important when we are going to work together so closely. I want to know where you were born and your family circumstances, your schooling, and career so far. Friends and acquaintances—" She sees Clémence's face drop a little; what a lot to get out all in one piece.

"*Non*," she adds, "I don't need it all now – we are, anyway, to be alone while the rest of them are in Transylvania

---

20   This will be great!

looking for vampires. You can fill in all the bits then. Just tell me, now, where you come from and about your career so far ...”

“Vampires?” says the new detective. “They’re going to Transylvania hunting vampires?” Now she looks as if she is going to laugh.

***

Colette has paid a visit today to the Romanian tourist office in Paris, to collect as much descriptive literature as she can. There is lots of general information saying that Romania is a very beautiful country, but also a lot about how interesting it is, in view of its long history and the Dracula.

She doesn’t understand why the creepy, gothic stuff doesn’t put people off – although it clearly doesn’t. She’d have thought the tourist office would have invested in “Don’t worry, it isn’t real”, but there is no sign of that. They appear to find it thrilling, as do *beaucoup de touristes*!

She finds herself wondering about fear, and what she herself finds frightening. She can think of only two things. One is from the time she has eleven years and sleeps in the grim attic bedroom of a school friend’s home. The friend is, like her, Parisienne, and lives in one of those tall, narrow houses, which have been little restored since the Baron Haussmann. It is large enough for her to have her own room, although she would prefer to sleep closer to Joséphine.

Colette is reading, in the chilly room, under the bedclothes, a French translation of *Jane Eyre* by Charlotte Brontë. It’s bad enough reading about poor Jane living with the horrible Fairfax children, but their bullying is not what upsets young Colette.

That belongs to the phrase, in chapter twenty-five, where seeing Bertha reminds Jane “of the foul German spectre – the

Vampyre". Of course, Charlotte Brontë had not had the benefit of Monsieur Stoker yet; Jane was published in 1847 and Dracula is still fifty years in the future!

The other frightening thing is a scene in the third film of *The Exorcist*, which involved something horrible chasing someone across the screen, waving obstetric forceps. It was so fast and so shocking that she became obsessed with the scene and repeatedly watched it, on video, to study her own unfamiliar reaction. She has *30 ans* when this happens.

She dismisses it from her mind. It still causes an unwelcome wobble.

The Transylvanian stuff is largely vampirish, forming around Bran Castle, "Dracula's Castle", although there is little evidence that it has much to do with either the Impaler or Monsieur Stoker's creature. She considers boycotting it for that reason. Alba Iulia, where Detective Melichian comes from, seems interesting, with Roman ruins and an amazing eighteenth-century star-shaped citadel. That, she would like to see. Maybe also from the air? She can imagine a bursting itinerary which may easily avoid Bran Castle and all its many attractions, invested with artificial creepy.

After she raids the Romanian tourist office, she visits a bookshop and buys a cheap paperback copy of Bram Stoker's *Dracula*, in French translation, as she is sure they don't have one in the house. She has never read it and doesn't think Patrice will have either. Part of her still feels that she will miss interesting information if she rejects all things Stoker. She also purchases what purports to be a biography of Monsieur Abraham Stoker, in English, although it is hard to see how such a reputedly secretive sort of fellow could have inspired such a house-brick of a book!

Colette recollects something she read years ago about *Dracula*, the book, occupying a particular place as a bridge between sentimental Victorian novels and a huge move into

modernity (meaning sex). And there are issues around Irish
Home Rule too, which she does not understand. She
wonders whether her friend Celeste Jolivet, who is a
graduate in political science, as well as a runway model at
Dior, has anything to say about that.

It is only as she is making a note of that, to ring Celeste,
she remembers that Romania, until 1989, had its own
real-life monster in power, Nicolae Ceaușescu. And wonders
whether that influenced the preservation of monster myths.
She suspects that real-life experience could well do this.

6

"And how is my new Detail coming along?" asks Monsieur
Delahaye, dropping by the *salle squad (temporaire)*.

"Quite well on the whole," says Patrice. "I have two
new staff members already: Mademoiselle Godard, an
accomplished technical expert, and Monsieur d'Aroque, a
junior detective. I am presently looking for a good forensic
psychologist, although they are hard to find."

"Why do you need a forensic psychologist?" asks Delahaye.

"In investigating a complex crime, there is a great deal
with which an experienced forensic psychologist can help
us: motivation and prediction of future patterns, locations,
and things of that nature. Although we may be able to
consult someone, it would be very much more straightforward
if we had one in-house. Which is, of course, your idea,
patron. It would also help with our training – keeping the
team up to scratch with developing techniques, improving
everyone's expertise."

"I see," says Delahaye, not convinced, although obviously slightly flattered. "I don't think we can pay for anyone full-time, though. It sounds expensive to me ..."

Typical, thinks Patrice; do it, but do it *à prix réduit*. He doesn't bother saying so at this stage. He doesn't want to start a fight yet; he may need to later. He will save his rhetoric until he knows he can win.

"I reckon," says Delahaye, "that Dr Rousseau might know someone we could use. You could ask him."

"I have thought of that," replies Patrice, "and I have instructed Monsieur Mercard to ring round the universities. They may have someone, perhaps recently qualified ..."

"You'll find Rousseau knows better," says Delahaye determinedly. "We don't want someone too young, *n'est-ce pas*? We'll need experience. But best part-time, don't you think?"

Patrice, who doesn't think that at all, mutters a kind of "humph" sound.

***

René has found a lecturer at the American University of Paris, who thinks he knows someone who would be perfect for what the detective is asking. She is tied up at present with teaching, so already qualified, but she will be looking for employment presently.

The lecturer will give her René's number and she will telephone him very soon. René, who would have liked to tie this up today, expresses his thanks and tries another university, which has no ideas whatever. This is, apparently, not the best time of the year to be searching.

Amazingly, Dr Petra Boulet, forensic anthropologist and forensic psychologist both, turns up at *le Trente-Six* at 14.30, asking for Monsieur René Mercard, who is *commissaire* of the Complex Crimes Detail. René, embarrassed that the lecturer he spoke to at the American University has got the wrong idea, goes out to meet the woman in the lobby.

***

"You know dear old Bram never went to Romania, don't you?" says Colette, marking her place in the book she is reading. "He did a lot of research in the British Library."

"British Library is good," says Patrice. "I've spent time there myself."

"But you wouldn't build a whole thing on just that!"

"I wouldn't. Probably. But I doubt if old Abraham did either; probably lots of other sources. And Edgar Rice Burroughs never went to Africa, you know."

"Don't you think you can see it in how he wrote *Tarzan*?"

"No idea. Never read *Tarzan*." He stretches and yawns. He's tired after a long day of plate-spinning with M Delahaye, Mlle Godard, and Dr Boulet, who has proven to be fascinating.

"You don't know anything about Dracula, do you. How did you manage to miss him?"

"I must have been away from school on the days they taught things which don't exist. Don't know a whole lot about religion either!"

"I think I'm going to have to read *Dracula*," says Colette, "so I bought a copy. We don't already have one, do we?"

"*Non*. Don't think so," says Patrice. "But I certainly don't want to look at it until we get back from Romania. I already need to bracket the things I think I know about the legends so I can look at the things themselves!"

"Of course. But I do have quite a lot to read," says Colette. "I need a little Romanian modern history, the abominable Ceauşescu, for example. I was thinking I might

47

ring Celeste; she may be able to recommend a book – or at least talk to me about the communist period. I did think about asking her, too, about the Irish Home Rule, but decided that was really a distraction … Bram, not Drac!"

"Sounds like a great idea," says Patrice. "I'm sure she'll direct you to something useful. I want to tell you about Dr Boulet, though. She's interesting, as well as accomplished."

Colette puts her book aside and looks at her husband encouragingly. He doesn't always tell her the more grisly details of his work; he protects her. But she is always avid for the personal, relationship stuff.

"Dr Boulet turns out," he says, "to have a doctorate in forensic anthropology, as well as a graduate degree in forensic psychology. We had a fascinating conversation but, unfortunately, she has teaching commitments in both specialities and there's no way she can come to us full-time."

"Oh, that's a nuisance. Is she prepared to consult though? If you need someone. I'm thinking especially about this Romania thing – some psych involvement there, I shouldn't be surprised …"

"Yeah. It would be useful to have her along, but there really is no chance of that. For the future, though, extremely interesting!"

***

"Celeste?" asks Colette, when the phone at Avenue des Magnolias is answered. "It's Colette. *Ça va?*"

"*Ça va?*" says Celeste. "I'm fine. Would you and Patrice like to join us for dinner one day next week? Pucelle is reputed to be coming home – for a proper bath. We thought we might have a kind of celebration!"

"*Non*, unhappily," says Colette. "We are off to Romania tomorrow! Patrice is helping the Romanian police with a case, and Amélie and I are going to do the tourist places while they're busy with that."

"Oh, that will be fun. It's supposed to be a beautiful country, apart from the vampires! Never understood why that's an attraction. Although, they have had their own monsters in real life."

"That was what I was telephoning you about," says Colette. "I remember you are a political scientist. I was thinking that perhaps you could recommend a book on the Ceauşescu years – or, if not, you could tell me something about them?"

"Um, well, there's quite an interesting book by an ex-spy who defected, Ion Mihai Pacepa – and I think you can get that one in French – and there's a journalist's-eye view one called *The Life and Evil Times of Nicolae Ceauşescu* by that John Sweeney, who says he tends to 'poke the crocodile's eye with a stick' or something like that. Although that's probably just in English. You can manage though, can't you, with Patrice and a dictionary?"

"I don't know," answers Colette. "And I won't have much of Patrice anyway, as the team is staying in police accommodation, and Amélie and I in a hotel. But I do have quite a good dictionary – I can probably get the flavour."

"It was an awful time," says Celeste. "All kinds of horrible things went on, although there was strange stuff mixed in with it. Things like reducing censorship for a while, then bringing it back in a worse form. Trying to float, and succeeding to a great extent, a personality cult around Nicolae and his toxic wife, Elena. Trying to pull away from the Soviet Union, including the rejection of glasnost and perestroika, but supporting, for a bit, the Prague Spring.

"Ceauşescu courted the leaders of the West – mainly to try to establish himself as a world leader who had been highly decorated by many countries. France even gave him the *Legion d'Honneur,* you know, but took it back again when he fell in 1989."

"One of the things I'm interested in," says Colette, "is why the vampire thing is so popular – apart from encouraging tourism – and is it connected to the idea of having had an actual real-life monster for such a long time? Don't you think that's interesting?" Celeste ponders for a minute, and then says yes, that could be interesting, but she will have to think about it; she suspects a metaphor.

"But we'll only be able to talk when you come back," she says. "It's a pity I didn't know before. I could have looked things up. I was interested in communist systems when I was at university – I must have notes somewhere ..."

"*T'inquiète,*" says Colette. "We can maybe get together when I come back. We are only allowed two weeks for it, which isn't Patrice's favourite way of doing things. But it must fit in before his new Complex Crimes Detail mission."

"He has a new Complex Crimes Detail? Good grief!" says Celeste. "Does Pucelle know she will be coming back to that?"

"Doubt it. It's to do with Monsieur Delahaye. A reorganisation, for some reason. I don't know what triggered it. But I suppose we'll see eventually."

"Let me know when you're back," says Celeste. "And send me a *carte postale* with something Dracula on it!"

7

Surprisingly, the whole party, policepersons and Lanier family, are sitting together in the aeroplane. Colette had kind of expected that she and Amélie would be seated in a different part of the plane from the police group. This is the direct morning Wizz Air flight from Beauvais Airport to Cluj Napoca, Romania. It only takes two hours and thirty-five minutes. But one must get to Beauvais – the shuttle takes one hour and fifteen minutes from Porte Maillot, almost half as long as flying to Romania! But easier than travelling at the other end.

Their arrival in the Transylvanian city of Cluj Napoca is without incident, and they exit the airport to be met by a police minibus, which will drop Colette and Amélie at their hotel in Alba Iulia, and the others at their police accommodation.

The police officer who meets them, young, dark, Romanian, seems to have been primed to go off as they arrive. He picks up Colette's hand, bends over it, and says:

"*Vă aşteptăm!*[21]" He kisses her hand and, although she doesn't understand the Romanian, she is quite comfortable. This custom has declined in France in recent years, to Colette's mixed regret.

The countryside is mostly rural, with small hamlets and farms. There are many vineyards, too; there is a prominent trade in Romanian wines. The Romans made wine here, a long time ago. It is a very pleasant day, with sharp sunlight, and dry. She supposes that the summer will give enough sunshine to ripen the grapes.

There are hills, though, even mountains. The heights, where there are villages sometimes, look almost unscalable. She has begun to read *Dracula* and digested the first few pages, which one could almost accept had been written by

---

21 We're waiting for you! – in Romanian (this means something similar to a reverse of "Au revoir" or the cliché "Missing you already")

an author who had been there. It's none the worse for that. A bit like a travelogue.

He had, though, started to write his book centring the action in Styria, Austria, copying his compatriot, Joseph Sheridan Le Fanu, who set his earlier *Carmilla* in that location. Colette has not read Le Fanu, hadn't even heard of him until she started internetting around Stoker. There is quite a lot of information on the internet and she wishes, just a little, that she had explored it more before she arrived in Romania.

The countryside is stunning, although Colette can see why it might be intimidating in the dark. And, presumably, there were more wolves and bears in the nineteenth century? She has read somewhere that most European brown bears live in Romania even today ...

As they approach their destination, there begin to be more cottages and farmhouses, occasionally some industrial conglomerations, with the usual weird-coloured smoke flowing from the chimneys.

At Alba Iulia, the weight of history swamps them. There are seventeenth-century, eighteenth-century and nineteenth-century buildings everywhere, but the city has been here since Roman times, so there are ruins too. "Iulian's White City" is situated on the banks of the Mureş river and, as the name of the place claims, many buildings are white.

Colette, impressed with the place, is pleased that they have come in March rather than the summer. According to the brochures, in the tourist season, Alba Iulia hosts gladiator contests and other re-enactments of ancient history. The kind of thing she loathes.

She notes the museums and libraries, and the fortress with seven bastions in a star shape, built between 1716 and 1735 by two Swiss architects. There will be much for Colette and Amélie to see here.

Patrice gets out of the minibus, with René, to help his wife and daughter with their bags. The men carry the two medium-sized suitcases into the hotel lobby, where Patrice kisses wife and daughter and promises to telephone them tomorrow.

The men rejoin the minibus; it drives away, leaving the female Laniers at the hotel.

It only takes a short time to check in and have their passports examined, then a member of staff carries the bags up to the second floor and into a large, airy twin room. Amélie throws herself on the closest bed, without speech, Colette unpacks first.

*****

The *PJ* team disembarks from the transport in two instalments: René and Benjamin in Pâclişa, Faye and Patrice in Bărăbanţ. The two younger male detectives are to be accommodated in a police barracks, but the *patron* and the young woman are boarding in a very nice house which belongs to the local chief of police. Someone has decided against a hotel.

One of the Romanian police officers, who had shadowed the minibus from Alba Iulia, leaves the squad car in the access of the house in Bărăbanţ, and catches the minibus back to wherever he is stationed.

Patrice and Faye meet the chief, who turns out to be a middle-aged female, who settles them in, feeding them a meaty Romanian stew and nice bread.

"This is really something!" says Faye Benoît.

*****

It is Fleur Olivier's first day in charge at the *Trente-Six*, with a staff consisting solely of the very new Clémence

Godard. Because she feels that it could be difficult to leave the office to eat, Fleur has brought in a bagful of sandwiches and asked the *brigadier* from the front desk to send a junior officer out for decent coffee.

This has now arrived, and the two women are settling to strengthen themselves for the day. Fleur explains, first, the important coffee situation – which is dire at the *Trente-Six,* consisting of a choice between the horrible detectives' supply and the horrible reception supply. For good coffee, they need to go to the *café italien* round the corner. She starts to consider work next.

"I don't want the *patron* to come home and find out that we haven't been doing anything," says Fleur, "so my idea is to pick up a few straightforward cases and go as far as we can to solve them. It seems to me that it would be an excellent idea to avoid René's car-theft ring – partly because we are not in a good place to run around, partly because it has all the appearances of being a long-drawn out thing, with perhaps no solution. What do you think?"

"You obviously know best," says Clémence. "But I imagine a car theft might be quite tricky ... There must be other things we can do.

"One thing, though. Don't be intimidated by the wheelchair. There are things I can't do, but there is a lot I can. I can interview witnesses and suspects – if I can access them in our interview rooms or in their apartments or workplaces.

"Naturally, I need an *ascenseur* for above the ground. But I am mobile because I have an adapted car and can get in and out of the chair by myself." She rolls up the long sleeve of today's light-green sweater and shows off her biceps, which are well developed.

Fleur is impressed by the muscle and asks if she is one of the Paralympic athletes. Clémence says she is not that good, but probably more than okay for a police officer. Fleur drinks some more coffee and picks up the top file from a pile on her desk.

"There is nothing especially urgent," she says. "And I expect the *patron* thought we would coast along until the rest of them come back. But I don't want to look like we girls can't manage. Not that the *patron* would think that."

"No, he doesn't seem that sort of person," says Clémence. "Exactly what sort of person is he, anyway? He seems unusual for a *commissaire*!"

"He is. He's a most kind and gentle man. But he is also a consummate policeman, with great integrity and attention to detail. I advise you never to lie to him – because he won't have it, and always knows anyway. His methods are a bit unusual, and you'll have to get used to how he does everything.

"He's a philosopher, a phenomenologist. That means he never takes anything for granted; he goes to the things themselves and looks at everything without prejudice. He examines the fine details – and that can sometimes frustrate officers, superiors even more. But he gets results – although he is known to take considerable time. People sometimes think that looking at things without prejudice is a simple matter but, for Patrice, it is not. He requires to suspend what he already knows, what he thinks he knows, what 'everyone knows' – 'the natural attitude'. It can be strange at first, but you get used to it!

There is a loud bang as something hits the *salle squad* window. Fleur and Clémence both duck down in their respective chairs, possibly expecting paving stones to come flying in. Fleur, recovering first, realises that the younger detective expects the worst, a terrorist attack, at least something through the glass. It isn't. Fleur is accustomed to it. It is an insane pigeon trying to get in, and happens two or three times every day since they were moved from their own office to the ground floor. Humph. She breathes, and gets back to her monologue without comment.

"Sometimes it seems that answers come *tout à coup*,[22] although that is never true; they come because he, and we, have worked hard to get to them. Also, he believes in coincidence, which many investigators say they don't. He says that, if there were no chance, which is another word for coincidence, there could be no evolution. And there clearly has been, so there is chance, there is coincidence.

"In short, he's a most interesting person to work for. The best *patron* I've ever had. And I've been with him for ten years now, ever since Vice let me go. Another story for another day!" She laughs and drinks the rest of the coffee.

"*Alors*, what is the first case we look at?" asks Clémence.

"It is something the uniforms should have dealt with," says Fleur. "It's pick-pocketing or similar, around the Rue de Sèvres. The gourmet shops are beginning to attract upmarket tourists at this time of year, and there is obviously a lot of money and jewellery around to be lifted easily. None of the wealthy people bother to defend their property, do they, so rich pickings. How do you feel about that?"

"*D'accord*. I am quite a good decoy for that kind of thing. Do you not think there are young refugees and such who do these things?"

"Usually, yes," says Fleur. "But in this case, it is unlikely. The *gamins* avoid the centre of the city because they look too *débraillé*[23] to fit in and get away. Unless they are begging, which they keep separate. They must be well-dressed thieves to fit in and get the best pickings. There seems no suggestion of weapons or threats, either, so, maybe it's safe ..." She

---

22   out of the blue
23   scruffy, mangy

shuffles the papers in the file and casts her eyes over the reports to see if there is any obvious reason the file has been passed on to the *Police Judiciaire*.

"*D'accord!*" she says triumphantly. "That must be why. There is someone who has been recognised!"

Clémence can only grunt, trying to guess what the older detective means.

"It's that man, uh, you know, Roger Rannequin, 'RR', the racing driver!"

"*Tu te moques de moi, d'accord?*[24]"

"No, I am not," says Fleur. "It's happened before. He has indulgent parents, his father is a senator, and plenty of racing fans. He doesn't need the money; he just likes stealing things. That's why we have the case. The last few times, I think it says five times in here, his father has pulled strings and no charges have been preferred. In other words, he's got away with it. It's fun for him. He's a pest.

"What do you think? Do you want to go for it?" She locates a photograph in the file and puts it on Clémence's desk. Clémence picks it up and examines it, saying she has seen him before, on television. He is expected to win the Grand Prix sometime soon, *n'est-ce pas?*

"He's a complete *beauf*,[25]" says Fleur, "and a *connard*.[26] Like to catch him, and make sure he is charged?"

"*Oui!*" says Clémence.

***

When Patrice telephones, around *21 heures*, he is happy with his accommodation. Is Colette happy with hers? And, perhaps more important, Amélie?

---

24   You are kidding me, right?
25   rude, vulgar
26   shithead

"We're fine, it's all very nice. As soon as we arrived, Amélie fell onto her bed and went to sleep. I think all that anger takes it out of her. She's still asleep!"

"But the hotel's okay, is it? You have not eaten yet?"

"No, although I got coffee and a sandwich brought up to the room. Rather large sandwiches, with some unfamiliar components. But rather good. I've wrapped one up for your daughter. When she awakens, I'll get her some Coca-Cola or something. What's yours like?"

"I have a pleasant room in the house of the chief of police, Maria Gadianu. She seems motherly on top of steely. But she can cook! She made us a stew with meat and vegetables. It was good and warming. And the bread was marvellous! Faye and I will stay here the whole two weeks, with a car to take us to the places we need to go – crime scenes and that. And a driver to find them when necessary."

"You have a lot to do tomorrow," says Colette. "You should probably go to bed. Sweet dreams, *dulciné*![27]"

"And to you, *chérie*. I love you."

***

Colette opens her cheap paperback of Bram Stoker's *Dracula* and reads a few more pages. She wishes it had an introduction or notes or something – she should have bought a better edition, *n'est-ce pas*? She is trying to recall what she learned when she read American Andrea Dworkin's *Intercourse* in the late eighties.

Dworkin's book is not exclusively about the Stoker novel, but it is one of the novels that the arch-feminist writer covers – and very interestingly, in Colette's opinion. She writes shockingly about sex, although it is less shocking now.

---

27   sweetheart

58

It is intriguing to think that the world has moved on in its conception of the oppression of women. At least some parts of it have.

Before she begins to read, she waits for the coffee and thinks of what she now knows about Bram Stoker. She knows he had a red beard and had been 1.88 metres tall and built like a bear. He was, perhaps, remarkable less for himself than for the people he knew. She lists some of them in her head: Oscar Wilde, Sir Arthur Conan Doyle, Sir Henry Irving, Ellen Terry, Walt Whitman, Hall Caine, W. B. Yeats, James McNeill Whistler, Lillie Langtry, Dante Gabriel Rosetti, Mark Twain, W. M. Thackeray, Alfred Lord Tennyson, A. C. Swinburne, Arthur Sullivan, John Singer Sargent and, possibly, Jack the Ripper! What an interesting time to be alive.

Abraham's biographers seem to have had a desperate need to read something about his sexuality into Dracula and his other works, probably because of barely veiled sexual content. How much is one able to understand the author from his works? How much do they give away through their characters and plots? Colette needs to think about this a lot more. And Stoker himself is not just reticent on the subject, he is completely silent.

He does appear to worship Walt Whitman (mostly from a distance, although they did meet eventually), Henry Irving (who exploited him unashamedly and appears to have always kept to the master–servant relationship), as well as the then-famous writer, Hall Caine, who seems to have been a true friend and is largely forgotten now. To most of these, Stoker was an addition, an assistant, an also-ran. He is, today, more famous than nearly all of them!

Stoker's relationship with Oscar Wilde included marrying Florence Balcombe, who previously looked as if she would marry Oscar – and who, before her death, received a letter, sent in 1881, from Oscar, to Ellen Terry. The actress wrote that it "by rights belongs to you (Balcombe)". Oscar closes the letter with the line:

"She thinks I never loved her; thinks I forget. My God, how could I?"

Bram and Oscar were certainly aware of one another, in Dublin, at Trinity College (although Bram was a little older than Oscar), and in London (where Wilde was a celebrity, and Stoker was Henry Irving's slave), but seem to have kept one another at arm's length.

As a quiet, Protestant, possibly straightlaced person, Bram may have been shocked by Oscar's bad behaviour – and much aware that should he himself give in to any homosexual inclinations he may have had, he could go the Wilde way. And there would lie ruin.

The concept of vampirism is ripe for metaphors of all kinds, thinks Colette, and although she has not read the scholarly writings, she can see their adaptation to cover the sucking dry of the people, or the culture, by communism, fascism, the aristocracy (*Vive la révolution!*), poverty, disease (especially syphilis and now HIV/AIDS), alcohol and drugs. There are multilevel shades of domination and submission in both *Dracula* and Bram Stoker's own life.

Sir Henry Irving was an emotional vampire and all but sucked Bram's blood. Colette can make a good case for Oscar Wilde's vampire credentials in relation to other people too. Although Lord Alfred Douglas (Bosie) fed on Oscar himself.

Her mind slides sideways to the matter of blood. There has always been mystery and imagination around the precious fluid, although science gives reasonably straightforward accounts. Some people have funny ideas.

There was resistance to being transfused with blood from a person of a different race. In some places, there still is, even though it is *stupide*!

She suddenly thinks that that cycle of life in the blood itself fits quite well metaphorically, although not physically.

There is such a lot of strangeness. Almost as much as siting emotions in the heart. Colette, a scientist, as dismissive of pseudoscience as Bram Stoker was accepting, refers to it as "piffle".

The first chapter of *Dracula*, Jonathan Harker's diary, is a travelogue of Romania, describing countryside and national dress, and giving the impression of the primitiveness of the people, the superstition (there is much crossing of themselves by peasants), and already, upfront class superiority is manifest.

Colette recollects that Monsieur Stoker indulged in journalism, as well as in novels. Um. The writing is okay, though; quite nice descriptions, although *un petit* old-fashioned.

Then Harker announces he's going to Castle Dracula. And everything changes.

The melodrama is stoked (no pun intended) up considerably – with wind and dark and storm and wolves. Colette underlines (in pencil, she does not make ink notes in books) a bit she wants to keep track of Jonathan Harker's quote about superstition:

> *"I read that every known superstition in the world*
> *is gathered in the horseshoe of the Carpathians, as*
> *if it were the centre of some sort of whirlpool; if*
> *so my stay may be very interesting."*

It is clear, when he has transited from the public coach to Dracula's *calèche*, that the driver, from his calming the circle of wolves, "the children of the night", must be the Count himself.

Colette looks around the light, bright hotel lounge and reflects that, were she reading the novel in a cottage, by candlelight (don't forget it's 1897), her feelings might be a little different!

8

The next file on Fleur's desk is called "Della Supermarché", and is the long, sad story of a particular grocery shop in the sixth *arrondissement* which, unknown to the police, regularly gets glass shards in its baby food for sale. It has tried investigating but has found nothing. The supermarket manager is suffering from a major depression, and the other staff are boiling their heads.

It is an unusual case to come to the attention of the *PJ* but, in this case, the crime has been going on for eight months, at least once each week. Store clerks have questioned customers, and no one has come under more suspicion than any other. Neither have they been able to trace all the jars which may have been contaminated.

There seems something unusual behind it – and that is why Serious Crimes has been given the file straight away. Fleur, who thinks that the case looks like it will run and run, explains the situation to Clémence, who says:

"How does whoever it is get the glass into the jars? Through the lid? Opened and resealed? Is it a locked-room sort of thing?"

"*Dieu seul sait!*[28]" says Fleur. "No one seems to have thought of anything which would work. There are no holes in the lids, and they appear to have been unopened."

"The factory?" asks Clémence. "Have investigators been there?"

"Only executives from Della," says Fleur. "They say that the factory, on the far side of the *Periphérique*,[29] prepares the jars and the food, and puts the one in the other. There seem no terrorists on the factory staff, but how can you tell? Going nowhere. No leads. That's why it's on our radar."

"Can we interview the person in charge now?"

"Tell you what," says Fleur, "ring him and make an appointment. See what you can ferret out. Police eyes and all that!"

"*D'accord!*"

***

René has woken again and checked his watch. It is 06.00. He has previously been awake at 23.45, 02.54, and 04.38. At all these hours, it remained very dark. He never sleeps well the first night in a different bed. He wonders what might have awakened him, but knows that it was likely just his own system trying to adjust. It will be better tomorrow.

He slides out of the narrow dormitory bed, puts on his robe (black Japanese silk, gold-embroidered, expensive) and goes to take a shower in the adjacent bathroom. There are ten beds in the mens' dormitory, but only four are occupied, including his and Benjamin's. On his return, he spots Benjamin still sleeping. The younger detective fell asleep as soon as he lay down. And hasn't woken up yet.

---

28   God knows!
29   the ring road around Paris

René dresses in black jeans and a light-grey shirt, with no tie, puts his gold detective shield and ID into the pocket of his black leather jacket. He left his shoulder holster and weapon in the gun safe downstairs in the office of the commandant. He walks to Benjamin's bunk and shakes him awake.

Benjamin, fresh from an exciting dream in which he captured several gangsters, agrees to get up, shower, and meet René in the canteen on the ground floor. They will wait there for orders, and/or the others to arrive.

It is 08.00 when Patrice and Faye Benoît drive into the car park and ask where they can get privacy for a meeting.

The small room, next to that of the commandant, seems crowded with the four of them, but the meeting will not take long. Patrice has paperwork, which he sorted out last night before going to bed, and has precise orders for each of them, as well as explaining what he himself is going to do. It is straightforward.

"René, I want you to stay in Pâclişa and talk to the officers who responded to the call that a Monsieur, er, Dobrescu, had been found dead. There are at least three of them, and you should talk to each on his own; oh, one is a woman officer. The names are Gavril Cuţov, Sofia Iordache, and Radu Balan. When you have done that, and written a preliminary report, please consult their original reports and look for differences. Then have your lunch ..." He smiles at René, who understands the joke.

"Benjamin," he says to Officier d'Aroque, "you go with Faye to the first crime scene – the address is in the file; I have a copy of the file for each of you – and gently interview the widow of Monsieur Dobrescu. The original report information is very brief and awkward. Please find out why it is awkward. And get a biography of Monsieur Dobrescu and his family. While you're there, feel out the atmosphere. This is the house where the local police appear to have got worked up, so I expect that it will be a little scary or sinister, or something. Are you both all right with that?"

Faye and Benjamin look at each other with nervous smiles and say they will be fine. Neither of them is superstitious. Patrice notices Faye fingering the crucifix which she wears on a silver chain around her neck. She sees him looking and slips the cross inside the crew neck of her scarlet pullover.

"I am going to interview, first, the officer who oversees the case. Or who had been doing so until we caught it. It is not, apparently, Monsieur Melichian, who was sent to us because he has good French. I shall seek him out another time. Before I go any further, I should tell you that you need to make sure that if you want an additional interview with anyone, it is very wise to specify it before you leave them – and make sure it is in both your diaries. Should they have one.

"Never forget that our time on this case is strictly limited, and we must be as smooth as we can. Always keep that in mind. *Se déplaçant le long.*[30] *Ah, oui,* the senior officer is *Madame Capitaine* Iulia Roşca, who is stationed in Alba Iulia. *Alors,* I shall be going there this afternoon. I can do that alone.

"Is everyone clear on all that?"
Everyone is.

***

"So, the woman in the apartment below is the only one who had been aware of anything about the Elephant apart

---

30 Moving along

from his, her, fearsomeness?" says Celeste as they eat dinner at Avenue des Magnolias.

"*Oui,*" says Pucelle, helping herself to salad, adding green leaves and dressing to her plate of spinach pasta with peppers and onions. "She is called Olena, another Russian, and she has spoken with the Elephant, although the Elephant did not, of course, speak to her. They do seem to have communicated though. Elephant appears to have used, occasionally, the sign method which she used with her son ... with a few other people."

"That still seems strange," says Manon, who is dispatching a lot of chicken grilled with garlic. "That you did not realise she was a woman ..."

"I saw what appeared to be there," says Pucelle. "It never occurred to me that she was anything other than a Russian drug dealer and enforcer. Why would she be a woman? There was no reason for me to suspect, and I was not in a position to be too curious."

Farah is sharing Pucelle's vegetarian menu and helps herself to her favourite chilli sauce. She contributes the idea that she herself assumes all the time:

"If I saw someone in a burqa," she says, "I would assume it to be a Muslim woman, although it could be a man. Or even an undercover Buddhist ..."

Everyone stops eating as they consider an undercover Buddhist. Then they put it to one side and continue with the meal. They need to finish the main course because there is one of Celeste's spectacular puddings for dessert.

"Did Olena give you any information about the Elephant?" asks Manon.

"Information, a little," replies Pucelle. "But where she might be? *Non.*"

***

Clémence drives her Renault Clio, sunshine yellow, rust trim, into the factory car park where Della *supermarché* sources its baby food, with glass in it. She parks in the executive section because it is closest to the main door. She slips out, hauling the wheelchair from behind her seat. Wheels herself to the ramp in front of the door. It is steep; obviously no one in a wheelchair has, before, checked it out.

In the lobby, there is a hatch, which is open for visitors to shout through to the woman about a kilometre away from what passes as a reception counter. The woman is on the telephone. Clémence yells that she is Officer Godard, from the *Police Judiciaire*, and that she has an appointment with Monsieur David Maurice, the chief executive officer.

The woman, hearing the incredibly loud voice of the police officer, comes forward, already saying that M Maurice's office is on the third floor and she will have to use the stairs. On realising that Clémence is hardly in a position to do that, she becomes flustered, tells her to wait, and hangs up the telephone, before dialling a single number and speaking softly to someone different.

Apparently, the police officer is to wait, and Monsieur Maurice will come down.

The CEO arrives with an arrogant look on his handsome face. He has light-brown hair and delicate white skin, slim scholar's hands, a winter wool suit in charcoal worn with a lemon shirt and dark tie. He does not want to talk to the police. But has been forced by the receptionist's bewilderment.

"Monsieur Maurice?" asks Clémence, wheeling towards him, "*Ça va? Je m'appelle* Clémence Godard, *Officier de Police Judiciaire.*" He disciplines his face into a slight smile of welcome and tells her he is David Maurice, going straight into the fact that he has already spoken to the police and has nothing further to say.

"*Nonobstant*,[31]" says Clémence, "I have several things I need to check with you. Is there somewhere private where we can speak?" He doesn't treat her to an answer but takes hold of one of the handles of her wheelchair and pushes her, lopsided, into a room off the lobby. She turns around to face him and says:

"Please do not do that again! I do not like it." Her tone is unequivocal. Even if he gets the chance, he will not do it again.

The small room is furnished as an office. Maurice takes the chair behind the desk and faces Clémence across it.

"Look," he says, "I told your colleagues that I have no idea how the glass came to be in the jars. Our systems are totally sealed and there is no opportunity. I have spoken extensively to the managers on the line, and in the warehouse. There is no possibility of wrongdoing. I have nothing else to tell you."

"Can you tell me," says Clémence, "exactly what is in the jars? When you start off with an empty jar, clean, I assume, what do you put in it, and where does it come from?"

"Of course it's clean!" he blusters. "The jars come from our sterilisation machines and are added to the filling line. The mixture comes through a filling nozzle, which is different for each separate flavour product and is cleaned at the end of the day, and halfway through the next day; that is, twice a day. We have a range of ten different superior flavours."

"I have no record of what the flavours are," says Clémence, "and whether the glass was found in all of them ..."

"I think it was in all of them," says Monsieur Maurice.

---

31   notwithstanding

"*Oui*, I am sure it was." He picks up some papers from the desk where he put them after he parked her chair. He looks through them as if he has left his spectacles upstairs. "Oh, apparently the glass was in every flavour except the one with lentil casserole."

"Please tell me the other flavours," asks Clémence. "I need to write them down. Unless you have a handy list?"

The CEO stares into space as if trying to recall Descartes's "Proof for the Existence of God", but then comes out with a list of the remaining nine flavours of the baby food:

"Um, beef, bean and sweet potato casserole; lamb, pasta and peas casserole; sausage and tomato pasta; cheese and macaroni; duck and rice casserole; Provençale vegetable casserole; salmon, potato and cauliflower; plaice, rice and peas; prawn, pesto and tomato pasta. I think that is ten altogether."

"Monsieur, you are making me hungry!" says Clémence, mainly because she thinks she ought to. "What are the ingredients of the lentil casserole, which was spared?"

"Green lentils, onion, nigella seeds, chopped bacon, celery. That is all."

Clémence underlines "bacon" in her notebook and asks if she can have a full list of all the ingredients of all the jars in this series. M Maurice asks, sardonically, whether she wants a list of all their baby desserts as well. She says that she doesn't. *Merci.*

***

René Mercard, in the police station in Pâclişa, has one of the three officers who attended at the home of Monsieur Luca Dobrescu when he had been found dead, three weeks ago.

The officer is a large, dark-haired, moustachioed man, who keeps his uniform hat on indoors. René tries to avoid

classifying him as *un beauf,* because he could be wrong –
and that is the easy way to miss something crucial. The
French detective explains why he is there, why the French
team has been assigned. The thug, no, not a thug, nods his
understanding. Then gives his name: Balan, Radu, in a gruff
voice matching the thug designation.

"I am René Mercard," René says in French; he has
checked that all three of the officers have some of the
language, although Madame Sofia Iordache has let it be
known that she would prefer to speak in English. "I
understand that you were the first on the scene at the house
of Monsieur Dobrescu. Please tell me what you found.
Please describe accurately."

Balan stares at the French detective in a hostile manner,
René thinks, trying to intimidate him. He will not be intimidated.

"I have a time and date," says René, "but need a description
of your arrival at the house, and what happened then."

"I was in the car with Officer Iordache," he says. "We
had been on night duty since 21.00 and we were tired."

"*Oui,* it was 07.00 when you got the call," says René.

"We arrived at the house at exactly 07.22," says Balan,
referring to his notebook. "The wife of Monsieur Dobrescu
was at the door, with her friend, Madame Dincă, who had
made the call from a nearby farmhouse. They told us,
between the two, that Luca Dobrescu had been killed in
the night.

"Officer Iordache entered first. It was a small peasant
house. That is, just one room, with a bed and some chairs.
And a fireplace to cook on. Monsieur Dobrescu was in bed,
on the side nearest to the only window. When I got to the
bed, after Officer Iordache had turned away *elle a vomi.*[32]
I saw the man lying there with his throat torn open. There

---

32   she vomited

was bright blood all over his torso, like a *bavoir enfant*.[33]

"When I turned around, Madame Dobrescu was standing behind me, muttering and crying. She said, '*S-au întors!*[34]'"

"And what did you think she meant by that?" asks René. The big man looks pale, which make his operatic moustache look more artificial than before.

"That they are back," he says. "That they are ... here again. That we are not able to recognise them."

"Would you care to give 'them' a name?" asks René.

"*Non*," says Balan. "I can write it down for you." René, amused, gives the officer a piece of notebook paper. The Romanian makes the sign of the cross, picks up a pen from the desk and writes something briefly, folds the paper, rises, salutes, turns and leaves the room without permission or further conversation.

When René unfolds the paper, he sees one word. It's Romanian, but the meaning couldn't be clearer: *Vampir*.

***

When Gavril Cuţov arrives for questioning, René is still reflecting on Balan. Surely, a grown man, about *45 ans*, can't believe in vampires; that would be ridiculous. René feels, anyway, that after such a long period of communist rule, superstition should have been laid to rest. But the big man had made the sign of the cross too. He invites Cuţov to sit down and introduces himself.

Cuţov is younger and more friendly than his colleague, clean-shaven, with reddish hair in a buzz cut. He removes his cap as he comes in and gives René a sunny smile, welcoming him to Romania. He adds the compulsory "Please enjoy our beautiful country".

---

33   child's bib

34   They have come back! – in Romanian

René asks him similar questions to those he asked Balan, and gets similar answers, after the younger policeman has explained why he did not get to the scene until *07.45* – he had been the more senior officer that Balan and Iordache had called in. He adds that Officer Iordache had not been willing to go back into the house, and that Officer Balan had been most concerned with keeping Mme Dobrescu and Mme Dincă out. He says this as if he is not convinced of M Balan's concern.

"Do you think it was an excuse on the part of Monsieur Balan so he did not have to return to the side of the body?" asks René. Cuţov's voice says "no", but his eyes beg to differ. He goes on to describe the scene pretty much as Balan did, until he gets to what Mme Dobrescu said at the end.

This time there was no refusing to say, crossing himself, or insisting on writing it down.

"She said it was a vampire," he says. "It must have come in the middle of the night and drained her husband of blood. It had not disturbed her, although she had been sleeping away from the window – it must have come through the window, *n'est-ce pas*? Because it had got to Luca first?"

René stares at the young man as he says this in a sensible, serious voice. He does not know what to think when the young man says:

"He must have come in the form of a bat."

9

On her way back to the *Trente-Six*, Clémence parks the Clio close to the Rue de Sèvres, puts her police pass in the windscreen. She strong-arms her chair out of the tiny car and makes for the gourmet shops. She is suitably dressed for the area, although reflects it may have been a better cover to have an assistant, which she does not need, to push along the chair.

She straightens the kilted skirt, in Ancient Red Gordon tartan (which has an overall pink effect and which she bought on a lovely visit to Edinburgh a few years ago), makes sure her creamy silk blouse is tucked in, and that her claret raincoat shows enough underneath to make her look well put-together.

The Rue de Sèvres is busy. Clémence stops in front of a very expensive *pâtisserie,* just to look at the cakes, which are exquisite. She chooses one, which she will not buy, because too expensive and she needs to control her weight anyway. Cake window-shopping is a pastime in which she often indulges. She looks, also, at the reflection of what is behind her in the display window.

There are many people passing and she cannot differentiate for the moment. It may be necessary to come back another day when it is quieter. If she does that, though, there will be fewer chances to catch any pickpockets or other thieves, let alone Monsieur "RR". She discovers that she wants him badly, although not particularly pitying his wealthy victims.

Which, in turn, reminds her of René's motor case, whose wealthy victims she does not care much about either. The notion that there may be a connection, she wonders about. The detective turns away from the plate-glass window of the *pâtisserie,* and wheels herself towards the kerb. Most people jump out of her way, even though she is not proceeding especially fast. A teenage boy blocks her way but, when she shows no intention of stopping, quickly moves. She wheels along the edge of the pavement, turning occasionally to watch the crowd. Nothing seems out of the ordinary.

Perhaps not today, she thinks.

Suddenly, someone, a man in a beige-and-brown-striped suit, pushes past the wheelchair towards the road. Clémence takes a firm hold on his hand and pulls him towards her.

He shouts, "*Lâchez-moi!*" and "*Dégagez-vous*[35]*!*" as he tries to prise her fingers from his wrist and shake her off. A couple of metres away, a middle-aged woman in a beautifully tailored dark-blue coat is gripping her right ear with her leather-gloved hand and shouting that someone has stolen her earring.

Clémence produces her handcuffs, snaps them onto RR's wrist, and clips his arm to the armrest of her wheelchair. The lady who has lost her earring, by having it pulled through her lobe, is bleeding profusely, and a man passing by produces a clean white handkerchief to staunch the flow. The woman discovers her other earring has also gone, as has her necklace – which had real pearls, officer!

The detective in the wheelchair, ignoring the pleas of her prisoner that it wasn't him, calls in her arrest and waits, with the victim and the man with the handkerchief, and several others, for a car to collect them. One of the crowd asks the prisoner if he is Roger Rannequin. All are shocked when he answers in the affirmative and begins signing autographs with his free hand.

***

René is delighted when Officer Sofia Iordache proves to be a slight, fair-haired twenty-two-year-old. Her blue uniform is smart and clean, unlike either of the two male officers', and she offers to shake his hand after she has saluted him.

---

35   Get off me! And piss off!

She seems businesslike too. He cannot imagine that she will believe in the undead.

"I'd like you to tell me," he says, "about what happened after you had driven to Mr Dobrescu's house on the morning in question." René's English is not remarkable, but it tends to be adequate in foreign countries where it is not the mother tongue of his witnesses either. If he has difficulty, he can always resort to the *patron*, whose English is exceptional.

Iordache tells him the same story as the others; she was with Officer Balan from the beginning, until she had to leave the house to throw up. She is a little timid about her weakness. René, always the white knight, tells her it's fine.

"I'm usually all right," says Iordache. "I have seen lots of blood before – just, this time, it seemed more horrible somehow. I am a little, what's the word? Claustrophobic. And the house is small. Very. Everything started coming at me ..."

"Don't worry," says René. "Different things affect different people. I can't stand heights. It's normal." He waits a moment before asking her to describe the minutes between her entry to the house and her throwing up back outside.

"I gazed around the house," she says, "before I looked down at the body."

"How did you know where the body was situated?" asks René, a good pupil of phenomenologist Patrice.

"The original call, from Mrs Dincă, said that he was in the bed," says Iordache.

"Okay, so you looked around the house. What did you see? Try closing your eyes and remembering exactly what you did." She does as she is told and closes her eyes. Her face becomes blank, and she starts with the smell.

"It is the smell that hits me first. I have smelled blood before, of course, but this is a lot of blood, a bigger volume than what I've smelled before. There is a smell of old people, too, and stale food. Cabbage. But that is usual.

"I look around the walls first. The house is just a shed, really. Poor, draughty. Wooden walls, with gaps. It's cold despite the fire. Who made the fire? I wonder about this because his wife discovered Mr Dobrescu before 07.00, when she woke up. Did she climb out of bed over her husband's dead body and make the fire?

"The walls are decorated with a lot of icons. Well, not real icons: posters, prints, of religious pictures. I was brought up Romanian Orthodox, although I'm not religious now. But I recognised a few of the saints on the walls, and the Blessed Mother, of course. I think they are very religious people. Then I look down at Mr Dobrescu, lying in bed, covered in blood. And my breakfast starts to come up."

"And you rush outside and deposit it against the side wall of the house?"

"Yes. I felt very upset." Iordache lowers her gaze and clasps her hands together.

"So," says René, "you only threw up the once, in the garden, not in the house?"

"Of course!" says Sofia, "I would not contaminate a crime scene."

René smiles and asks her what she thought immediately after she recovered from vomiting? About the case?

"That their religion didn't protect them against the Devil."

***

Fleur responds immediately to a call from the front desk at the *Trente-Six,* asking her to get over there immediately as *Officier* Godard has brought in a prisoner. Fleur arrives to see Clémence, with a man bending over, firmly attached by his wrist to her wheelchair.

"Fleur, it's Roger Rannequin," she pants. "I caught him *en flagrant délit*, in the Rue de Sèvres. I've arrested him and booked him in."

The *brigadier* comes out from behind the desk, with his assistant, and unlocks the handcuffs from the wheelchair, putting the half not on RR onto his assistant's wrist. The young police officer takes the racing driver away, down to the cells in the basement.

"What were you thinking?" asks Fleur. "I thought you were on baby food today!"

"I did that as well," says Clémence. "I just thought I'd stop at Rue de Sèvres on the way back and have a look around. I was lucky. There he was!"

"*Mais*," says Fleur, "do you not think that was incredibly dangerous? He could have had a knife. Or a gun. You could have been killed! The public could have been killed."

The younger detective looks regretful for a split second and then asks if she should not have arrested the suspect.

"*Non*," says Fleur, "you shouldn't have gone there at all. It was too dangerous on your own." She stops for breath and raps out that they will go to the *salle squad* right now.

When they get there, Fleur does not tear a strip off Clémence, she just pours them coffee from the pot of horrible and sits down at her desk. She is counting herself down to calm, because she has imagined a picture of the girl, shot, on the pavement, her wheelchair turned over, its wheels spinning on their own in the wind. It has scared her considerably.

"Tell me about the baby food," she says.

***

"What sort of thing would you like to see today?" asks Colette, when she has managed to awaken Amélie after about eighteen hours' sleep. They are having a room-service breakfast, with *plăcintă aromână* – a spinach pie with lots of eggs in the filling – sliced ham and cheese, followed by jam-and-cream doughnuts, *gogoși*. And, naturally, thick, sweet Turkish coffee. They have decided against cornmeal porridge as too heavy – although have already found out that the spinach pie is remarkably dense.

"I suppose," says Amélie, "that you want to do old churches and museums …"

"I do. But we can do shopping too if you like. We can at least have a look at some shops. I've no idea what things are unique to Romania, but it might be fun to find out?"

Amélie looks over her doughnut with a grimace, but there is a touch of excitement around her eyes. Their glint is not as stunning as it used to be, but it is there. A little.

Colette has several leaflets showing the Catholic Cathedral of St Michael, built eight hundred years ago, the ramparts of the citadel wall, the Unification Cathedral (built 1921 – ugh!).

"Apparently, the Cathedral of St Michael is thought to be the third religious building on the same site, built from some of the stone blocks from the walls of the Roman camp at Apulum!"

"Aw, *maman*," says Amélie, "just an old dry church."

"Aw, Amélie!" says Colette. "It has witnessed many remarkable events such as the entrance of Michael the Brave in 1599. In 1565, at the Reformation, the people turned Protestant, and it went back to the Catholics in 1716. How about that? And it's considered the most important monument in Alba Iulia!"

"Isn't there anything less dusty?" asks her daughter.

"The fortress is supposed to be very interesting," says Colette, wondering where she can find anything at all which would interest a teenager like Amélie. "There are museums and galleries, the Prince's Palace, the Orthodox Cathedral, the university."

"I'll have enough of universities next year!"

"The first monarchs of the Unified Romania, King Ferdinand I and Queen Marie, were crowned in the cathedral on 15 October 1922."

"Oh, wow!"

Colette finds that old Dorothy Parker satirical verse going through her head and is sure it's going to be an earworm for the rest of the day:

> *"Oh, life is a glorious cycle of song,*
> *a medley of extemporanea,*
> *And love is a thing that can never go wrong,*
> *and I am Marie of Romania."*

"*Écoute*," says Colette, suddenly finding an entry in one of her pamphlets, "there is an 'escape room' in Alba Iulia. It appears that you must use your brain, in a team, to get out. There are lots of good reviews of it. Why don't you look on your phone? There will be more about it. It is near here. They recommend you go for up to two hours, and it's open from *15 heures* to *22 heures*. I can go to the cathedrals and meet you from there for a good dinner."

"That sounds great," says Amélie, a little reluctantly. "I'll read what it says on my phone and get back to you."

***

Accompanied by a little husband, the victim whose jewellery had been stolen by Monsieur Rannequin has been brought to *le Trente-Six* by another police car. Her statement is taken by a uniformed officer and Fleur wonders, after looking at it, where the other earring is. It is not in Rannequin's pocket with the first one, covered in blood, and the double string of recognisably good pearls.

She wonders if it is a case of increasing the haul for purposes of insurance. She says this to Clémence when she returns from the *toilettes pour dames*. The younger detective thinks that could be correct.

"No one tells the truth any more," she says. "And this woman is rich, she doesn't need to defraud her insurance. It's just greed." Fleur sighs in agreement. Says she'll mention this to Mme Barthélemy when she telephones her to give her the information for her insurer.

"I have been thinking," says Clémence, "about the baby food. I need to go onto the factory floor and talk to the people doing the job. Monsieur Maurice was no use. I am interested, though, in the fact that the lentil casserole has never been contaminated. *Pourquoi* do you think that might be?"

"The ingredients are interesting," replies Fleur. "Who doesn't eat bacon, or other pork products? None of the other flavours have those in them ..."

"Muslims," says Clémence. "Jews. People who don't like pork products."

"*Oui*," says Fleur. "Another anti-Muslim or anti-Jewish conspiracy?"

"Could be."

10

Benjamin and Faye arrive at the Dobrescus' house and discover that there is no one there. It is a small, poor-looking shack of wood and tar paper, and is surrounded by an abbreviated vegetable garden, with a few cabbages and beets. There are a few other shacks a little way off, but this is not a proper village, nor even a part of one. It looks more like an emergency build; where people have had to set themselves up because they have nowhere else to go. Definitely in the country.

As the *PJ* stand, looking around, a female voice shouts something unintelligible at them and an old woman comes hobbling over as if trying to scare trespassers off. They both produce their credentials, asking if the woman speaks French or German (Benjamin has some German). She has a few words of French and tells them they should get away from the Dobrescus', and that she is the closest neighbour, Madame Dincă.

"Perhaps you can tell us where Madame Dobrescu is?" asks Benjamin. "We need to speak to her about her husband's death."

"*Non, non, non*," says Mme Dincă. "She has already told the police everything. She is not well. She is afraid. She is staying in my house."

"I'm afraid we must insist," says Faye, asserting her police mission for the first time.

The peasant woman gives in quickly, unused to talking back to policepersons. She has not tried to unravel the obvious fact that they are French police, not Romanian. She stamps towards her own shack, which might be called "next door", and Faye and Benjamin follow her. They enter behind her, through the flimsy door, which seems to be made of packing cases.

There is another woman sitting hunched in an old chair by the fire, wrapped in a dark shawl. She gives the impression of extreme age and deep depression; her head is low on her chest, hair covered in a dull headscarf. Mme Dincă makes no attempt to introduce them but remains standing by the door.

"*Salut! Êtes-vous* Madame Dobrescu?" says Faye loudly, to make sure the woman hears. She looks around as if she has just awoken from sleep. She blinks several times and does not confirm whether she is that person or not. Benjamin, joining in, gently explains that they have come to talk to her about what happened in February, to her husband, at their home. She changes her glance to him, as though she hadn't seen him at first. The remarkable thing is not what she says, but the way she says it:

"What is it you want to know?" she asks in perfect French, with only a slight foreign accent. She is obviously not the peasant they had expected. Both *PJ* look stunned, until Faye manages to speak.

"I'd like to know," she says, "what you thought when you awakened and realised that something had happened." Diana Dobrescu takes a deep breath.

"I had been dreaming," she says. "Deeply asleep. I do not usually sleep so deeply. Sometimes I do not sleep at all. But that night I did. It was late, for me, not to awaken until almost seven. And I was surprised that Luca was still in bed too. He usually gets up at six and takes a walk. But he was still in bed. A few seconds later, I realised that he was cold. I sat up and looked over at him. He had blood all over his chest.

"I put my fingers on his neck and there was no pulse. I put my hand to his mouth and there was no breath. He was dead. I had no way of knowing how he had died."

"I'd have thought," says Benjamin, "that you would have seen that his throat had been torn ..."

"*Oui, mais certainement.* I meant that I had no idea who had done this thing. I had seen and heard nothing."

"Very well," says Faye. "Perhaps you would be good enough to tell us something about yourself and your husband? Like where you came from, how long have you been here, what employment you have? Things like that."

"Are those important?" the woman asks.

"They are," says Benjamin. "The context always helps the investigation." The woman looks at him thoughtfully and begins an efficient narrative about their lives.

"We have been here five months," she says, "since the end of September last year. We came from Bucharest when Luca retired from his office job. We have two children, Maria and Eugen, who have children of their own now and don't need us. There are no other relatives, so it was easy to come up here, where Luca's family originally came from.

"I myself have not worked since we married; I have supported my husband and children in other ways. I had three miscarriages and could have no more children after Eugen. My husband had a pension, and we supplement it with our own vegetables and selling goat's milk. We have a nanny goat around the back. We did. Before."

"What job did you do before you married?" asks Faye.

"I was a secretary in a government office," says Mme Dobrescu, "very junior. But that was a long time ago and can have nothing to do with what happened."

"We shall be finished very soon," says Faye, trying to reassure someone who seems to need little of that. "The last thing I have to ask is if you are aware of anyone who could wish your husband harm? Did he have enemies, would you say? Anyone who may want to hurt him?" Mme Dobrescu looks dismissive.

"*Non*," she says. "Not at all. Everyone likes Luca, he is a friendly man!"

"May we look inside your house?" asks Benjamin, seemingly from nowhere.

Mme Dobrescu looks surprised and disinclined but, almost immediately, asks Mme Dincă something in Romanian. The old woman indicates that she will take them.

In the other house, it seems even more shack-like. There is a cold wind blowing through and no fire is lit. The Romanian woman does not enter with them but stays outside the door. Both police officers notice her crossing herself as she opens the door for them. Faye feels compelled to slip her fingers into the neck of her sweater, touching the cross.

There is little to look at. A double bed with a tired old *contre-lit*[36] and two thin pillows. Over the window, passing on the darkness from the March day, a piece of raw-edged cloth is pinned up. The blood has obviously been cleaned away. There is a home-made rag rug on the dirt floor, and cooking utensils close to the rough stone fireplace. There is a water tap, from a pump on a home-made wooden cupboard at the back of the single room. Everything is clean, but poor. The prints on the walls are excessively religious, in Benjamin's opinion. Faye, who is closer to her own Roman Catholic upbringing, is not so sure. They don't dispel the atmosphere of threat much at all, though.

***

Colette spends the day in Alba Iulia, in the rain, closely examining museums, artefacts, and listening to guides, whose French is not of the highest order. She has found that some of the English commentary is better – and she can cope best of all with using both at once. She finds the whole experience interesting. Occasionally, she spares a thought for Amélie, probably shopping in the town, when she has finally got out of bed.

Happily, the beds are quite *confortable*.

When she has had enough of the museums, Colette sits in the hotel lounge, with coffee, and reads a bit more of

---

36   counterpane, bedspread

the Stoker biography. She is going to read this alternately with the *Dracula*, to give a measure of academic respectability.

She reads quite a lot about Stoker's childhood, when he had a mysterious illness for seven years from birth, with an overanxious mother (who had been through the Irish Potato Famine and the big cholera outbreak, which had still not then concluded), who was always pregnant. Abraham, named for his father, was one of seven children, in a Protestant family, trained to be afraid of Catholics.

Colette contemplates how all this might have produced a very peculiar child – perhaps it did? Being suffocated by *Mama*, largely ignored by an unambitious and distant *Papa*, threatened by a Catholic majority, whether realistically or not, and, perhaps, not expected to live long?

No one seems to know what caused Bram's illness, although it appears that it was treated by whiskey and opium in liberal amounts. Madame Charlotte Stoker was a tough cookie, who championed good causes but was also deeply interested in the occult and the supernatural. Plenty of material there for fantasy, not to say nastiness of various kinds. Happily, Bram got better and turned into a strong, healthy athlete, although he retained his love of fairy stories.

Tonight, her daughter is going to the escape rooms, and Colette will meet her from there for dinner.

***

Patrice has spent much of the morning reading a book about Romanian history, which seems to have been remarkably restless and violent. He reads through and brackets the Dracula stuff, with a "humph", and finds himself fascinated by the monstrosity of the Ceaușescus. He notes a few things which he wants to remember in the context of his current enquiry. The police in the communist era, *Securitate*, appear to have been just as appalling as he had expected.

In the afternoon, he goes to Alba Iulia to meet with *inspector principal de poliţie,* Iulia Roşca. Her rank – he has a list – is inferior to his, equalling *capitaine*[37] in the *PJ*. She is a dark-haired, forty-year-old, wearing a burgundy business suit, and receives him in a friendly manner, offering coffee or tea as he wishes.

They chat about the cold weather and Patrice asks whether she lives in the city or does she come in from somewhere else? She and her young family live in the city but have a nice flat out towards Bărăbanţ. He says that he is staying near there – with Chief Maria Gadianu.

"I need to talk to you," says Patrice. "As Senior Officer in the case of the murders in Pâclişa and Oarda, and the two in Bărăbanţ itself, I'd like your impressions."

"Of course," says the *capitaine*, in excellent French. "I was also the first officer on the scene at the first murder in Bărăbanţ, although not at the second one, which was discovered the following week. The first was the case of Monsieur Gheorghe Dabija, a local butcher. His was the first we found of all four murders.

"The second was that of Monsieur Artur Mitrea. He was a very old man, who lived alone. It is established that Monsieur Mitrea was killed before Monsieur Dabija. His body may have been lying for quite a while, according to the pathologist. It wasn't even the smell which alerted the neighbours. Someone just randomly realised that she had not seen him for some time. The decomposition was long over."

"I have sent members of my team to Pâclişa, to begin our investigation there," says Patrice. "What can you tell me about the killing in, where is it, Oarda?"

---

37   chief inspector in UK

Capitaine Roşca sighs and tells him that little has been done in Oarda, that was the last killing – at least they hope so. She travelled there – it isn't far, only about fifteen minutes. The body is still with the doctor, for post-mortem. Patrice asks if he can visit to see the body. Are the other bodies being stored there too?

"They are," she says. "We would usually have allowed the families to bury them by this time, but there are, well, difficulties."

"Difficulties?"

"*Oui.* We cannot allow the families to bury them as they wish ..."

"*Quoi?*"

"They want to carry out the old rituals. They want to bury them at the crossroads. With a stake of holly through their hearts."

***

Clémence Godard is back at the baby-food factory, which also makes other canned or bottled vegetable and meat products. She has not called ahead this time; she intends to go in and induce workers to talk to her without the intervention of their *patron*. Instead of approaching via the executive parking spaces and the main door, she parks the Clio as far as possible from the door, wheels herself around the back and locates a large delivery door with no need for a ramp.

There appears to be no security at all, and she goes in following a forklift truck. She is aware that such a vehicle can do lots of damage to any frail human body, not just hers.

There is a marked changing room on the left-hand side, and she wheels into it. No one is there as she adopts a blue plastic overall, bootees, hair-covering mask, and gloves. If no one recognised the wheelchair, she could get into the French Crown Jewels in the *Galerie d'Apollon*! She looks like a worker – if they have any who use a wheelchair.

She approaches a production line which is filling glass jars with something, although she cannot swear that it is baby food. It is beige and semi-liquid. There are two bundles of human-controlled blue plastic attending the line, and she joins them, copying what they are doing – swiping out the occasional empty jar which appears to be cracked, and flinging them into a bucket under the rubber belt. She has little time to reflect on the interest this causes her before the nearest worker shouts out:

"*Allô*, Lucia!" Clémence hopes that a loud grunt is answer enough because the woman is obviously speaking Italian. There seem to be lots of cracked jars; she has only been there a few minutes when a man arrives to remove the box immediately in front of her. He stops to talk. She hopes he is French.

"*Ça va*, Lucia?" he asks, and then says, "You aren't Lucia, though, are you?"

"*Non*," says Clémence, "I am from the *Police Judiciaire*. I am *Officier* Godard. Is this the place where you usually work?"

"*Oui*," he says, surprised, "but I go all over the factory."

"*Quel est votre nom?*"

"*Je m'appelle Paul Frisch*," he says. "I am the senior assistant of this department."

She thinks, in view of his age, around twenty, that he is probably increasing his level of seniority but might be useful anyway.

"I am investigating the presence of glass shards in jars of baby food. I have already spoken to Monsieur Maurice, but he does not work on the line, and I feel someone like you would have better information." The young man blushes a little but is eager to help. "Can you tell me whether all the jars of baby food are produced on this line?"

"*Oui*," he says, "except when we have an emergency." Clémence imagines, for a moment, what a baby-food-factory emergency would look like, before asking him what kind of emergency.

"We might run out of jars if they haven't ordered enough. Or of spludge to put in them."

"Spludge?"

"Oh, that's what we call it," he says. "We don't bother to know what it is; it could be anything. So, instead of finding out what it's supposed to taste of, we just call it 'spludge'. It does well enough."

"How many jars come along the line broken?" she asks.

"I don't know," he answers. "Quite a lot, I'd say. We had *un mec*[38] come to count them last year, but we never heard back. I suppose management did. I estimate that probably about a quarter of the jars are cracked when they get here."

"And how many, would you say, are completely in pieces, shattered?" asks Clémence.

"Some. There is a different person who removes any pieces of glass before they get here. He works over there." Paul raises his arm and waves at someone at the other side of the huge workspace. The bundled-up person saunters over, taking his time. Paul introduces him as Pierre Duflay, *un pote*.[39]

"How are the jars packed when they arrive at your workstation?" asks Clémence.

"They are on pallets," he says. "The forklift brings them

---

38   a bloke, a guy – in Verlan
39   a mate

and sets them on my counter, six pallets high. They are covered in plastic, and I must remove it and place the jars at the pick-up point at the end of the filling line. I take out any bits of glass I see. I have to be very careful, because sometimes they are small and it would be dangerous to leave them in … there is plenty of time, though, because only one pallet can be loaded at once."

"How good are you at spotting the glass?" asks Clémence, sure that this is a weak point in the system. How well does this person see? she asks herself. "Can I see you doing it, *s'il vous plaît*?" He nods and takes her to his workstation. There are three covered pallets on the counter, one on top of the other. Perhaps he was selected for his height; he is tall enough to see the whole of the pallet.

"See," he says, "there is glass in this one. I could see it from the side anyway." He hauls the top pallet down to the space next to the tower of three, produces a sharp knife and removes the plastic. Shards of glass are settled in the right-hand row of jars, between the two marking the halfway point. Pierre removes both jars and extracts eight tiny pieces of glass. Clémence notices that he is wearing not the fragile rubber gloves that she and the others on the line, and Paul, are wearing, but a heavy pair of specialised sharps gloves.

The glass Pierre has removed goes into a bucket under the counter, and he manhandles the whole pallet onto the top of a separate counter, where four more, unplasticked, pallets are stacked.

"I have to reject the whole pallet," he says, "if there is any loose glass in it. The rest will be unpacked by Magdalene this afternoon. She comes on at *13 heures* and she will check each jar for cracks before placing them on the line."

"How much does she find?" asks the police officer.

"Not much," says Pierre. "I'm very good at what I do!"

***

Pucelle is talking in the streets today, searching for people who have a need for food or accommodation, as well as asking them how long they have been in Paris, been around here, have they families, have they seen a large person who is Russian?

She is kneeling, she thinks, almost as much as she did in the convent – approaching bundles of clothes huddled in doorways, chatting with them in a friendly manner, in French, or Russian, or halting Kiswahili. She has given out several cards with the location of the immigrant hostel and the telephone number of the organisation office. She cannot be sure that they will ever use either; it is hard to trust anyone. Pucelle tries to make a beginning on developing this.

She talks to passers-by but hears nothing of the Elephant.

***

"*D'accord,*" says Patrice when they are settled in Madame Gadianu's pleasant dining room, "what do we have? Faye?" The civilian officer is surprised to be called first, when René and Benjamin, as well as Patrice himself, are seated at the table. She starts to speak, gets confused, ruffles her notes, and stops. Patrice tells her to take her time. She is grateful.

"Officer d'Aroque and I," she manages, "interviewed Madame Dobrescu and Madame Dincă, who is the neighbour – Madame Dobrescu is staying with her. She came out to chase us off when we were looking at the Dobrescus' house. She said that Madame Dobrescu was too ill to speak to us, but she didn't insist."

"She took us," says Benjamin, "to her house and we spoke to Madame Dobrescu, who wasn't much like we expected, Faye?"

91

"True," says Faye. "She was wrapped in a shawl and, obviously, upset and grieving still – but she was, well, not quite the peasant we had thought. She described waking and finding her husband dead in the bed. She had slept later than normal …"

"We wondered about her being drugged by the murderer," says Benjamin. "She usually gets up early, as did her husband. But there would be a problem in getting her drugged, *n'est-ce pas*? She said that he had no enemies, everyone got on well with him. He was a friendly man."

"How long have they lived there?" asks René.

"Five months," says Benjamin. "They came to Pâclişa from Bucharest at the end of September, after Monsieur Dobrescu retired from his office job. Their two children, Maria and Eugen, are grown up with children of their own, so there was nothing holding them there. Monsieur Dobrescu originally came from Transylvania."

"He has a pension, from his job, and they supplemented with home-grown vegetables and goat's milk," says Faye. "Then Madame Dincă took us to look at the crime scene."

"She stayed outside," says Benjamin. "Just let us in."

"What was the house like?" asks Patrice, keen not to miss any fine detail.

"Basically, a shack," says Benjamin. "Rough but clean. She crossed herself as she opened the door …"

"Who did?" says René.

"Madame Dincă."

"*Alors*, what was it like inside?" says Patrice.

"Far too many icons!" says Benjamin. "It was quite sickening. Saints and Mary and stuff. Ugh!"

"It was very cold," says Faye. "It had been cleaned, of course, and the bedding replaced. It looked very poor: a dirt floor, a water pump, a fireplace with cooking things. It was quite creepy. Grimms' Fairy Tales."

"*D'accord*. Anything else? Impressions?"

"It would be quite easy," says Faye, "to get creeped out in there, especially if you were on your own. But there was one other thing – apart from the general creepiness and Madame Dobrescu not being quite as we expected.

"She mentioned that she had had three miscarriages after her two children were born. I wondered why she told us that – I don't suppose it has any relevance, does it?" Patrice looks at her for a moment and says that everything is relevant, that is why he asks for on-the-ground impressions. Then he says:

"The answer to that is in Romanian history – not ancient, fairly recent, up to 1989."

"Why 1989?" asks René.

"That was the year the Ceaușescus fell, and the communist regime. Nicolae Ceaușescu's government policy was to increase the numbers of 'pure born' Romanians, so he banned contraception and abortion, and insisted that women have as many children as possible. It was financially viable to have five or even ten children. It is just as the Nazis did, except they insisted that only Aryans have the children."

"That is why," says René solemnly, "there were so many orphans, lots of them physically or mentally handicapped. The Nazis euthanised those instead, *n'est-ce pas*? And the state of the orphanages for unwanted children in Romania was *dégoûtant*.[40] It was an international scandal!"

"I remember reading something about that," says Faye.

Patrice gives them a few moments to process this and then asks René to talk about what he learned from the police officers at Pâclișa.

The detective is well used to doing this; he knows exactly what Patrice wants, and can give it to him precisely:

---

40   disgusting, nasty, abhorrent

"*Patron,*" he says, "I interviewed all three of the officers who attended after Madame Dincă had called in that Monsieur Dobrescu was dead. Radu Balan, the oldest, and first on the scene, hadn't said very much at all – just that Dobrescu had been killed by bleeding out from his throat. He reported that Madame Dobrescu had said, 'They have come back'. When I asked him what he thought that meant, he refused to say the word, but he would write it down for me. He wrote the word 'Vampir' – clear, I should think."

"But *ridicule*!" says Patrice. "Go on. What did the second officer have to contribute?"

"She was Sofia Iordache," says René. "And she had to leave the scene promptly to vomit."

"What was interesting in what she said?" asks Patrice.

"Um," says René, "there wasn't a great deal, although I did make the point that she had only vomited once – and ran outside to do so. Monsieur Balan said that she vomited inside the cottage. I draw from that that there can be discrepancies between participants at the scene.

"She also described the smells. Old people, cabbage, a lot of blood. She seemed to think it was the smell of a lot of blood. Don't quite follow that. And she was wondering who had made the fire, as Monsieur Dobrescu had been discovered by his wife at 07.00. Had Madame made it? Seems unlikely. Maybe the neighbour – but with Monsieur lying there with his throat open?

"But just as she was finishing, she commented on the large number of icons on the walls, said they must have been very religious. Then she said that their religion didn't protect them 'against the Devil'. That struck me because why would she think 'devil', if others immediately think 'vampire'?"

"*Intéressant,*" says Patrice. "But the name 'Dracul' has been mistranslated to mean 'devil' as well in Romanian. It could be that the words are used interchangeably. Or not. The accepted meaning is 'Dragon', both Vlad Ţepeş and his father before him were members of the Order of the Dragon, Dracul in Romanian. Dracula is 'son of the Dragon'."

"Then we have the third officer," says René, "Gavril Cuţov. He was interesting, largely because he did not believe that Balan was really concerned about keeping Madame Dobrescu and Madame Dincă from going back into the house – he didn't believe in his colleagues' concern for them. He thought Balan didn't want to go back in. Neither did Iordache.

"Cuţov himself, of course, was quite okay with that. He was younger, although more senior, much pushier. I thought he would be proof against believing in the supernatural. But just before he left, he commented on how the killer had got in: through the window, so as not to disturb Madame Dobrescu as she was sleeping on the side of the bed away from the window. He said, and I quote verbatim, 'He must have come in the form of a bat'."

Patrice looks at René as though he has gone mad.

"It looks, then, as if we are expected to accept that everyone thinks it's vampires," says Patrice. "Are we expected to go along with that? Um … René, did you think that the officers thought that – or had they been instructed to say it?"

"I think the latter," says René, "although not necessarily all of them. I have a strong feeling that Radu Balan was really frightened. Cuţov wasn't, though. His bat thing was an afterthought. I am sure."

"*Se déplaçant le long*, what do we have now?" Patrice stops, then begins to summarise the case so far, waiting until the end to list the "essences" of the Dobrescu killing. "Monsieur Dobrescu was murdered by a person unknown, who did not disturb Madame Dobrescu, even though she was on the outside of the bed. The victim's throat was opened and, we presume, he bled to death over a period, undetermined. We also assume that he did not wake up while he was dying. Madame Dobrescu awoke unusually late, to find her husband dead.

"Madame, their neighbour, or another person, unidentified, lit the fire between 07.00, when Monsieur Dobrescu was discovered, and the police arriving, which was 07.22. Officer Balan and Officer Iordache, at the end of their night duty, lightly examined the body, although there was no doubt of death and of its surface cause.

"Officer Iordache, even though experienced, leaves to vomit outside and does not return. Officer Balan says that the killer was a vampire. Officer Iordache blames 'the Devil' – or possibly Dracula. Officer Cuţov, although seeming sane in every other way, says the killer must have come in bat form. Which we think was a bit off.

"What are the things we need to attend to, especially?" He looks around the table, waiting for someone to start the list of essentials.

"We need to merge the accounts of René and Benjamin and myself," says Faye.

"*Oui!*" says Patrice, "What things?"

"From René," she says, "the fire, the Vampir, Devil and bat. The reason why Madame Dobrescu mentioned her miscarriages, the position of the window, the oversleeping, or not waking up of both Dobrescus – were both drugged? If so, how? Who lit the fire? Everyone loved Monsieur Dobrescu. How long did Monsieur take to die?"

"*D'accord,*" says Patrice, "we need to talk to the pathologist regarding time of death, cause of death, whether any drugs, and how long it may have taken the victim to die. We shall think about possible motives when we next meet – we shall have more information then, especially about the other victims. We can consider comparisons and commonalities.

"Faye is quite correct about what she has taken as essential, although there is one more thing which she has not mentioned. Madame Dobrescu was not what you expected. She did not appear to be the sort of woman who would be happy living in a shack. She was well spoken and seemingly well educated. What is she running away from? Did it find her? Or him?"

The team keeps silence while it thinks about that.

"In the meantime," says Patrice, "I want copies of the bank accounts of all the victims and their wives, if any. As soon as you like."

11

Amélie has really enjoyed her first visit to an escape room. It is huge fun, and she finds she has a great feeling of satisfaction as her group of six teenagers, formed on the spot from people who didn't know each other, won the prize. It is only a box of chocolate, but they all share it and make plans to meet again and do the same thing.

The teenagers are one French (Amélie), two Transylvanian Romanians (Stefan and Anca), one Wallachian Romanian (Simoneta), and two Germans (Wilhelm and Jan). Amélie has arranged to meet with Anca and Simoneta for coffee tomorrow morning. She is feeling much happier.

Colette and she go for a nice dinner at a nearby restaurant, and Amélie eats a great deal for the first time in an age. Colette is delighted to see her daughter's appetite and smiling face. *Dieu merci!*

"I am going to the icon museum tomorrow," says Colette. "Would you like to come with me?" Amélie's look says her mother has gone too far.

"That sounds exciting," the girl says with a straight face.

***

Monsieur Zabi, *le juge d'instruction*, collects the details of the two cases from the pile of files on his desk and separates them into their relevant places before him. Roxanne, his indispensable assistant, has given him everything he needs to consider the charges which the *Police Judiciaire* wants to bring. He is waiting, only, for Madame Olivier and the new officer ... what is the name? *Oui,* it is Clémence Godard. He doesn't know her. He has only just begun to read when the two *PJ* women arrive. Roxanne brings coffee in immediately. She awaits in ambush.

They exchange greetings and Zabi asks how Edgar is. Fleur's husband had *la grippe*[41] last time Fleur was here. She says he all right now. Juno Zabi, Micah's wife, is also well.

"*Alors,*" says Zabi, "I have not met Mademoiselle Godard previously." He, still standing from greeting them, moves over to the wheelchair and shakes Clémence's hand. Back in his own chair, he asks Fleur for a rundown of the two cases they have brought him.

Fleur, who is well accustomed to this, knows he doesn't want the facts, he has read them already; he wants her reasons for wanting to prosecute, so that he can present them to the *Procureur de la République.*

"The first case," she says, "is that of the baby food from

---

41   the flu

supermarché Della. There has been glass in all of its casserole range, with the exception of the lentil and bacon, for several months. We have investigated and Mademoiselle Godard has discovered that there is very little chance that this has happened in the factory. Their precautions are quite extraordinary."

"So, where do you think it happened, Mademoiselle Godard, and why?" Zabi looks at her in his hawkish mode, and she thinks he must be quite something when interviewing suspects – especially those who are not telling the truth.

"It can only have happened in the supplementary factory, where they get supplies from when they run out of spludge, jars, or lids for jars. It is the premises of Roccier et Cie, near Beauvais. I went there yesterday and discovered several possible faults in their system. I should like your permission to close the factory down and prosecute them on charges of wilful neglect.

"That would stop the glass from hurting children immediately. There is, though, another thing, which we shall have to address after more investigation ..."

"And what is that, mademoiselle? And what, for the love of God, is spludge?"

"Oh, spludge is the stuff they put in the jars. That is what the workers call it. So that they don't have to attend to what flavour it is." Zabi looks revolted but gestures to encourage her to continue.

"I do not yet know who should be charged at Roccier," she says. "There must, I think, be some person with a grudge responsible. But I have not yet identified that person. It seems interesting that it is only the lentil one, the one which is always spared, which contains bacon – there are no other pork products. *Alors,* I suspect—"

"That the glass is aimed at Jews or Muslims, or others who avoid pork?" says Zabi.

"Possibly," says the detective, a little shamefaced because it's silly, isn't it? Zabi's look, like Fleur's, says "Not at all".

They turn to the case of Roger Rannequin, and Zabi raises his eyes to heaven, showing clear whites in the very black face.

"I am pleased," he says, "to see this. At least, I was pleased until I realised what problems we are going to have with his father. You know he is a politician, a senator? *Oui*, well, he's a ... never mind what he is. It will be difficult. Are we okay with that?"

Fleur and Clémence say that they are. Fleur says a good deal more about being glad they've caught him this time – the offence is serious, and she thinks the five times his father has helped him get away with it are entirely sufficient.

"We have, this time, a very good witness," she says, "quite apart from Mademoiselle Godard, who caught him *en flagrant délit*."

"Excellent," says Zabi. "We shall take what enjoyment from this that we can! By the way, was Mademoiselle Godard in charge of both these cases, Madame Olivier?"

"Not really," says Fleur. "She went out to the baby-food place and came back via Rue de Sèvres and happened to see Monsieur Rannequin steal Madame Barthélemy's earrings and pearls. You have her first-person statement in the file."

"Ah," he whispers. "And Mademoiselle Godard brought him in?"

"She did. She took a risk," says Fleur. "A big risk. I have scolded her about doing such things alone. Although I am sure she will still do them."

"Perhaps you should train her better," says the *juge d'instruction*.

Oui, Monsieur *le Juge*," mutters Fleur, leaving the cases with him and rising to leave. On their way out of the building, Clémence says:

"Fleur, there was something wrong with what you said to him about Roger Rannequin. I only saw him take one earring, and there was only one earring, covered with blood, in his pocket."

***

Colette has been looking forward to today's trip out in Alba Iulia. She has booked a tour and an icon workshop at the Museikon. She will stay until *17 heures* and be fairly sure that Amélie is out with her new friends. She realises that she will have to begin to let her daughter go a little bit at a time. Have they brought her up well enough? Time will, as always, tell.

Although the icon museum is situated in an old military building, it has been completely renovated and is clean and bright, with various rooms showing richly decorated paintings of saints and virgins. It is the sort of place Colette really likes, although not strictly a believer. This museum is not devoted entirely to Romanian art, but also has icons from Greece and Bulgaria, and from non-Orthodox faiths.

There are several tours, but she chooses the one which takes in what she would call "the undercroft", an underground space lined with patterns of brick which please her greatly. She walks around by herself when the tour is over; everything is quiet and calm and restores her soul.

In the afternoon, there is an icon workshop, which combines theoretical information and practical experience. She does wonder, though, whether it might be called "making a beautiful mess". She is not gifted in fine art; she has other talents. It is all very enjoyable, even so, and she learns a great deal.

Icons, they say, are not just representations of Jesus, the Holy Mother, and the saints. They are much more than that. They are there to make an almost physical connection between the faithful and God; it is not only the saint who is the bridge, it is the icon also. It "anchors some of the spirit on earth", and carrying out the actual painting of the icon represents a "conversation with God".

It is in this spirit that the practical work is undertaken, and Colette finds it is, indeed, an uplifting experience. Their tutor explains about painting icons on glass and how the technique works – on the reverse of the glass sheet, the highlights are put in first and the "lower" layers in turn, working backwards. It is amazing!

When she gets back to the hotel room, Amélie is asleep again. She wakes enough to say she has had a good time with her friends and will come around for dinner in the restaurant with Colette.

***

The county morgue at Alba Iulia is pretty much the same as any in France. It is in the basement of a government building, it is extremely cold, and smells of death and disinfectant. Patrice, René, Benjamin and Faye arrive there to meet the forensic pathologist, equal to the French *médicin légiste*. *Capitaine* Iulia Roşca meets them there and introduces them to Doctor Elena Apostol, pathologist in charge, who does not have any French. *Capitaine* Roşca stays to interpret.

Apart from the victim from Oarda, whose post-mortem is still in progress, all the bodies are being kept here, in the fridge. The second-found, M Dobrescu, has been here for three weeks. The doctor checks her list and pulls out the relevant drawer. Monsieur Dobrescu is lying, clean, under a white sheet. Dr Apostol draws the sheet down to his waist, revealing the Y-shaped post-mortem incision, well stitched. The wound on his throat, dry now, can be seen to have been catastrophic.

"He partly bled out, although there is blood – hence livor mortis on the underside – so I expect hypovolemic shock," she says, through *Capitaine* Roşca, "and doesn't seem to have woken up between incision and death. Obviously, the wound has been caused by a knife, very sharp, with a flat, non-serrated blade. Simple, single, deep slash. No practice cuts. Probably a man. Could be a strong, experienced woman. Will turn out to be right-handed.

"The toxicology is back, of course, and reveals that he was drugged with a lot of fentanyl. He probably took an hour or so to die. The body temperature was not useable in determining time of death. We might lengthen the time because the house had been very cold, but shorten it because a fire had been made – perhaps to deliberately shift the time of death. But maybe not. By the time I got there, rigor was well established. My report tells you everything else you need to know."

She gestures to Roşca, who nods that she has it. The doctor moves to another drawer and opens it on the well-decomposed remains of Artur Mitrea, the old man who lived alone. Who was killed first?

"Although Monsieur Gheorghe Dabija, the local butcher from Bărăbanţ, was the first found of our corpses," says Dr Apostol, "Monsieur Mitrea would have been the first killed. His decomposed body was found in his bed, but it had been there for a long time – my estimate is not less than two months but unlikely to have been more than six. Decomposition was well advanced, and rigor had passed, obviously. All the technical details are in my report. Tox could not identify drugs, but they are likely to have been absorbed if he were still alive for a while after the injuries. Before death intervened. This might mean that he was alive for longer than the others. Or not. Perhaps not such an efficient killing? That is the question.

"Cause of death was identical to Monsieur Dobrescu, as far as I could tell. As it also was to Monsieur Dabija, the other corpse found in Bărăbanţ. Dabija was probably killed between Mitrea and Dobrescu, although the timing of finding them makes it seem different. Do you wish to see the final stages of Monsieur Nichita Bunea's post-mortem?

"*Oui, s'il vous plait*," says Patrice, before looking around at the others to see whether each is willing. He sees immediately that, although René is fine, both Benjamin and Faye are already pale green. He suggests they go for a coffee. Outside the building. They thankfully depart.

Patrice, René and *Capitaine* Roşca follow the pathologist into the large autopsy room, which seems even colder than the refrigerated section. There are six tables altogether; two are taken: one has a mortuary technician sponging a body, one a pathologist and technician engaged in dissection. The newcomers walk over to the first, which is closer to the half-windows into the street.

The young woman with the sponge is introduced as Audry, who speaks some French. Everyone smiles, nods, and assumes protective clothing. The pathologist, who is already wearing scrubs and bootees, adds a long rubber apron, a head covering, and surgical gloves. Audry steps back, taking her sponge and pail.

"I have already dictated the first part of this," says Apostol. "You can have the transcription when it is typed. It was the usual, well-nourished male of sixty-eight, et cetera. Cause of death, like the others. No vampires, by the way; no sign of teeth marks. No saliva for DNA test. Traces of fentanyl also found. I had the tox screen expedited. Have you spoken to the police who were first on the scene yet?"

"No, they haven't," says *Capitaine* Roşca, not translating for Patrice and René, although they can easily guess.

"This one was a teacher, apparently. The hands and nails fit with that: soft, not manual work." She turns and addresses the policemen:

"It's going to be difficult, this," she says, "because we shall obviously have all the stupid, superstitious fools saying other things. But you are looking for a right-handed person, with access to drugs. Quite strong, although not excessively. How he picks them, I've no idea. *Du-te cu Dumnezeu!*"

Outside, Patrice asks for a translation of what Dr Apostol said when they were leaving.

"Um," says Roşca." She said, "Go with God!"

***

Fleur and Clémence need to discuss both the baby-food situation and the cold case involving the abduction of Nikolas Pellisier from his mother's car two years ago. It is now ten days since the child's glove, complete with name tape, was found in the litter bin.

"I am in some difficulty with this," says Fleur, showing the glove in a plastic evidence bag. It is red, with black-and-white patterns knitted into it, the right size for a smallish eight-year-old. "It demands that something is done about it – right now. But, until the others come back, we have no spare officers, unless we hand it over to another team.

"We have plenty to do, with the baby food and RR, with René's motor thefts in the background. And someone should start looking at the fraud cases. I'd like to have an overview before the *patron* returns. Can we do this too? Or should we hand it off?"

"We can't really do much with René's case just now," says Clémence. "And we thought we could wait until he

105

comes back, *n'est-ce pas?* True, there is more work at the baby-food place, but I think we're nearly there, don't you? And RR is fairly straightforward, yes? We can't do the frauds, can we?"

"*Alors*, you think it's fine? That we can do it all?" Fleur looks at her colleague in alarm. She's young, isn't she? She has great energy. Fleur's own energy is long gone; she works hard, still, but more slowly than she used to.

"I can go and interview people in Beauvais tomorrow," says Clémence. "It shouldn't take too long. And then we'll need to think about what they have told us. Rannequin will be going to the *juge d'instruction* soon, won't he? Has Monsieur Zabi fixed the date yet? Because we will interview the victim before then. Do you want to read the fraud papers and make a summary, while I visit the parents of the boy – Nikolas, is it?"

Fleur, who never looks down at people, does so now, and asks Clémence if she wants to be *commissaire*. The younger detective regards her knees and becomes very red in the face. She is embarrassed. She knows she has gone too far.

"*Je suis profondément désolée*," says Clémence. "I have gone too far."

"I am sorry too," says Fleur. "But you must realise that I am not your friend, I am your superior officer. I hate saying this …" She stops, reluctant to continue. "But, for your own good, remember it. You have the exact problem I have had all my career. It is the reason I am not more senior. I have always gone my own way, done my own thing. The *PJ* is not yet ready for that. There must be discipline.

"Happily, Monsieur Lanier gives us much latitude, and we get more done. But it is vital that you, we, remember who is in charge." She stops again and lets Clémence stew for a count of thirty. Then she says:

"Well, now we've got that over, I can tell you that you are quite right and that is precisely what we shall do. I shall start on the fraud papers; you go and interview Monsieur and Madame Pelissier and see whether there is anything new there."

***

When the team members arrive at their temporary *salle squad* in the Pâclişa police station, Patrice has already drawn up the list of victims, and the police officers who have attended them, on blackboards.

Victim	Police attenders	Family members seen
Artur Mitrea, 84 Retired, Bărăbanţ	Avram Florescu Maria Meleghi	None *Voisin*: Mme Caranfil
Gheorghe Dabija, 66 Butcher, Bărăbanţ	Pavel Theodorescu Avram Florescu	*Femme*: Irina Dabija *Fille*: Maria Dabija
Nichita Bunea, 68 Teacher, Oarda	Roxana Lupu Eugen Danti	*Femme*: Daciana Bunea
Luca Dobrescu Farmer, Pâclişa	Gavril Cuţov, Radu Balan Sofia Iordache	*Femme*: Diana Dobrescu *Enfants*: Maria & Eugen *Voisin*: Elena Dincă

"Strange," says René. "Nothing in common, as far as can be seen on the surface."

"Perhaps further down, though?" says Benjamin. "We only have ages, current locations, and occupations. There must be many other things."

"*Certainement*," says Patrice. "And how shall we find those out?"

"By researching local and national records," says Faye.

"By interrogating wives and neighbours," says Benjamin simultaneously.

"We did learn a few things at the post-mortem of Monsieur Bunea," says René. "That Monsieur Bunea and Monsieur Dobrescu were both drugged; that Monsieur Mitrea may have been, but it was too late to tell; and Monsieur Dabija, we don't know about and will have to ask."

"*D'accord*," says Patrice. "René, go immediately to Bărăbanţ, and interview the two officers who attended Monsieur Dabija and talk also to Madame and Mademoiselle Dabija. I shall telephone Dr Apostol and ask about drugs in Monsieur Dabija.

"Faye, I have a special job for you. How would you feel about travelling to Bucharest alone? I need someone who knows what they are doing to search the national archives for any information about these four men. I shall get Chief Gadianu to get the police databases searched for any mention of their names. Although I suspect there will be no mention of them there."

"I am fine with going to Bucharest," says Faye. "I have been before. My husband and I went last year for a holiday, and I know it quite well. Not the archives, though. But I'm sure I can manage."

Benjamin is looking crestfallen. He is the only one not given a job. Patrice glances at him and says that he needs Benjamin to assist him in some other things, *s'il te plait*.

12

Unsure of whether Monsieur Pellisier is still working at the restaurant Allons Grande in Neuilly, Clémence makes an opportunity to telephone him. He is excited, at first, and she is sorry to disappoint him by recounting that the police have only found what appears to be his son's glove. In a miserable tone, the sous-chef tells her that he can arrange for his wife, Yvette, to be at the restaurant at *15 heures*, when he has a break from his preparation.

Clémence arrives a few minutes in advance and takes the time to flirt with a waiter who oversees serving coffee between meal service. She learns little except that the Pellisiers are still hoping every day that somehow their son will be returned to them – even though it seems unlikely. When Roland Pellisier comes out of the kitchen, his wife is with him, and they join Clémence at a table near the door.

She enquires how they are, expecting they'll say just the same, which they do. She produces the plastic evidence bag with the red glove, and Madame Pellisier bursts immediately into tears. She sobs way down in her gut. Her heart is broken, absolutely. There is no remedy, except the unlikely return of her son. Her husband, also close to tears, says hesitantly that his son will now have *8 ans*.

Clémence regards the couple, seeing that they look older than their years; they are only in their early thirties, and ill, thin, colourless, desperate. Her own heart twists for them. How would she cope, she wonders, if she had a child who had been taken? Imagination fails.

"Monsieur Pellisier, I must tell you that this glove was the only thing found. In a litter bin close to the Tour Eiffel. It has been established that the bin is emptied and cleaned regularly, and it was done in the hour before the glove was found. So, there is no chance that it has been there since" – she hesitates before saying the name – "Nikolas disappeared. It has clearly been put there. What we are asking ourselves is, why?"

"Is someone trying to communicate with us?" asks the mother, between the wrenching sobs. "Is it Nikolas? Has he got away and ...?"

"*Désolée*, madame," says Clémence. "I am really so very sorry, but if Nikolas got away, would he not have come home?"

The mother, face lowered, tears flowing, nods her head several times. Her husband puts his arm around her shoulders, and she rests her head, uncomfortably, on him. Clémence, nearly overwhelmed, prepares to ask another question.

"I have to ask you," she says, "has anything come up in the last two years which may be of help to us? I know that officers have checked up on you every now and then, but nothing has been found during that time."

"What do you mean?" asks M Pellisier sharply. "No one has checked up on us in all that time. We have never lost hope, but obviously you people have. You don't care; you are doing nothing! We have engaged a private detective. Although he has found nothing, at least he is trying!"

Clémence's exclamation of "*Bon Dieu!*" is only in her own head.

***

Colette is extremely tired this morning, having pounded marble floors for the last three days and taken quite a demanding icon course yesterday, and decides to stay in the hotel and read *le Dracula*. The hotel has a pleasant lounge and inexhaustible supplies of coffee and tea, as well as pastries (which are not like home, but fine). She does not want to read in the bedroom; Amélie has taken to living by night and is mostly asleep there.

Colette settles herself at the end of a sofa, close to a window for the light, and places her complaining feet on a velvet ottoman. She orders a pot of coffee and some cake, opens the cheap paperback to the relevant page.

It is becoming clear that there was a lot of interest in phrenology and physiognomy in Victorian days, although by the time Stoker was writing *Dracula*, it had been mostly discredited, officially. *Nonobstant,* he spends a fair amount of time describing the Count's physical features, as if preparing (possibly) to consider him degenerate (or is she going too far forward – because she knows what is going to happen later?):

> *"Hitherto I had noticed the backs of his hands as they lay on his knees in the firelight, and they had seemed rather white and fine. But seeing them now close to me, I could not but notice that they were rather coarse, broad, with squat fingers. Strange to say, there were hairs in the centre of the palm. The nails were long and fine, and cut to a sharp point. As the Count leaned over me and his hands touched me, I could not repress a shudder."*

Colette reminds herself that it was thought, in the times when the novel was written, that fine, white hands were a sign of good breeding. Umph.

Harker's diary describes a gold breakfast service (of immense value), rich hangings and other costly fabrics, but no mirrors. And no servants! Time *sentir un rat,*[42] Harker!

***

Clémence, back in the *salle squad (temporaire)*, tackles Fleur about Monsieur *et* Madame Pellisier having been ignored by the *PJ* for most of the two years since their son was taken. She is angry.

---

42   to smell a rat

"Whose responsibility is it?" she asks Fleur, and Fleur looks puzzled. She thinks for a moment and says that she doesn't know.

"Who will know?" asks the young woman. "I want to know now, so I can yell at them. You have no idea how awful they look, how awful they feel. It is *épouvantable*.[43] The parents are still inconsolable, after two years. They have not had a chance to mourn or to move on. It is just ... I don't know what it is. *Je suis dévasté!*"

"*Désolée*," says Fleur. "I am so sorry that you had to discover that. Although I am glad you did. Now, we shall find out what happened in the aftermath. But I have to say, it would be better if we could actually find Nikolas and return him to them."

"But it's likely that he's dead, *n'est-ce pas?*" says Clémence. "The statistics say the chance of finding an abductee alive diminish rapidly after the first twenty-four hours."

"I know," says Fleur. "But why don't we ignore the statistics for a while? They only operate anything like well on big numbers, they only give us an idea. In this one case, maybe, just maybe, they're wrong?"

"There is something new," says Clémence. "The Pelissiers have hired a private detective and I have his details here. He has found nothing. But it is certainly worth speaking to him, isn't it?"

"*D'accord*," says Fleur. "You know what they are usually like – useless, as well as expensive. But one never knows. Call him. Ask him to come in as soon as possible."

***

Before she calls the private detective, Clémence wheels herself over to the missing persons' department and talks

---

43 appalling, terrible

to the only person there – who, kindly, looks up the Pellisier case file for her.

"You appear to have most of the details correct," says Gilbert, a lieutenant with long blond hair caught into a substantial ponytail down his back (although not a lot on the top of his head). "Not that there's much, you understand ..."

Clémence stares at him furiously. Of course there isn't, you haven't followed it up, *imbécile*! She doesn't say any of this – it isn't likely to get her anywhere.

"Why," she asks, "did you not follow it up?"

The other officer looks down as if the answer will be found lying around his feet.

"We didn't think it was a real case," he says. "There's something funny about it. It should have reached your department over a year ago."

"Well, it didn't." says Clémence. "Why did you think it was suitable for us?"

"Because Lanier's Detail always takes over the funny cases," he says. "And we didn't think the boy was really kidnapped."

Clémence continues to stare as if she doesn't believe this is happening. She doesn't.

***

The *Arhivele Naţionale ale României,* is headquartered in Bucharest and is organised under the Ministry of Internal Affairs. It has forty-two regional branches, one in each county throughout Romania.

This building, in Boulevard Elisabeta, is impressive, and Faye is eager to begin work. This sort of thing is more familiar to her than the quite frightening police work she has been doing. *Oui,* it is exciting, but there is much to be

113

said for the comfort zone. She presents herself at the desk. There is no one attending it, but she is accustomed to having to wait in the French bureaucracy; it may be worse in the Romanian.

Although the office block is not modern, the inside seems clean and organised. It gives hope for a neat plan of what it contains. She does not yet know exactly what she wants, but she has a starting point in mind. If only she can begin to get an idea of the internal organisation, she will, eventually, uncover what she doesn't know she's looking for. She waits.

About twenty minutes after she has arrived, a young woman in a grey knitted dress appears from the room behind the desk and asks her something she doesn't understand. Hardly surprising. Happily, Faye learned a tiny bit of Romanian when she was planning their family trip to Bucharest last year. She knows how to say, "Do you speak French?" That, it seems, is quite enough. The other woman says she does. And asks Faye to enjoy her beautiful country. *Certainement.*

"What may I do for you?" she asks in good French. "Do you know exactly where you want to look in our records?"

"I am hoping," says Faye, "to look at lists of government employees in the last, say, thirty years. Or maybe from about 1980 onwards. Would that be allowed?"

A subtle look of concern passes over the woman's face, to be replaced almost immediately by a look of serious cooperation.

"Of course," she says. "We are open about all those things now. I suggest you start at ..." She looks down onto a piece of yellow paper taped to her desk and reads off a catalogue and room number. Faye writes it down on the back of her hand and asks directions of how to get there.

There is a large plan of Boulevard Elisabeta, 49, on the wall, and the receptionist comes around and points to the reception desk and the place Faye is to go. She smiles and directs the Frenchwoman to the *ascenseur. Tout va bien!*

***

In pursuit of the case of Monsieur Dabija, René travels back to Bărăbanţ to interview the two officers who attended: Pavel Theodorescu and Avram Florescu. Because Monsieur Florescu also attended the deathbed of Monsieur Mitrea, along with Maria Meleghi, he intends to speak to him about that also. When he has seen the police officers, René will visit the widow Dabija.

Pavel Theodorescu is quite a young officer. René would estimate him to be about *25 ans* or so, with a young man's moustache of a thin pale ginger, and matching hair trying hard to keep from its own inclination to slip backwards. He speaks only rudimentary French but has a little German.

René wonders what he will miss if he concentrates on the German language. Then the young man asks if he should get his partner in? Apparently, Avram Florescu speaks French! René is delighted. Maybe he should speak to them together – although this is usually frowned on by the *patron*'s method.

"What can you tell me about the day you were summoned to the home of Monsieur Dabija, the butcher, with the news that he had been killed?"

Theodorescu looks sideways at his partner, who says:

"The family home is in a flat over the butcher's shop. We climbed the stairs and Madame Dabija was standing in the doorway. The daughter does not live there, over the shop. She is married and lives a few doors away with her husband and two children. Madame Dabija was very

115

distraught. The killer had come in the night. Her husband had come home drunk the night before and had fallen asleep on the sofa in the *salon*.

"The sofa was covered in blood. At first, she thought it might be animal blood and he had gone down to slice up some meat for the morning. Then she realised there was too much, and it was his blood, that it came from his throat, that he was dead and cold. She telephoned their daughter, and she had come with her baby in her arms. She was trying to comfort her mother, but the baby kept crying – it was annoying, so the mother sent her away.

"We asked whether Monsieur Dabija had any enemies, and his wife said that the other butcher in Bărăbanț hates him; they are in furious competition – a Monsieur Tabardici."

René sees both the Romanian police officers pale a shade and wonders if M Theodorescu really does speak French but is too shy. Avram Florescu makes up his mind and suddenly blurts:

"But she said it wasn't Monsieur Tabardici who killed Gheorghe; that it was a punishment, from Them!" Despite the movement towards paleness, both policemen seem to be treating that idea with some scepticism. Both laugh slightly uncomfortably – even though Theodorescu claims not to understand French.

"What else?" asks René. "Had the flat been disturbed, the furnishings, anything like that?"

"*Non*," says Florescu. "It was tidy. It looked fine."

"What kind of place is it?"

"It's okay," says the policeman. "Nicely furnished, good but old furniture. Pleasant enough. They are not rich but, I'd say, comfortable."

"Nothing out of place, then," says René, "even though Monsieur Dabija came home drunk the previous night? Does that seem right to you? Or had Madame tidied up?"

"I don't know," says Florescu.

"While I have you here," adds René, "I understand that you also attended the death scene of Monsieur Artur Mitrea, with Officer Meleghi?"

"I did," says Florescu slowly, remembering. "He had been dead some time and was mostly decomposed. There was no smell, well, almost no smell – food in the kitchen had gone bad, so, that was horrible, but almost none of the usual death smell."

"Obviously no doubt that he was dead," says René. "But how did you think he had died? First impressions?"

"Oh, it was clear," says the officer. "There were many bloodstains on the pillow and on the blankets, all around the head, but especially on the level of the throat. You could tell that his throat had been ... er ... torn."

"When you say 'torn'," asks René, "what do you mean?" The officer looks anxious for a moment, then says:

"Perhaps he had his throat cut with a knife? Or maybe he was garrotted?" The tentativeness of the officer betrays that he probably believes neither of these things. René makes a note of the possibility.

"I need one of you to take me to visit Madame Dabija," says René. "I have your report. Is there anything you would like to add?"

"*Pas vraiment*," says Florescu. His colleague, nodding, agrees.

∗∗∗

"I am wondering," says Patrice, in English, when he is connected to Dr Apostol's assistant, Audry, "whether you have any toxicology back for Monsieur Gheorghe Dabija? I need to know whether he contained any drugs ..."

"*Non*," says Audry. "No sign of any drugs, except

alcohol. There was a great deal of that. The killer would not have needed to drug him. We are only surprised that he could walk home – which his wife says he did, apparently. Although he was very accustomed to being drunk. There has been much violent argument and even some fighting between him and his local rival. Odd, though, if the other butcher killed him, that the modus operandi was the same as the other victims ... We are assuming the other butcher did not kill them?"

"*Non*," says Patrice, "that doesn't seem right. Thank you." He hangs up the telephone and turns to Benjamin.

"*D'accord*, Benjamin, what is our next task?"

13

It is, Clémence has discovered, *Commissaire* Frossard's team which dropped the ball in the Pellisier case. She wonders whether it is worth yelling at him – he is on the brink of retirement and, after a long career of waiting, is somewhat overjoyed that it will soon be over. After a long examination of her own feelings, as well as those of M *et* Mme Pellisier, she decides she needs to know anyway.

This does not go well. He nearly cries and she is left feeling like a bully. According to Frossard, there seems to be no particular reason why the neglect happened; it was just crowded off the end of the team's work schedule. He mentions nothing about it being "funny", as Lieutenant Gilbert had said. Clémence returns to the *salle squad* to assist Fleur with the interview of the private detective, M Antoine (Tony) Serres. She will attend the second baby-food factory *demain*.

Monsieur Serres's office is in an old, dirty building at the border between the "respectable" city and the *banlieues défavourisées*. Very down-at-heel gumshoe. He has been asked to call at the *Trente-Six* because his building has no lift – Clémence could not access it, and Fleur would be unsure of her own ageing legs.

When the younger detective opens the door, in answer to his peremptory knock, the private detective swaggers in, dressed in old jeans and a distressed grey jacket, combat boots and a tweed cap. He ignores the woman in the wheelchair and goes over to Fleur's desk. He knows her, apparently.

"Madame Olivier?" he says. "It's been a long time … Tony Serres, remember me?"

Fleur looks at him for a moment and then it gels.

"Of course!" She met him years ago when she was in Vice. He had been looking into something – she can't recall what. They shake hands, ask one another how they are. They are fine.

"What I want to talk about, Tony, is the Pellisier case," says Fleur. "We have a tiny new bit of evidence, and my colleague" – she indicates Clémence – "has been to speak again to the parents. She discovered, to her fury, that they have not been contacted by Missing Persons for almost the whole two years. And that they have hired you to investigate – because we are not doing our job."

"Indeed," says the detective. "They were, are, desperate. What is the new piece of evidence?" Clémence has rolled up behind him and now says:

"It's a glove, with Nikolas Pellisier's name in it. It turned up in a litter bin close to where he disappeared. There was nothing else in the bin."

"May I see it?" Tony asks. Fleur removes it from the top drawer of her desk, still in its evidence bag, and hands it to him. He turns it over a couple of times and asks whether the parents have identified it as being their son's. Clémence confirms that they have.

"What have you discovered in your own investigation?" asks Fleur.

"Not much," says the other detective. "There is nothing to go on. I have followed up a few flimsy leads; talked to several people, coming out of prison, who have this sort of thing in their background. But nothing. I feel as if I am taking the Pellisier's money for nothing. I have recently written down a date when I'll stop investigating. I have told them that if I have nothing promising by the last day of April, that will be the end. I don't want to do it, but it's getting ridiculous."

"That's probably for the best," says Fleur. "Although I'd be pleased to hear any ideas you might have for why this glove may have just appeared, after almost two years ..."

"Um," he says, "I don't have a clue. What could it possibly mean? If it were a gang or something, could someone be trying to reinvigorate the investigation? Could it have been the child, asking for help? No, that's stupid ..."

"It might not be," says Clémence. "I was thinking about the Stockholm Syndrome. Could it be that the child is still alive and has identified with his captors? Going along with them, but sending his parents a message?"

"Not very likely," says Tony Serres. "With the idea, which is borne out by experience, that an abducted child will be dead if not found in twenty-four hours, *petit* Nikolas probably died some time ago, no matter what his mother thinks she knows."

"Does his mother think he's still alive?" asks Fleur.

"She does," says Tony. "She says she is sure he is. She says she would know if he were dead. I can't dissuade her from that."

"What about the father?" asks Clémence. "What is your impression of him?"

"*Plus difficile*," says Tony. "He keeps his own counsel, not much talk, not much emotion. I don't like him, but then, I don't have to."

***

Benjamin d'Aroque, working in the squad room of the police station in Pâclişa, against his will, feels that he did not sign up for paperwork like this. It is a well-known cliché for policepersons to say that they hate paperwork, but he doesn't care about that. *Le patron* has set him to search the Romanian police criminal databases for any traces of any of the murder victims: Dobrescu, Dabija, Mitrea and Bunea. So far, there is no sign of any of them. But there is a lot more to do.

He thinks that at least one of the men must have a previous criminal record. His inexperienced guess is the butcher, Monsieur Dabija. By all accounts he seems to have been a brutal drunk. The precise type. But there is nothing.

***

Today, Colette has decided to read the compulsory chapter of *Dracula* that she has set herself, and then go out on a little trip to Bran Castle, twenty-five kilometres south-west of the city of Brasov. She has booked a guided tour, after all, so that she can get a feel for what the "official" story of the Dracula's Castle is.

Bran is in Transylvania, although very close to the border with Wallachia – which, she thinks, was the area where the original Vlad III Dracula lived in the fifteenth century. Colette knows that Bran is usually referred to as the original of Dracula's Castle, outside Romania. At least, that is where

121

Monsieur Stoker is reputed to have set his story.

Bran, apparently, is the only castle in Romania which matches Abraham's description of Dracula's Castle – although this surprises Colette. Surely not the only one? The castle is a museum for art and furniture collected by Queen Marie in the nineteen twenties and, as such, quite satisfying. The tour group tries to get the guide to talk about Dracula, but she is very resistant.

As the tour breaks up, Colette decides to dine in the restaurant. She selects the almond-flake and seed-crust schnitzel, which is pork, mashed potato and baked garlic, with mixed salad and redcurrant sauce. This, and a glass of Romanian red wine, is entirely the best thing about Dracula's Castle. She thinks that Patrice might, though, enjoy the dungeon!

***

René is driven, by Avram Florescu, to the shop and flat in Bărăbanț, where M *et* Mme Dabija have lived for several years. He asks Avram, specifically, how many years it is. It is the kind of question that Patrice will ask him. Avram says that it is six years, since the butcher had *60 ans*. He adds that Dabija retired from some admin job in Bucharest. Apparently, he had originally trained in butchery when he was young.

René finds this most peculiar. What have butchery and administration in common? Unless the administration job involved some butchery of its own? Could that be? He files it away for further thought.

Mme Dabija has almost nothing to say. She confirms the policemen's story of the death of her husband. She doesn't think the competing butcher killed him either. Her husband was not very good at business, they are quickly

122

going bankrupt. The other butcher is doing well enough. She is not especially sorry Gheorghe has died.

***

Faye's research at the Romanian national archives hasn't borne fruit yet, although she has, for some reason, heard the hunting horn in her ears, which arouses her instinctive sense that there is something to find. She has no idea, at this point, what it might be. But it is strange that all the employee records she has found begin in 1989. This is, she knows, the year when the communist regime ended with the execution of Nicolae and Elena Ceaușescu.

She has made a friend of the receptionist, who is a qualified archivist called Gabriela Balauru. She has been enormously helpful, and Faye has a plot to encourage her to be even more so. The two have taken to having afternoon tea together in a small café close to the archive building.

Today, Gabriela is sympathising with Faye's so far unsuccessful investigation, until the Frenchwoman says:

"I was wondering if it would be permitted to look at some of the government records dating from before 1989? It's possible that the people I am looking for may have been in their jobs before the fall of communism."

Faye expects that Gabriela might pale or flush in embarrassment, but she doesn't. She just takes a deep breath, before saying that that will be fine – but they must go to an annexe in the next street, where some of the overspill from the general collection is housed.

"No one really goes there," she says. "The records from that time are not well kept, a little muddled, a little mixed up. There is, or was, a special archivist who worked there, trying to sort them and put the data on computer. But he died last summer and hasn't been replaced." She looks slightly sheepish, then seems to make up her mind. "I expect I can find the key. Best not to say anything to anyone though. It's just for your own research, isn't it? Just for your book?"

"*Mais certainement!*" lies Faye.

14

Odd, thinks Clémence, driving her sunshine yellow Clio into the car park at Roccier et Cie, to be visiting a second factory in just a few days, when she has never been in one before. This is very similar to the first, although smaller. She follows the same procedure she followed before and gets to a similar place: the conveyer belt where jars are filled with food.

It is not, however, either as efficient or as clean as the factory she visited previously. She looks for the worker who checks that jars aren't broken and discovers that there is no one there. Clémence is unable, at this distance, to see what is being put into the jars. It has a different colour, not the beige-yellow colour that all the *supermarché* Della spludge seemed to be; more orange. She suddenly realises it is little carrots going into the jars. So, probably not baby food then.

What is probably a woman, bundled in a hygienic outfit, stomps up to Clémence and demands to know who she is. The young policewoman reaches for her badge and identity card, displaying it to the woman. Who takes a step back, as if expecting Clémence to take out her gun and shoot. The detective says she is not looking for criminals, only wanting to talk about the production line.

"Why? Who has done something wrong?" asks the woman. She seems pugnacious. There could be trouble.

"I am investigating," says Clémence, going for openness, "the glass in baby-food jars at Della *supermarché*. I understand that you sometimes help them out with extra jars when they are in short supply. Is that true?"

"*Oui*," says the woman, pulling down her face mask, revealing a fierce, middle-aged face. "They are short at the month end often. They do not order enough because they are trying to save money. This is usually costing them more money anyway. *C'est stupide!*"

"I see," says Clémence, "that you are filling jars today with carrots. Do you do baby food on different days?"

"We don't do baby food at all!" says the woman. "We only provide them with the jars when they have none. We pack vegetables and pickles. We are not involved in this broken glass business. They are trying to implicate us to conceal their own guilt!"

The young detective has little idea what to ask next; the woman's answers are a barrier and an end. Is there anything else she can reasonably pursue? She doesn't think so. She is suspicious about the anger.

***

Patrice, alone because all other members of the team are occupied, goes to Oarda to follow up on Nichita Bunea. He knows some things because of having attended the latter part of M Bunea's post-mortem.

Although Oarda is, structurally, part of the city of Alba Iulia, it is essentially a small village with, Patrice remembers from Melichian's notes, under two thousand of population. It does not take long to find the address, which is a small house, in a small street.

Madame Bunea, a tall woman in her well-preserved fifties, with dark-blonde hair, a pair of green slacks and a baggy beige pullover, opens the front door. She stands back for Patrice to enter as soon as he has identified himself.

She leads him into the sitting room, which opens straight out of the street. He politely removes his shoes without being asked. The place is tidy, clean and bright, with neutral colours and pleasant furnishings. Nothing is expensive, but displays excellent taste. There is a scent of furniture polish; sandalwood, says Patrice's nose.

"Madame," he begins, "I am very sorry for your loss, but it is important that the circumstances around your husband's death become clearer. Because of the situation, the local police have asked my team, from Paris, to work with them under the agreement between our two countries.

"First, I need to ask whether your husband, or both of you for that matter, have anyone who might wish to do you harm? I know it is a difficult question, but it is always the first we must ask."

"Yes," she says; her English is very good. "The police, the Romanian police, asked me that. I'll tell you what I told them. My husband and I have lived here for over fifteen years, since we found employment in the schools. Different schools. I am head teacher in the Oarda High School; although my speciality used to be geography, I don't get much opportunity to teach it these days! My husband taught English and general subjects in the Middle School. His job was a little further away at the edge of Alba Iulia.

"We are, were, well settled here and everything was working out well. We took part in village events and issues, although never got involved in politics – that isn't good for a teacher. We have many friends and neighbours, and I can venture to say we are, were, quite popular. We have always helped people where needed and got on well with everyone."

"Then you would say that neither of you had any enemies?"

"Yes, I should say that. I can't think of anyone who would have any problems at all with us."

"There is no parent of a pupil who is angry with you about his child not doing well at school? Nothing like that?"

"Nothing like that."

"May we go on," says Patrice, "to your life before you were here in Oarda? Where did you come from? Have you travelled the world? Have you lived in other countries?"

"Not really," she answers. "We both travelled when we were students. And of course Nichita spent some time in England. I visited there but my English is mainly school-learned in Bucharest. We both worked in Bucharest before we came to Transylvania. We had jobs in high schools."

"Were you native to the capital?"

"No," she says. "Neither of us were. My husband came from Constanţa, on the Black Sea. I am from Moldavia. But we were both at university in Bucharest; that is where we met."

"Do you mind me asking if you had any children?" asks Patrice, a sudden possible insight moving in the back of his head.

"No, we never wanted children," she says. "I suppose we had enough at school!"

***

In Bucharest now, Faye and her friend Gabriela are walking to the annexe where there are some records – "Don't expect them to be complete" – from pre-1989. Gabriela seems concerned that Faye will not be able to find what she needs, and seems to experience that as a failure in her hospitality. Faye hopes this will mean that Gabriela will give her all the help she needs.

They arrive at a grey concrete building of two storeys, with a hefty door in the front. The door is painted Romanian-flag blue and has fearsome hinges on the right-hand side. The building does not have any windows on the streetside. Gabriela says something resembling "Here goes" and takes out a heavy iron key which looks as if it would open Dracula's Castle itself. Faye does a delighted little shrug and follows her friend inside as she snaps the strip lights on.

The annexe, it appears, is quite well lit. The centre of the long room is filled with double-sided desks, with an individual lamp on each, but the tables under the far-side windows are piled with papers and files and the occasional bound book – muddled and dusty, as if someone has been looking for something, walked out in the middle and left everything all over the place. There is no sign of any technology.

Gabriela sets her handbag on the closest desk and says there is not likely to be any coffee; she will go and get some later. In the meantime, can Faye give her any idea as to where she would like to start? Faye does not know, makes a flying guess.

"Let's begin in July 1987," she says. "And let's look at government officials. Are there lists of them? I'm thinking of, possibly, the Ministry of Internal Affairs. Was that a thing back then?"

"*Non*," says Gabriela. "The Ministry of Internal Affairs existed after the war – from 1946 to 1972, when the director was executed for spying for the USSR. The whole thing was purged after that and became the Interior Ministry, known to be filled with Communist Party activists.

"It was responsible for internal security, so for the police and the *Securitate* – that was the secret police – as well as things like uncovering foreign espionage and domestic political threats to the regime, supervising routine police work, and local fire departments."

"A lot of responsibility then?" says Faye.

"Definitely. And after, for about ten years, they padded the police departments with activists and Ceauşescu loyalists, so that they could consolidate the regime. In the process increasing the numbers of officers from around two thousand to twenty thousand."

"Wow!" says Faye. "So what had I best look at first? Have you any thoughts? Noting that I'm looking for four men who were in Bucharest pre-1989, but I don't know from when ..."

"I was wondering," says Gabriela, "whether you know if the four men were Ceauşescu loyalists, or maybe dissidents?"

"I really don't," says Faye. "Just that they were here, and that they moved away, to various places in Transylvania, and that they are recently dead."

"I do have some information about the situation of the Ministry of the Interior in the year 1989," says Gabriela. "It was, of course, a very important year, when Romania rose up against the Ceauşescus, and the communist regime was overthrown." She walks over to a desk piled with junk and extracts a dark-blue plastic binder, bringing it back to the desk where Faye is sitting.

"Look," she says, opening the binder. "This tells us all about the *Securitate* being, in that year, the largest part of the Ministry of the Interior. So, I think it may well be that we'll find the names of your men in those records – although I'll have to find the records first." She stops and looks thoughtful, then says: "It isn't really to anybody's advantage for anything like names to be easily found ...

"And they were the largest secret police organisation in proportion to the general population of a country. Agents were everywhere, and civilians were also supposed to report irregularities to them, as well as people's ordinary opinions – in case they could be classified as illegal or disloyal.

"My mother told me that they were always entering houses and businesses to check on anyone they suspected – which was everyone! And police and judges were so corrupt that justice disappeared completely. There was censorship of all mail, and typewriters had to be registered. Oh, and the *Securitate* collected samples of handwriting, so people who had written seditious words could be identified."

"They worked on all kinds of levels then," says Faye. "Are they thought to have been successful, or is it known that they were sloppy? Some secret police are."

"They were certainly successful in frightening the people," says Gabriela. "My parents and grandparents were deeply afraid – and I don't think any of my relatives was particularly seditious. But they weren't rabid communists either ..." She looks vague, as if thinking whether she could describe anyone in her family as either pro or con. "I don't think I can say anything about that; they just wanted to get on with their lives. Unhappily, it was difficult in those days to have any kind of life, unless one was political. In the correct way."

"What happened to all those officers?" asks Faye. "All the ones who increased the numbers in the Ministry of the Interior? All those in the police?"

"Oh," says Gabriela, "many of them are still about. NATO and the European Community requested that *Securitate* personnel be purged before Romania was taken into both organisations, but many are somehow still there. Newspapers and the television channels show us scandals regularly. But, of course, some of them are retired ..."

***

Patrice is weighing in his mind whether Madame Bunea's comment about not wanting children is to go on his lists of "essentials" for this case. His stomach, as well as the back of his head, says that it is. He wonders about the other two widows' situations on such – although he recollects that, on his blackboard in the *salle squad* in Pâclişa, Monsieur *et* Madame Dabija did have a daughter. And they have no way of knowing, currently, whether M Mitrea had either wife or offspring. How could it be relevant? There is something, though, which might make it so.

Still in Oarda, he calls at the police station to speak with Officers Lupu and Danti, who attended M Bunea's death scene.

He asks to speak to the officers one at a time, and Mlle Roxana Lupu arrives first. Patrice imagines that her last name means something like "wolf", and he can see the family resemblance. She is short and solid, with thick grey hair roughly pushed under her cap, and a police uniform which has seen better days. He would estimate her age at around fifty. He has the assistant *commissaire* for an interpreter, as Mademoiselle Lupu does not speak either French or English.

"I am investigating the death of Monsieur Nichita Bunea," says the French detective, "and I should like you to describe to me what happened from when you arrived at his house until you left. I shall be talking to your colleague, Monsieur Danti, later."

Commissaire Paduche translates, and Lupu begins to describe what happened. She is well accustomed to reciting her findings and does so in a slightly sing-song narrative voice.

"My junior colleague and I arrived at the Bunea house in Oarda within ten minutes of the call of Daciana Bunea, the victim's wife. She met us in the doorway, and we went in and straight to the bedroom, where Nichita Bunea was lying in bed with his throat bitten open. There was a lot of blood, which I couldn't understand, because why would there be blood when the killer would have wanted to drain it all? Cases of this, which I have seen before, have had their blood drunk through the incision in the throat, wasting none.

"Mr Bunea was obviously dead, and I ordered Officer Danti to telephone the coroner and scene-of-crime team immediately. Then I left the room and told Officer Danti to guard the bedroom door until the SOCOs and pathologist arrived.

"Then I spoke to Mrs Bunea. She was, of course, upset, but she is a strong woman, and answered my questions quickly and completely. I asked her whether she had been in the house all night. She said she had. I asked her whether she had heard anything. She said she had not. I asked her if she had woken up during the night – was there any disturbance? She said she had not awoken. And there had been no disturbance.

"I asked her if her husband had any enemies. She said he did not. They are part of the local community and have been accepted there for many years. That is all. Sir."

Patrice, a little dazed by her rhythmic recitation, asks the officer whether she had met Mr and Mrs Bunea previously. Officer Lupu says that she has seen them in the village, but she didn't know them to speak to. That appears to be all she has to say. *Commissaire* Paduche says that she will have the tape transcribed and email him a copy as soon as possible.

When Lupu has saluted and left, Paduche says she is sorry that he got so little from the officer. Patrice, who got one thing, says he is fine but asks whether many of Paduche's officers believe in vampires. He says this lightly, as if joking, but the *commissaire* looks serious and says that there are still many people who believe in the old stories; this sort of thing doesn't easily go away.

"Even with the length of the communist regime?" he asks. "I'd have thought that forty-two years would have been enough to have laid superstition to rest ..." He is suddenly aware that he has allowed his French rational mind full rein when he perhaps should have bracketed it.

"In a country which traces its history back beyond the Romans?" asks Paduche.

***

"*Papa* rang," says Amélie when Colette gets back to their room in Alba Iulia. The girl is dressing to go out and Colette immediately clips her good taste and consideration of what is appropriate to a short lead.

"When?" asks her mother. "Is everything all right? Is there something wrong?"

Amélie rolls her eyes. Typical of *Maman* to think there's something catastrophic.

"This afternoon, about *16 heures*. Nothing is wrong. He just wanted someone to talk to."

"That would be you, then?"

"*Mais certainement!* No really, either of us would have done. He's feeling lonely."

"Oh, the poor lamb. Did he want ringing back?"

"*Oui.* Any time this evening, he said. Unless you were going out. We had our conversation when he rang."

"Did he say anything ... er?"

"About anything? *Non.* He kept absolute silence." She looks at her mother, as if wondering if she has gone too far. Decides she hasn't, laughs to cover it. "He said he's working hard and it's quite a slog."

"Despite being in another country? I'd have thought he'd be enjoying the differences."

"Um. He did say that some people here still believe in vampires. Even after forty-

two years of communists, and twenty-seven years since that ended. I think twenty-seven years is more than enough time to grow back into superstition, don't you?"

"Hard to say. I am very slow at reading *Dracula* – and it isn't even the right book, I don't think. I need something about the Ceauşescu regime to give me a more modern idea."

"I thought you said that the writer of *Dracula* never went to Romania," says Amélie. "I'm surprised you are bothering with his book."

"I know," says Colette. "And there are other books, and papers, about vampire lore, in lots of countries, and even some outbreaks of real vampirism in various places. I should be reading them, shouldn't I?"

"You should," says Amélie firmly. "I must go now. I am meeting my friends to go to the youth club. Do you like my outfit?" She knows this is daring, her mother will think it horrible.

"It's interesting," says Colette. "And the scarf is very colourful." It is true, the scarf is very colourful. It is green, and red, and pink, and magenta, and sky blue, and black. Unhappily, it is tied, tightly, around Amélie's bare thigh.

∗∗∗

Roger Rannequin is just as arrogant and privileged as he looks on the television in his racing exploits. His hair is cut and styled by one of the most prominent hairdressers in Paris, and Clémence is certain it is also dyed. The colour,

134

a pinkish biscuit-beige, is one she has never seen on anyone else. The racing driver's skin is also a weird colour, only found in a tanning booth. Is everything about him artificial? She suspects it is.

"Tell me," she says at the beginning of the interrogation, "what you were doing in the Rue de Sèvres on the day you were arrested?"

Rannequin looks down at her, which is not difficult as he is tall and she is sitting down. His face has a sneer built in.

"I was not there," he says. Clémence is surprised that he lies; he knows that she knows that he was. She handcuffed him to her wheelchair.

"You were there," says Fleur. "We know that already – although we do have three witnesses who say so, in addition to the arresting officer, Mademoiselle Godard."

"Do you know Monsieur *et* Madame Barthélemy?" asks Clémence.

"*Qui?*" he asks.

"The lady and her husband from whom you stole some items," says Clémence.

"*Non,*" he says.

Fleur produces an evidence bag from under the table and indicates, through the plastic, a rope of pearls and a gold earring shaped like a shell. She asks him whether he recognises the jewellery. He shakes his head. Never seen it before in his life.

Clémence tells the tape recorder that the prisoner is indicating that he does not recognise the jewellery. She removes it from the bag and lays it out on the table. She says that there is a pearl necklace, numbered A1, and an earring, numbered A2. These will be trial exhibits should the case go to court. He says:

"I have never seen them before. You have planted them on me!" He looks directly into Clémence's eyes, accusing her. "It is you," he shouts. "It is you who has done it. This is corruption in the police. In broad daylight!"

Neither of the detectives can easily believe he is saying this; it is stupid. Fleur tells him to calm down, and that he is charged with the theft of gold and pearl jewellery, to the value of thirty thousand euros. The uniformed officer standing by the door takes him down to the cells.

15

In the *salle squad* in Pâclişa, Benjamin d'Aroque is trying to find himself something to do. Everyone else is out, he alone is office-bound. He has done as Patrice asked and searched for the names of the murder victims. Found nothing at all. Now what?

He decides to write the case out as a plan. This is a way he was taught at the Academy. It may help him to see it in some context. He knows that most police officers, detectives anyway, have some method of seeing things more clearly. He does not quite know what is Patrice Lanier's method. He himself feels confused.

There is the list of victims, their wives and families (if any), as well as the police first responders – on the blackboard, where *le patron* wrote them. He makes a title on the top of his notepad. Underlines it. *Bon!*

A quick list of all the names from the blackboard. He doesn't need it because it's up there, but for completeness, *oui*. As he does this he thinks of Faye, in Bucharest, wondering how she is doing in the archives. It is not the sort of job he would like – all that dusty paper or, possibly, smeary computer screens. Yuk. He picks up his cell phone and rings Faye's number. She answers on the second ring:

"*Allô, c'est* Faye Benoît."

"Faye, it's Benjamin. *Ça va?*"

"*Ça va?* I'm fine. I'm in the National Archives in Bucharest with my friend Gabriela."

"Have you found anything yet?" asks Benjamin. "Or is it difficult?"

"*Non,*" she says, "it's fine. We're getting on well, as everything is open now." As she says this, she knows it is not true, and that Benjamin won't believe it any more than she does. About Gabriela's beliefs, she's not sure. She asks Benjamin what he is doing currently.

"I'm helping," he lies, "to interview witnesses and the police who originally did that. Also, I have checked the police databases for the names of our victims – but found no trace. So, none of them have police records. Or else they have been removed ... I am just writing out some of the things we already know so that I can give a report when *le patron* returns from Oarda later."

"You're busy, then?" says Faye.

"*Oui*. As are you by the sound of it."

"I am. I'll probably be back where you are in a day or two. *À bientôt!*"

"*À bientôt!*"

As soon as Benjamin hangs up his cell phone, there is a call from Patrice, asking him to go to Bărăbanţ and knock on doors, together with Officer Meleghi, who will meet him there. They should ask as many neighbours of Monsieur Mitrea as possible for whatever they know about him. They should focus on whether he had a wife, ever worked in Bucharest, had any children. And how long had he lived at the address where he died?

"*D'accord, patron,*" says Benjamin.

***

"How are you doing with the fraud papers?" asks Clémence as she looks up from the Rannequin file on her desk. Fleur is staring into space as if she were *en rêverie*.

"*D'accord*," says Fleur, then stops. "*Non*, I am doing nothing. I can't understand any of this. We need a specialist."

"Do you know one?" asks Clémence.

"*Non*," says Fleur."

"Who might, though?" says Clémence. "An accountant or lawyer or someone?"

"Going to have to be one of those," replies Fleur. "Do you think maybe *Juge* Zabi might know?"

"He could do. When are we going back to him with RR?"

"Tomorrow," says Fleur. "The preliminary hearing is set for *10 heures*, and the *Procureur de la République*[44] will be there too. So, he might prove another source? *D'accord*, we'll see what we can find."

***

There is someone else who has seen the Elephant. Pucelle is, by now, surprised, as she seemed to have disappeared totally. Only a couple of Russian immigrants from their old building, the twins, Olena and Oksana, living with their boyfriends and assorted children in the one flat, remembered seeing her there – in her original role as a very large drug dealer. Male.

This new person is an African, with halting French, possibly from West Sahara, who swears he saw the large person a few kilometres away, when he lived in that area. He tells Pucelle the name of the street, which she has not

---

44   prosecutor

138

yet explored. She is halfway there when she realises that he may have lied, hoping for money – although she did not give him any. She cannot afford to refuse even dubious leads.

Pucelle walks all the way – the charity has not given her any travel allowance – and talks to several people. No one has seen Elephant. She hands out cards for their possible benefit and asks them to leave a message for her about *l'Éléphant,* should they see her or hear anything about her.

***

Faye and Gabriela are searching through files that the archivist has turned up in her first search. What has proven to be a list of names from a local newspaper which, in 1987, published details of *Securitate* members, still in the secret police but who are supposed to have been purged previously, is halfway down the file. The newspaper article is photocopied and pasted to a blank sheet of copier paper, in turn punched and filed in a green folder about something quite different. Sheer chance appears to have led Gabriela to it.

There is no trace of any of the names they are looking for – but they reason that there must be other folders with similar lists, as well as anything official, which they have not yet located.

Gabriela has a few ideas of where there may be things like the newspaper tell-all article, turns to the far side of the room to see if she can find them. Faye is concerned that that sort of thing may well help, but that official paperwork will be better. She is, really, still trying to orient herself amongst the jumbled papers. There is no possibility that she can go through all of it in the restricted time she has available. Even if they were in proper order, it would take someone like Gabriela to locate what the Frenchwoman needs.

They have not yet found any organising principle which would help. If all the folders for, say, 1972, were purple ... Faye decides to attack the piles of what seems like junk and hopes to uncover two things which appear to match. At least in colour.

She chooses blue files. Immediately finds that there are three different shades of blue – dark, medium and light. Her next choice is dark blue, and she selects the nearest two dark-blue files randomly. One says it is for 1984 and one for 1978. One is about deployment of police in the village of Micești, which is close to, and administered by, Alba Iulia. The other is about secondary schools in Oradea, up near the Hungarian border.

Problem in her logic, Faye tells herself. Just because the files say they are about one thing, it doesn't mean that they are about that thing. Anything could be hidden in the middle. Gabriela's newspaper list was concealed in the centre of something entirely different. It doesn't help that all the text is in Romanian, and way beyond Faye's capacity.

She was hoping that, because Romanian numbers are Arabic or Roman, like French, she would be able to discern the year of the files' compilation. It is her only hope. She calls Gabriela, who walks over to where she is standing, surrounded by bewilderment.

"Gabriela," she says, "I think I may have a *petit* way into this. I think it's all I've got."

"I haven't found anything else yet," says the Romanian, "so, please, if you can think of something ..."

"It's just exploiting randomness," says Faye. "All I can really understand, without you to help me, are numbers, probably they will be years. I am thinking that, if we both rush at all this mess and find folders which are either the same colour or carry the same year, we might be able to organise a bit. I thought that all the files for one year might be the same colour, but they aren't. And, of course, as we saw with your newspaper thing, random subjects are inserted in the wrong file anyway …"

"*Oui,*" says Gabriela. "I am concerned that we shall have to examine every bit of paper in the whole archive to find what you want. I suppose, though, if there are coincidental matches, we might just find something?"

"I'd much rather examine every bit of paper and make absolutely sure," says Faye. "But I have no time. Do you believe in luck?"

"*Mais certainement,*" says Gabriela. "We are a Latin people, we all believe in luck!"

***

"Monsieur *le Juge,*" says Fleur, presenting Roger Rannequin to *Juge* Zabi. Both Clémence and the *Procureur de la République* are seated behind them, closer to the wall of Zabi's office. Roxanne, his indispensable assistant, is assiduously taking notes. A defence lawyer no one knows sits by the window, saying nothing. He is most likely a placekeeper.

Fleur reads from her notes, including the unlikely story of Clémence's capture of the thief.

Zabi, stunned, looks under his long eyelashes at the young detective and asks her if she has anything to add to Madame Olivier's story. She doesn't.

"There will be witnesses?" asks the *juge.*

"*Oui,*" says Fleur, "the victim and her husband, Monsieur *et* Madame Barthélemy; a Dr Benet, who was passing by and wiped the blood from Madame's ear; and Detective Godard herself, of course."

"And you have no problems with any of these witnesses?" asks the *juge*.

"Not at all," says Fleur. "Although there is a slight difference between what Madame Barthélemy says she lost, and what Monsieur Rannequin had in his coat pocket."

"Ah," says Zabi. "And what might that be?"

"Monsieur Rannequin had a double string of pearls in his pocket, and one 22-carat gold earring. Madame says she lost both her earrings as well as her pearls."

"*D'accord.*" Zabi focuses on Roger Rannequin and asks him whether he is ready to make a confession.

"*Non, putain de pas,*[45]" Rannequin almost screams.

"*Non, putain de pas,* Monsieur *le Juge*!" instructs Zabi loudly. Rannequin looks sheep-faced and mumbles "*Désolé*" under his breath. Even he realises it is a mistake to swear at the magistrate.

"I did not do it," mutters Rannequin. "Why would I? I am rich. I don't want her vulgar jewellery! I plead not guilty."

"Are you ready, Monsieur *le Procureur*, to proceed against Monsieur Rannequin?" asks Zabi.

The *procureur* says he is.

***

René writes his impressions of the Dabija flat and of Mme Dabija, and finds he has nothing, except the after-image of a not very successful marriage. He expects that Mme Dabija will not stay in the town very long. She will be off, possibly with a lover. But on reflection even that is fantasy. He has nothing. He tries to clear his mind and wishes that Patrice was back, or Fleur was here, or something.

Avram Florescu dropped him off at the station house in Pâclişa, after they had interviewed Mme Dabija. The burly

---

45   No, I'm f***ing not!

policeman had said very little all told. He had, however, been somewhat reluctant to enter the flat, the crime scene. René had spotted him making a super-speedy sign of the cross, thinking he was not observed.

He perches on the side of the bed in the dormitory and gets his notepad out. What did I achieve today? he thinks. Where are we now? He writes "Irina Dabija" and notes his impressions of her in a free-form description. All the things he noticed. That the flat had a temporary feel, as if Mme Dabija has already packed her bags. That she is several years younger than her late husband. And quite chic. That she is convinced that his competitor, the other butcher, has not killed him, implying, perhaps, that another known person had? That he, René, had been struck by the oddness of Gheorghe Dabija having held an administrative job in Bucharest and then becoming a not very good butcher in Bărăbanţ.

That the phrase had occurred to him:

"What have butchery and administration in common? Unless the administration job involved some butchery of its own?"

Interesting.

***

"What exactly do you think you were doing last night?" asks Colette, when she has managed to wake her daughter from the undead.

"Um, *Maman* ... we went to a club, or something. It was very loud!"

"*Tu plaisante!*[46]" says Colette. "Were you drinking?" She

---

46 You are kidding me!

goes on, not waiting for a reply. She can smell alcohol on the sixteen-year-old daughter from here.

"You have *16 ans*, Amélie! You should not drink when you are away from home!"

"But you have let us have wine and water since we were little!" shouts Amélie. "Why change your mind now?"

Colette, who had known that the common French practice would one day rebound on her, is not sure what to say. It is illogical.

"What were you drinking with these friends of yours?" she asks.

"Vodka," says Amélie, not thinking to lie. Colette, surprised that she is surprised, has never thought to forbid spirits. She just never expected her children to be aware of them. Wrong.

"Thank you for telling me the truth," says Colette. "Were there any drugs at this club?"

"Yes," says Amélie, "there was, at least, Ecstasy, but you know I don't do drugs!"

"And how would I know that?" asks her mother.

"Because I have told you!" says Amélie.

"And you never lie. Of course."

"Do I?" asks the girl. "Do I? No, I don't lie. I try not to lie. Oh, never mind. *Va-t-en!*[47]" She turns over in bed and faces the wall. Colette is steaming with anger such that she could, for the first time in her life, slap the daughter. She turns, picks up *Dracula* and her notepad from her own bed, and stamps out of the room.

***

In the lounge, she settles in a bucket chair, crosses her legs, and starts to read chapter three. As Jonathan Harker begins

---

47　Go away!

to feel he is a prisoner in Castle Dracula, Colette's concentration slips back to her daughter, and she looks away from the very small font size of the cheap text, staring at her feet.

She is wearing her bedroom slippers, strident magenta and fluffy (a Christmas present from Jean-Pascal). She blushes and wonders whether anyone else has seen them. They would if she stood up and walked to the *ascenseur.* She attracts the attention of the waiter and asks for coffee. Bluffing it out.

Colette is already a touch bored with Monsieur Stoker's stilted language. He never uses one word where twenty-five would be more baffling. And his efforts to make the Count's English sound as if it were spoken by a foreigner is *bof.* Her coffee arrives, with a sweet pastry, brought by the young woman who has served her before.

The Romanian's intuition is right; Colette's anger has made her forget she really wants something sweet. She is grateful. It occurs to her that she might get premier information from the girl if she were to speak to her about Dracula. She asks if she can have a word. The young woman, staying standing, asks Colette what she can do.

"You are Romanian, aren't you?" she tries in English.

"*Oui,*" says the waiter, in French.

"I am reading Monsieur Stoker's *Dracula,*" says Colette, even though the waiter can probably see that well enough.

"*Oui.* Are you enjoying it?"

"I have hardly read enough yet," says Colette, "but I am wondering about what native Romanians might think about the book. With Monsieur Stoker never having come to Romania and that ... Is he representing the country well? Or is it a laughing stock for your countrymen?" The young woman drops into an adjoining chair, introducing herself as Lidia.

"I think we have mixed feelings," she says. "Some are, like, it's a parody, it's awful, it misrepresents a modern country in Europe. Like, we don't have superstitions, we aren't primitive peasants!"

"You don't hold with it, then?"

"I didn't say that. Others say leave it alone, it's good for tourism, isn't it? I am an economics student. I know we need all the foreign tourists we can get! But I am not so young or naïve that I don't know that religion and superstition, what they call 'the old ways', go back millennia. No nation throws that off easily, even with extreme restriction during Ceauşescu. That just replaced one monster with another. Afterwards, maybe it just reversed?"

Colette, who hadn't expected a short lecture from an economist, signals her understanding, and Lidia picks her tray up and goes back to the kitchen. Colette opens the book to page twenty-four. On the next page, as she reads the words describing Dracula making Harker's bed (confirming that he has no servants), and then setting the table for dinner, she cannot help but hoot with laughter.

16

Benjamin d'Aroque drives, in the borrowed police car, to Bărăbanţ to meet Officer Meleghi. He sees the *petite* officer standing outside the station, in a brand-new dark-blue uniform and hat still showing signs of its recent blocking in manufacture. She has been waiting patiently for him and is into the passenger seat like a streak of lightning.

He tells her who he is, and she introduces herself as

"Maria". She is rather pretty, brunette, and has a turned-up nose. He is enchanted. She also speaks good French. He asks her to direct him to the street where Monsieur Artur Mitrea was found dead – they are to knock on doors and ask neighbours about him.

The first person, of course, is Madame Caranfil, an elderly, very, next-door neighbour, who has obviously spent her life lifting old-fashioned lace curtains and spying on the people next door. And next door to that.

She asks them in and gives them instant coffee. They ask for sugar as a disguise, and settle in to listen to her narrative. She tells them, in the first thirty seconds, that M Mitrea lived there from before the fifteen years she has been there herself "after my husband died". Maria rapidly translates her Romanian.

"He never had a wife that I know of," she says. "And no one ever came to visit him. He kept to himself. He was quite gruff, sometimes shouted at the kids in the street. He always did his own shopping, at the supermarket in Alba Iulia, not the little shop near here. I thought that meant he was stingy. Perhaps not well off. He certainly didn't buy decent clothes. I suppose he had nowhere to go ..."

"Do you know what he did for a living?" asks Benjamin, through Maria Meleghi.

"No. No idea at all. He didn't have a job any time he lived here. Maybe he was too old? I don't know how old he was; he always seemed decrepit. I think he came from Bucharest, but I don't know for sure. That's all I know."

They knock on the doors of four other neighbours, all older women, and received absolutely no further information. Benjamin suggested they get Coca-Cola from the little shop close by. He desired ice cream but deemed it too unsophisticated for a police officer from Paris. They drink the fizzy in the car.

"How long have you been in the police?" Benjamin asks Maria, who says only six months. But it's all she's ever wanted to do, ever since she was a toddler. The Frenchman wonders how aware she is of the history of the police, and security police, in Romania. Maybe she is young enough to be entirely innocent?

"Do you come from around here?" he asks. "From Alba Iulia or somewhere near?"

"No," she answers. "It's usual policy to post new officers well away from home. I was born in Vaslui. It's in Moldavia, nearly five hundred kilometres away from here. I don't get home much."

"I am so sorry," he says. "You must be lonely?"

"*Oui*," she says, and looks at him with big eyes. He suddenly becomes alarmed and realises he will be leaving Romania with the team next week. Not good to make any commitments. When they have finished their drinks, they knock on a few more doors and get exactly no cooperation whatever.

***

"I may have found something!" Gabriela almost shouts from the far side of the archive room, "There are three files here which have two things in common." She almost skips over to where Faye is disconsolately sorting through files which mean nothing to her, and slaps three wine-coloured cardboard folders on the desk in front of her.

"This one," she says, flourishing the top one, "says it is from July 1989 and to be about the meeting of the Political Consultative Committee, that means the Warsaw Pact, in Bucharest. The agenda and concluding remarks are on the top.

"Concluding remarks say that the speakers had discussed the future of socialism and agreed that reforms were unavoidable, and outlined possible changes in the political, economic and social realms, including liberalisation as well as political and civil rights."

"*Bon Dieu*!" says Faye, astounded. "They said that? What was the context? What was going on at the time?" Gabriela looks thoughtful, drags up a chair to sit on.

"It was when Solidarity was providing the prime minister of Poland," she says. "The big cracks in communism were showing. Ceaușescu didn't like it because it was ruining his personal plans to become a world power. He was suggesting, so they say, that the Warsaw Pact join together to stop Poland liberalising, 'with all means necessary'. He clearly meant armed attacks. Which would have led to World War III. Happily, Gorbachev and the others were not that insane!"

"Who knew?" says Faye, amazed and alarmed in retrospect. "Did the rest of the world know?"

"I suppose so," says Gabriela. "At least the governments would have. There is a story that Ceaușescu and Gorbachev had no time for one another and that, at Ceaușescu's country cottage, where he had taken the other leaders for drinks, Gorbachev's wife, Raisa, had to calm them both down."

"*D'accord*," says Faye. "So, what exactly is it that you have found?"

"Underneath the agenda and remarks sheets are some things not related to the substance of the meeting. It is lists of assistants and officials who attended – or, presumably, were to attend, as it would have been written before the meeting. In the middle of those lists, there is another. A list which is within the other list."

"What does that mean?" asks the Frenchwoman, mystified.

"It is a concealed list. Quite a common Romanian trick," says Gabriela. "You write something relatively innocent but conceal something not so innocent at all in the middle of it. It isn't even as if it is a separate piece of paper – it's cross-written over, or indeed under, the ordinary list!" She shows Faye the sheet in the middle of the file. It just looks like a jumble of rubbish to Faye – until suddenly she sees that they are two completely different pieces of writing: one printed, one in written script, diagonally across the first.

"What does it say?" asks Faye. "What is it?" She is excited to find something, anything, secret.

"It's another list," answers Gabriela, "but in the form of prose. No obvious list structure, no punctuation, no capital letter, no spaces between words – it just looks as if it rambles on and on about nothing. But it is really a list of names."

"*Jésus!*" says Faye. "And are there any of our names in it?"

"That would be way too easy," comments Gabriela. "But it is something. It tells us that there are others. To some extent, we shall have to guess what they are, but I think I may be able to make educated guesses sometimes. The other two folders have similar lists. My plan is to separate as many wine-coloured folders as possible to start with and see if we can see other similarities. Perhaps you can choose another colour?"

"You say there are two things all three files have in common, *n'est-ce pas?*"

"*Oui.* There is a name written inside each folder, underneath all the papers. It is the same name, Nistor Vadulescu, and it is the name of the man who was third-in-command of *Securitate* in 1989!"

"*Oh, Bon Dieu! Alors,* we are looking for that name?"

"I think we are, *oui!*"

***

In the evening, Jean-Pascal telephones from Paris, and Colette and Amélie both have wordy conversations with him. Both are wanting to know if Sartre is well (he is), if Jean-Pascal is getting plenty of studying done (he is), if there is any interesting news (there isn't). Colette also wants to know if her son is eating properly. He says "Aw, *Mama*!" but that doesn't mean anything. They only have ten more days away, he will hardly starve in that time, not in Paris!

He asks how is his father, how is the case? Is Romania fine? They tell him, in unison, that it is a very beautiful country. He wishes he were with them – school is a bit boring, but he is seeing plenty of his friends. In fact, he had a little party last night.

Colette takes a very deep breath and stops herself from asking what they broke. He will come to it eventually. Now she thinks she sees the reason for the unexpected telephone call. She gives the phone to Amélie, so she can tell her brother about what she has been doing, goes to have a shower – where she can't hear what they are saying. She knows she won't like it.

When she returns, Amélie has hung up the phone and talks, lightly, about going out together for dinner. Colette's stomach turns slightly. Must have broken something major.

***

At *le Trente-Six*, Fleur and Clémence are discussing what remains of their caseload now that Roger Rannequin has gone to the prosecutor.

"Although," says Fleur, "we haven't, yet, heard from the senator. We may well have a visit from him before RR goes to court."

151

"Won't he be, rather, trying to influence the *juge* or *procureur*?" asks Clémence.

"Not if he's ever come across Zabi before," says Fleur. "He won't get anywhere with him. Don't know about the prosecutor, he's new, but I think being in Zabi's sphere of influence may have cleared any doubts about that. *Alors,* I am expecting the senator at any time in the next few days. He will come in like a whirlwind and shout at us.

"All we need to do is nod our silly heads and say '*Oui,* Monsieur *le Senator*' occasionally. Mainly, just ignore him. We can't do anything, and he knows it. You could be influenced against giving your direct evidence, could you? No, didn't think so. He'll run out of steam, say he has the ear of *le Président de la République,* and then charge out again. And that will be that.

"He must have known this can't go on with his stupid son. He's probably sick of it himself. It's just his head boiling. Not to worry. What about the baby food, though?"

Clémence looks sick and puts her elbow on the desk to prop up her head. She doesn't know what to do next; everything to do with the baby-food *débâcle* has come up with nothing.

"There must be something I'm not thinking of," she says miserably. "Missing. Something. Can you look at it with fresh eyes? Can I swap you for the fraud documents?"

"*Avec plaisir!*" says Fleur. She is delighted to surrender the papers of evil. She is still waiting for Roxanne, at the office of the *juge d'instruction*, to get back to her. She had no idea who could help but had offered to make some calls.

The telephone rings as Clémence wheels over to Fleur's desk and a uniformed officer, in the main *salle squad*, tells her that a sock has been found in a litter bin near the *Arc de Triomphe*. It has the name "N Pellisier" stitched into it. Fleur asks the officer to bring it in.

Clémence puts on rubber gloves before touching the plastic evidence bag. She opens it and removes the sock. It is brown, light brown, with a yellow band around the top, about one *centimetre* broad. It is a school sock. The uniform sock of the school Nikolas attended. The name tape, within the band, is the sort sewn by mothers of clever children being sent to good schools. The foot is very worn.

***

Faye separates as many wine-red folders as she can see from all other colours. There are many colours; she wonders if that is deliberate. More confusing. Needing a break, she notes the three kinds of blue, yellow, brown, buff, purple, green (pale and dark), pink, lilac and orange. She asks Gabriela, who is deep in one of the wine-coloured files from Faye's pile, whether she needs coffee. Faye herself certainly does.

Gabriela looks up, her brain still in another place entirely, and says "*oui*" vaguely. Today, she has brought a thermos with coffee, although they have already drunk most of it, starting at six in the morning. Faye rinses the mugs at the sink in the tiny kitchen off the main room, and spoons in the horrible instant coffee with which they are currently fuelling their theories.

They have made it their practice to stop searching while they drink a cup of coffee and, maybe, discuss anything which seems useful. These breaks are getting shorter and shorter as they approach the deadline by which Faye's visit to Bucharest is to end.

Neither woman is sleeping, and both are looking pale and drawn. They are nervous, as if expecting someone to come in and catch them doing something they should not be doing, even though there is, supposedly, no legal sanction these days. Gabriela is now officially on holiday and not

153

going into the main national archive at all. Faye, grateful for her enormous assistance, tries to spend as little time as she can wondering about Gabriela's motive. Sometimes, she cannot help it.

Is Gabriela so deeply committed to championing her home country in front of foreigners that she wants to help so much? Or is she just bored with her job? Or is there something sinister going on? She suspects her own motive for wondering. Can't the other woman just be naturally friendly? Why not? Because she's a foreigner? Is Faye really that prejudiced?

"I haven't found anything more in the red files," says Gabriela, sipping her coffee. "I think perhaps that we should choose another colour?" Faye gazes at the stack of around fifty wine-coloured folders by her right hand and sighs. The choice is between plodding on, hoping that the red files produce something useful, and putting them aside and making another choice. She doesn't know. She asks Gabriela what she thinks.

"I am not sure," says Gabriela. "We could change just before we would have found something ... or there could be nothing. And we could be lucky ..." She twists her face in indecision. Faye gazes out of the window for a moment. Perhaps she will use the magical thinking *le patron* discourages.

"We shall look at the files which match the colour of the jacket of the next person who passes the front door."

"We'll have to go and stand outside!" exclaims Gabriela, excited.

"*D'accord*. We must introduce an element of chance!" They stand and walk to the door, unlocking it, opening it wide. Just as they do, a woman walks past. She is short and bent. Elderly, grey. With a large shopping bag. She is wearing a bright-green, springlike coat.

The conference room in the police station at Pâclişa is set for a large meeting. Patrice has called for all the detectives involved in the murder cases – he refuses to call them the Vampire Murders, although he is sure that others are doing so. He has arranged to meet Colette and Amélie for dinner at 21.00 before he returns to Bărăbanţ with Chief Maria Gadianu.

The meeting is scheduled to begin at 10.00, Chief Gadianu and Patrice himself are there yet. Still, it is only just past 09.45. There is still time. As Patrice forms this thought, the entire contingent from Pâclişa enters the room: *Capitaine* Roşca, René Mercard, Benjamin d'Aroque, with Officers Cuţov, Balan and Iordache. Faye simultaneously joins them on Zoom, from Bucharest.

It is 10.05 when the remainder of the contingent from Bărăbanţ arrives. Theodorescu and Florescu nod at the others and take seats at the large rectangular table. Maria Meleghi goes over to the coffee trolley and gets three cups. Patrice notices that Benjamin d'Aroque is watching her every move. He makes a mental note of that.

It is only about three minutes later when Roxana Lupu and Eugen Danti arrive from Oarda. They are almost the last. A round of introductions has started before the very last invitee, not expected to come, arrives. Clearly, Silviu Melichian likes to make an entrance. He is in full uniform. *Très smart.* Patrice, who has checked, notes that he has a large star and laurel leaves on his shoulders. He is *chestor de poliţie*, the equivalent of the French *contrôleur general*. Phew! He nods to everyone and says hello to senior officer Chief Giardanu. Sits down at the foot of the table, opposite Patrice.

"*Bonjour, mes amies*," says Patrice, "and welcome. I shall be speaking in French and, as several of you will not understand it all, I shall leave time for translation. Please, anyone who doesn't understand should let either myself or the translators know immediately.

"Today, we are going to consider the killings of *Messieurs* Dobrescu, Mitrea, Dabija and Bunea. I have gathered you all together because I believe each of you has an exclusive piece of the puzzle. You may not agree. But I insist that this is so. You are officers and senior officers stationed in the villages where the crimes happened, plus my team from Paris, plus Monsieur Melichian, your ultimate superior officer. Every single one of you knows something the others do not know.

"I am relying on you to speak out – via a translator if required. *Se déplaçant le long.*[48] You will see that we have already a blackboard with the names, ages, locations and known relatives of each victim – plus the names of the first officers attending, who have now all been interviewed by my team.

"There is another board next to it – which is blank." He gestures towards this. "You should write anything there which occurs to you, not just during this meeting but afterwards. Those of you who are not frequently here in Pâclişa should telephone and have your insight written up for you. Madame Roşca, you will provide someone whose task it is to do this?"

"I have already done so," says *Capitaine* Roşca, "I have asked Officer Iordache to do this." She repeats this in Romanian. Sofia Iordache nods in agreement, moves her seat closer to the board.

"*D'accord,*" says Patrice, "we have all asked the basic questions. Who were these men? Why were they killed? What is the connection between them? These may be

---

48 Moving along

called the social aspects of the case.

"The technical aspects of the case are the scene-of-crime officers' report, and the report of the *médecin légiste*. I shall give each of you a copy of these, in Romanian, when I have finished my short comments."

Patrice is too experienced in this business to hand out reports before he speaks to them – people will try to read and listen at the same time. "SOC tells us of the pattern of blood spatter – of course, when the throats were cut, except in the case of Monsieur Mitrea, whose body was too badly decomposed for the pathologist to describe this. I shall return to that in a moment.

"Much blood went into the mattress and pillows in each case. Around the head and neck, as well as that on the clothes – the nightclothes. Some blood soaked under the head in the three cases, under the skull for Monsieur Mitrea. The blood travelled by capillary attraction from the throat almost to the waist, like a bib. The floors were innocent of blood.

"Dr Apostol's report of post-mortems is clear that each victim died from similar wounds in the throat. In each case there was a single slash of an extremely sharp knife, left to right, by a right-handed person standing over the victim. There were no hesitation marks. There were no teeth marks, or traces of saliva.

"In the case of the badly deteriorated Monsieur Mitrea, Dr Apostol has deduced that he would have had a similar knife wound, as she could observe traces of the cut marks on the skeleton.

"In the case of all these men, none died of bleeding out as such, but probably of hypovolemic shock, due to lower volume of blood – it was all over the beds – which drastically lowered their blood pressure and caused their organs to shut down.

"There was, in each case, livor mortis in the lowest parts of the recumbent bodies, where blood collects after the heart stops. There is also a possibility of having been overdosed with the drug fentanyl – which works very quickly and resembles morphine in depressing the respiratory system. There were no defensive wounds, of course, due to having been drugged."

"You do not think there were vampires involved?" asks Melichian, surprising everyone in the room. Patrice thinks that the very senior officer has come especially to introduce the topic and, perhaps, dispose of it once and for all.

"I do not," Patrice says firmly, dismissing the entire ridiculous possibility.

"Because," says Melichian, "we have had vampire killings before!" Some of the cops sitting around the table nod their heads and murmur to one another. Both *Capitaine* Roşca and Chief Gadianu shake their heads and look fierce. Patrice stops for a moment and decides he himself needs to dispose of this now.

"I realise that there have been some," he says. "And I have read a report of such being carried out by a group of young men last year. They, naturally, were only pretending to be vampires. Trying to divert the blame."

"They did drink the victims' blood, though," says Sofia Iordache in a timid voice, from her position by the blank board.

"Doesn't make them vampires!" her *capitaine*, Roşca, almost shouts. "Just stupid kids, playing about, who decided to cross into very nasty crime. They were quickly arrested and charged. They went to prison for the murder of three people they selected at random. It provided a lesson for any other stupid people wishing to take revenge on others."

"Was it revenge?" asks René, making notes rapidly on his pad. *Capitaine* Roşca looks as if she has eaten something sour and says no:

"It was random, as far as we could see. There were six boys: one, seventeen, was the leader; there were two at fifteen; one at thirteen; one, twelve. The youngest was only ten, the brother of the seventeen-year-old. Three of them, including the ten-year-old, swore they were vampires and had been initiated by drinking the blood of the Lord of Darkness. The young one is now confined to a psychiatric hospital. He is diagnosed with schizophrenia. The rest are in prison for life."

"How sad," says Faye from the Zoom feed.

Patrice asks Renć to hand out the copies of the two reports and asks the group what is the connection between the victims?

"They are male," says Roxana Lupu, the Wolfwoman.

"They are old!" says Maria Meleghi, the just-qualified.

"They are not native to Transylvania!" says Radu Balan, courtesy of *Capitaine* Roşca.

"There is no connection!" says Avram Florescu, who should know better. Eugen Danti, also not long qualified, agrees with him. Faye Benoît clears her throat and says:

"There must be at least one connection between them, perhaps more. They are not just selected at random; they cannot be! Although they live in three different places, one in Pâclişa, one in Oarda, two in Bărăbanţ, they are all from other places, and they, perhaps, all came from Bucharest to Transylvania. Two of them were retired from full-time work, but the other two were old enough to retire but still worked as a teacher and a butcher.

"My allocated task is to look in the National Archives in Bucharest and find out where any or all of them might have worked. If, for instance, they all worked together in Bucharest, that could be a useful connection – which might help with why they were killed."

"Please, Mademoiselle Iordache," says Patrice, "write on the original board that Madame Benoît is searching the archives in the capital. Officer d'Aroque, what task have you been working on?"

"I have two tasks, *patron*," says Benjamin. "One is to check the police databases, both in Romania and in the European Community, to see if any of these four men has a criminal record. None has. There is no mention of any of them, either as a perpetrator, or as a witness.

"The second task was to interview, along with Mademoiselle Meleghi, the neighbours of the late Monsieur Mitrea – who had no wife or children to speak for him; only his dead body."

<h1 style="text-align:center">17</h1>

Colette is, for once, shopping for a new outfit, not in Paris. She and Amélie are joining Patrice for dinner at a plush restaurant this evening, and she wants something nice to let him know that she appreciates him taking time off from the very rushed investigation to be with his family.

She almost never shops for clothes outside her home city. Why would she?

There is a tiny boutique just around the corner and she sees a couple of things she likes in the display window, which is artistically contrived. She goes in and finds the elegant assistant speaks English. They take little time to plump for a gentle turquoise silk suit, which fits beautifully and brings Colette's fair colouring to life. The Frenchwoman selects high-heel pumps to match and is well satisfied.

Back at the hotel, Amélie has gone out with her friends. Colette returns to her favourite chair, favourite coffee (by the pot), pastry, and the *Dracula*. She is enjoying the ridiculous book more than she thought. It is a mirror which well illustrates Victorian prejudices and highlights enormous class consciousness – even now, not totally gone from Europe. She contemplates its literary position and thinks about whether one can truly separate literature in English to before and after *Dracula*. It is at least a possibility.

Why is it that, when frightened out of his mind, Mr Harker chose to wait until after Dracula's "lizard-crawling" down the side of the castle (why can't the Count go through the door anyway?) and then decides to explore? With a guttering oil lamp. In the dark. With the distinct possibility that Dracula will come back. Anytime. They always do, don't they?

***

They have an early sandwich lunch at Pâcliṣa, and M Melichian makes a point of collaring Patrice to semi-complain that, perhaps, he is making the straightforward homicides more complicated than they must be?

"You want us to go home?" asks Patrice.

"Not at all," says Melichian. "I am just wondering whether your method is quite suiting us here."

"In what way?"

"You have to remember," says Melichian, "that my rural officers are not quite as well educated as those you have in Paris. Of course, it is different in our cities, but there are even a few – who have been police officers for quite a time – who are not especially literate. Your philosophical method may be beyond them ..."

"Your Swedish contact at Interpol did not explain my methods to you?" asks Patrice.

161

"Well, no," says Melichian. "He just said you were superb at your job and could take all the stupid stuff in your stride without it affecting you."

"And I can," says Patrice, handing him a plate of something which he cannot identify. Melichian takes a piece of whatever it is and melts back into the crowd with it in his hand. Fifteen minutes later, it is time for Benjamin and Maria Meleghi to take the floor.

"*Se déplaçant le long*, Monsieur d'Aroque, Mademoiselle Meleghi, tell us about the neighbours and life story of Monsieur Mitrea. If any."

"We spoke first to Madame Caranfil, who is old but curious and misses nothing," says Meleghi. "Mitrea has lived in that house for at least fifteen years, but she doesn't really know anything much about him. She has seen no visitors or family of any sort. She didn't like him; he was self-contained and gruff and yelled at kids."

"She thought he was stingy," says Benjamin, butting in, "but, possibly, not well off. He didn't work as long as he lived there – but seemed 'decrepit'. And she didn't know how old he was."

"She thinks he came from Bucharest," says Meleghi.

"The other neighbours we spoke to, ten altogether," adds Benjamin, "didn't add anything of value. Oddly" – he stops and looks around the room – "they didn't appear to want to talk about the murder, or about Monsieur Mitrea. People usually do."

Melichian raises his head from the table, where he has been contemplating grains of salt left over from lunch, and says:

"Perhaps they do in Paris."

***

Faye is just finishing her "presentation so far" at the Pâcliṣa meetingnd describes the difficulty because of the jumbled mess in the archives, as well as the usual cry of much of the information not yet being on computer. She tells them that it isn't that at all; the state of the information is such that it cannot yet go on computer.

"I should think," she says, "that it will take about twenty years to make any inroads to it – and that would be with qualified archivists, of which there are few. *Alors*, all we can do, my friend Gabriela (who is a qualified archivist) and I, is to plough through as fast as we can and hope that we find something helpful. All we have is hard work and good luck!"

"Do you believe in luck?" asks Police Quaestor Melichian, head on one side in pity. Faye colours; she said it without thinking, although she realises that this is the second time she has invoked luck regarding the Romanian archives.

"I thought," says Chief Gadianu, "that you French had given up superstition along with religion. You brag that you are a secular state, *n'est-ce pas?*"

"We do." Patrice pitches in to save his civilian assistant. "But like you, we have not had the time to shrug it off altogether." He smiles warmly, trying not to be a crocodile. *"D'accord,"* he says, moving to stand before the second blackboard, which is still blank. Mlle Iordache is still sitting in the nearest seat. The French detective picks up the chalk, the scent reminding him of school in Pont-St-Esprit.

"Alors, what do we have? What I should like you to do now is to, each of you, give me the thing which most strikes you about what you have seen of this case. For example, Madame Benoît feels she needs a lot of luck to get anywhere in the archives. That is significant. Why?" No one replies and Faye flushes once again.

"Because she has said it twice!" says Benjamin, who is

beginning to see what Patrice has in mind. Patrice smiles and says, "*Oui.* That is exactly right." He writes the words "*La Fortune*" on the board. Looks around at the people at the table. M Melichian, grappling, against his better judgement, with the unfamiliar method, says:

"The wives are younger and smarter than the men who were killed."

"They are also more educated," shouts Radu Balan, through Roşca. Patrice writes these up, and then gives the chalk to Iordache to continue. He returns to his seat and begins to draw default penguins.

"It is the same killer!" says Florescu, not having quite understood. Iordache writes that down, it is okay.

"Right-handed killer!" says the Wolfwoman.

"No perpetrator DNA!" shouts Florescu.

"*Capitaine* Roşca mentioned 'revenge'," says René, who is practised at mopping up the loose ends in this exercise. Roşca looks flustered and quickly says she didn't really mean that as such. There is a moment of silence while they all think about that.

"However," says Patrice, "it was said, and that is interesting. This exercise is to bring to light anything which any of us knows intuitively, rather than what is on our conscious mind, *quoi*? Why did Madame Roşca bring this to the surface? It was in her mind ... Are we thinking of, or even just mildly aware of, certain revenge murders? Madame?"

"Of course," says Roşca, having regained her poise. "We have had revenge killings before, in the early nineties especially. There was lots of anger about what the *Securitate* did during communism, the Ceauşescu regime. It was a terrible time ... but not now. It's a long time ago. Nearly thirty years."

Gavril Cuţov, the reddish young policeman who had attended Monsieur Dobrescu's crime scene with Balan and

Iordache, mutters, intending to be heard, that Romanians have long memories. Various Romanians look sniffy at that, until Gadianu interrupts:

"What else do we have?" she asks, cutting in before Patrice can take charge. He is listening to things others may not be able to hear.

"One of the things which intrigues me," says Patrice, "is that the neighbours of Monsieur Mitrea – who had lived in Bărăbanţ for at least fifteen years, was elderly and seemed to be poor, financially and in terms of family – had no sympathy or interest in the murder. I have never known that before. People always want to talk about such things and venture their own suspicions and solutions. It seems very peculiar."

"But Monsieur *le Contrôleur Général* said that might happen in Paris but not in Romania!" Faye butts in from Bucharest. Melichian looks uncomfortable for a split second, then returns to his usual urbane, sophisticated attitude.

"And why is that?" asks Patrice.

***

"I cannot tell you," moans Patrice, "*comme j'en ai marre*[49] about the vampires!"

Colette sits opposite, in the new turquoise silk, which extracted a pretty compliment from her husband when he saw her. Amélie is wearing some form of teenage rags, and both parents are slightly avoiding looking at her while engaging her in conversation.

"Thought you were dismissing them out of hand," says Colette, "refusing to give them an entry into the conversation."

"*Oui*," replies Patrice. "But, unhappily, that is not working. It sounded good in Paris, but here, not so much."

---

49   how fed up I am

"How do you mean, *Papa?*" asks Amélie. "I've been hanging out with loads of Romanians and none of them has ever mentioned Drac or vampires!"

"Maybe the youth is different?" says Colette. "They certainly are at home …"

"Aw, *Maman*, they just see things that should be thrown away. They're more advanced is all!" Colette looks at her daughter under her eyelashes and says that that isn't necessarily so.

"I have to say," says Patrice, "that it is much more complicated than I had realised. I thought, I assumed – which I should not have done, I know that – those forty-two years of communism, including a lot of repression and horror, would have purged the superstitious nature of the population."

"And you have discovered that it did not?" says Colette.

"It's not just that," says Patrice. "I was wrong on a lot of things. I thought that churches were closed, priests persecuted, et cetera, like in Russia and other communist regimes. But it wasn't like that here."

"It wasn't?"

"Not at all," says Patrice. "The Romanian Orthodox Church, apparently, cooperated with the communists by means of a church constitution, approved by the regime in 1948, which neither the Roman nor Greek Catholics did. This meant that the government provided money to build churches, and train and pay priests, and survived in better shape than they'd been before.

"In fact, it has been said, by their then Patriarch, of all people, that the communist regime provided an opportunity for spiritual growth, and the Church became even more vigorous and 'lively' – his word. It's no great surprise, knowing that, that superstition is alive and well in Romania. Around eighty-five per cent of the people are Romanian Orthodox and attend church.

"Apparently, Amélie, even most young people go to church, even girls and boys on a date!"

"Oh, I don't think so," says Amélie. "They never mentioned it to me!"

"You are making the Church and the Dracula into one big superstitious thing," says Colette. "Are you sure you want to do that?"

"Well, it is the same thing," says Patrice. "If you believe in all the hocus-pocus of religion, you are ripe to take on the tradition of the folk myths, *n'est-ce pas*? Especially if it's tied up with your history and love of country. Don't forget Vlad Dracula was a military hero ..."

"So was Charles de Gaulle," says Colette. "And I didn't like him much either!"

18

"It isn't going to be colour-coded, *n'est-ce pas*?" says Faye on returning to the archives on the Monday of their second week in Romania.

"*Non*," says Gabriela. "We shall just have to look inside the folders, although there may be some attraction of one colour over the other. Suppose they aren't just random. Proper randomisation can be difficult; it's easier just to pick what's to hand. Even suppose that Monsieur Third-in-Charge of *Securitate* liked green? He might be inclined to use more green files."

"I guess it's as good a guess as anything else," says Faye. "At least it gives us somewhere to go. Do you think it might be green?"

"Why not?" says Gabriela. "It's the colour of love and peace. And hope." Faye does not know where her friend gets this from, but it doesn't matter anyway. She grabs several bright-green files and makes a pile on her adopted desk. *D'accord!*

One of the folders carries the name of Nistor Vadulescu, written low down in the envelope body part, where no casual observer would see it. It is in his beautiful italic handwriting. Faye wastes no time looking through the papers, trying to decipher the impossible Romanian. She puts it on a separate pile for Gabriela's examination. Almost immediately she finds another.

By lunchtime, the two women have located eight files carrying the *Securitate* signature; only two of them are green. It is three in the afternoon when Gabriela sees the word "*lucadobrescu*" in one of the lists of what look like long, nonsensical words.

***

Because Patrice is away and Fleur does not have sufficient seniority to set up a surveillance operation, they must call in a replacement *commissaire*. The officer sent by *Divisionnel* Delahaye turns out to be *Commissaire* Robert, Pucelle's deeply unpopular, sometime undercover control.

"*Alors,*" he says, "what is it you want to do, then?"

"We need to set up surveillance at a variety of sightseeing places around the city," says Fleur, suddenly realising what a huge undertaking this is going to be. "We have recovered, in two different places, the glove and sock of a boy who disappeared two years ago. The case was cold until the glove appeared." Robert looks bored; such a banal case!

"Do we know whether this glove is the boy's?" he asks as if he couldn't care less.

"Of course," says Fleur sniffily. "Both glove and sock have a name tape in with his name. His mother says she sewed them in; she recognises not only the items but also her stitching!"

"Humph. I suppose you want to put out a detail of men on every Paris landmark, then?"

"No," says Fleur, looking down. "That would take a huge number of resources. I think we need to pick where to do it. But I do think the child is trying to communicate with us. As we have never had any actual leads in this case, it is very important."

"But you have no idea where the next item, if there is one, will arrive. I am assuming you don't expect that another knitted thing will come to, where were they found? Tour Eiffel? Where else?"

"Arc de Triomphe," says Fleur. "But we cannot abandon them in case they are the only places Nikolas has access to."

"Ah, so where are you thinking of? The Bois de Boulogne? The Luxembourg? The Notre-Dame? Twenty others?"

"*Non*. I feel we should start with the two we have already picked up, plus Sacré-Coeur, Notre-Dame, the Louvre, and Les Invalides. Six in all."

"And where do you think I will get the men to go and stand at these six places on the chance that your boy will turn up at any of them?"

"Two officers at each are twelve men," says Fleur firmly. "I do not think we need to have more than one shift; I doubt they will bring the boy out at night. I expect it is just for a bit of fresh air, so probably in the morning or afternoon. Not even at mealtimes."

"It seems obvious," says Clémence, who has said nothing so far, even though she is very committed and emotional about finding Nikolas Pellisier, "that he is being held somewhere around the centre of the city. So, while we are there, we can keep an eye out for him at the same time."

Robert turns towards her, and his eyes drop to engage the woman in the wheelchair.

"When you say 'we', mademoiselle, don't think for a moment that you will be taking part in this – if it happens at all. You are not in any fit state to work on the streets of Paris. I thought so when you were, unfortunately, appointed, and I still think so. Forget it! I don't know what *Commissaire* Lanier is thinking, appointing people like you ... this ludicrous diversity drive, I suppose."

Fleur and Clémence look at one another, stunned to silence. Fleur has not experienced enough of M Robert to know that this is normal for him, with his unreconstructed attitudes, and Clémence has never met him before.

"I am adequate for many jobs," says Clémence, squeezing the words out like her future firstborn. "There are some things I can't do. This is not one of them!"

"She single-handedly arrested and brought in Roger Rannequin," says Fleur between clenched teeth, "and has handled everything both *le patron* and I have thrown at her since she got here. She is an exemplary officer!"

Robert doesn't look pleased at this and turns away from the officer in the wheelchair.

"Well, if you can get someone to lend you enough men," he says, "put them wherever you think it will work. But this officer" – he points, rudely, to Clémence – "is to stay here manning the telephone. I do not want her on the street. There would be hell to pay if anything happened to her. Do not disobey me, or neither of you will have a job!"

He stamps out of the room, leaving the two women stunned. Fleur says that they have no choice but to do as they are told. Clémence, accustomed to disability discrimination, says, "*D'accord,*" against her will and intention.

***

"What is that?" asks Colette when Amélie is getting ready to go out with her Romanian friends. She points to the girl's neck, where there are two tiny red dots, far too small to be cuts, on the left side, below her chin. Just like Mina Murray in the book.

"Aw, *Maman,*" says Amélie, "it's just a joke! Last night's game was vampires. It was so silly! Even my friends think it was silly. It's only for the tourists. The vamp bite was drawn by one of the staff on the way in – we all got them. It was about trying to escape from Dracula's Castle – and we all did, it was easy!"

"Didn't you say," says her mother, "that the young people had no time for superstition or anything like that?"

"I did," says Amélie. "But I think it was my fault, asking them about Romanian vampires and stuff. They decided to take me to play this game so they could say, 'See, it's stupid,' when we came out."

"They don't believe, then?"

"Not at all!"

***

In the middle of the week, Pucelle drops by the office of the Immigrant Health & Support, to discuss her work so far with Frieda.

The German woman is making coffee in the tiny kitchen and shouts to enquire how the new staff member takes it.

"A little milk, if you please," says Pucelle, "but not too weak. I wonder if you have had any messages for me?"

Frieda, today hurriedly assembled into a dark-red full

skirt and a summery blouse, unsuitable to the cold weather, says that she thinks there is one. She hands Pucelle a mug of coffee milkier than the other woman had expected and, placing her own mug on her cluttered desk, rifles through some papers.

"Where is it?" she mutters. "I cannot find anything … ah, *là*, here we are. A person who would not give her name telephoned for you – she asked for Domi, that is you, *n'est-ce pas?*"

"*Oui*," confirms Pucelle, surprised that anyone has referred to her as that, the name she went by when she was first entering the field, undercover, when she is "Pucelle" now.

"*Bon*. This unnamed person left an address. It is not her own address. It is an address where you might be able to find someone you are looking for. She did not say the name of the person. She said you would know. How mysterious!" Frieda looks at Pucelle as if waiting for a story.

Pucelle takes the piece of paper from her new *patron* but does not venture an explanation.

***

The young waiter, Lidia, who Colette feels she knows quite well by now, tells her that the heating has broken down, so it is very cold in the guest lounge. If guests want to read or chill out, she is suggesting the writing room, which is off the lounge and has a fireplace with a cheerful wood fire. They are serving complimentary beverages and snacks in there. When Colette enters, there are no takers but much heat. She finds a corner of a comfortable sofa and appropriates a footstool. Lidia brings her usual coffee and pastry, asking how she is doing with the book.

"Oh, it's fine," says Colette. "Although the print is very small!"

"What about the text?" asks the young woman. "Is it living up to your expectations?"

"More than," says Colette. "It's quite funny, actually. I am seeing lots of things other people haven't remarked on – whether they've seen them or not. One bit I read yesterday concerns the idea that Jonathan Harker, who must be the wettest Englishman who ever lived, 'looks to his diary to help soothe him', and reflects that the only way to safety is through Dracula – who will protect him until he has no more use for him. Imagine that! All that horror, and Drac is the best he can do …"

"Fascinating," says the woman. "You might think about substituting Ceauşescu for Dracula – and think about why Romanians allowed him to stay in power for forty-two years, despite everything."

***

The address which had been left for Pucelle is that of a flat in the poorest part of the city. It is on a street with apartment blocks which have seen better times – grimy and rundown, old property scheduled for demolition, but when?

The flat she is looking for is on the third floor; happily, as the *ascenseur* is, as usual, broken. Pucelle climbs to the second floor reasonably comfortably, but her leg is seriously troubling her as she leaves the second landing for the third. The flat is the fourth door on the right side of the corridor. The door is painted, olive green but gone scabby. There is graffiti on the walls and some of the doors, in multiple languages.

In answer to her knock, the door is opened by a large white man with a grey beard, in a vest, his old jeans suspended by shoulder braces. His visible skin is grey with inground cement or plaster dust. He says, '*Ça va?*' with suspicion.

"*Bonjour*," says Pucelle, "I am looking for *L'Éléphant*. Do you know her? She is a rather large Russian, who is usually dressed like a man ... I have been recommended to try this address. *Je m'appelle Domi.* I used to visit with Elephant and the Peacock ... were you here when they were around?"

The man is staring at her, not speaking. Pucelle decides she will have to let him know she is not looking for the Elephant with vicious intent.

"I am looking for her because she was very kind to me, before her son was killed, and I want to thank her and see that she is all right. I am not meaning her any harm."

His face clears a little, a bit less tension than before, turning to go back into the flat but leaving the door open so she can follow. Inside, he sits on one of three deckchairs which appear the only furniture. He says something, clearly in Russian, which she must ask him to repeat because of his strange accent. Her subconscious furnishes the location "Siberia" without her consciousness knowing she knows it.

"You might," he says, "ask for Irina Alexandrovna. That is her name."

19

By home time on the second Monday, Gabriela and Faye have turned up three of the four victims' names in a variety of coloured files. Dobrescu is in green, Dabija in purple, and Bunea in light blue, along with many names they do not recognise. There is no sign of Monsieur Mitrea, but they have probably not gone back far enough. They acknowledge that they could have to search for the rest of their lives.

They realise, too, that Monsieur Mitrea was rather older than the others – by twenty years or so. His details could be buried even deeper and signed by a different *Securitate* third-in-charge with a different method.

They spread out the contents of the three files and study the other names around those of their three victims.

"They seem to be men," says Gabriela, "at least in the lists which have our names. I can see no obvious women."

"What else is there," asks Faye, "in the way of other information on the sheets with actual names? And are they all cross-written like the first one?"

"They are all cross-written," says Gabriela, "and there are a few bits of other things on the same sheet. There are some numbers against each name – not just Monsieur Dobrescu's."

"Let us have a look. What do you think they are?"

"Just numbers? They vary quite a lot but are all six or seven digits. Could be a code, I suppose?"

"*Merde!* Another layer of complication," says Faye. She gets out a handkerchief and blows her nose. "I don't know how much more I can stand."

"Let's go out and get something to eat," says Gabriela, "in the nice coffee shop. Then we can come back and be inspired in the morning." Faye thinks Gabriela tends to be inspired rather more than absolutely necessary.

As they pay for their meal, splitting the cost equally between them, Gabriela realises something. She divides the change in half and hands one half to Faye, putting the rest in her purse. Faye notices her friend is pink and excited. They have enjoyed a pleasant dinner, but this seems excessive.

"It's money!" Gabriela says shrilly as they get to the street.

"What is money?" asks Faye.

"The numbers!" Gabriela says. "The figures by the names. Look, it's to do with the collapse of Bancorex!"

"What, *au nom de Dieu*, is Bancorex?" asks Faye.

"Was, not is," says Gabriela. "It was a great big bank, owned by the Romanian government. It went bankrupt in the nineties, closed in 1999." Faye is puzzled; what could this have to do with their murder victims?

"It's quite long," says Gabriela, "and quite complicated. But I think it's the thing we are looking for! Come back to my flat and I'll tell you all about it."

***

Patrice and Benjamin sit together in a small café in Pâclişa to discuss the progress of the case without the presence of the Romanian officers. Benjamin is interested in why the *contrôleur général*, Melichian, sat in. Patrice says he expects the senior officer is just keeping his eye on what is happening.

"He may well have other reasons. What he said was interesting, *n'est-ce pas?*"

"Which part?" asks D'Aroque. "The part where he suggested that it might be vampires?"

"*Oui*. Although I thought at first that he had just come to get it out of the way, to help us. Now I wonder whether it was something else he had in mind."

"He is a very senior officer," says Benjamin. "I can't believe he would be interested in a case like this – rural, primitive … whatever."

"Indeed," says Patrice. "But there is more here, *n'est-ce pas*? I am having difficulty getting my head around this stupid vampire thing. I need some help. You recall that I talked, before we left home, with a forensic psychologist from the American University?"

"*Oui.* Dr Boulet. You said she was very interesting … but she was committed to other work and could not come to work with us."

"*Exactement*," says Patrice. "But I think she may be willing to give me some advice. I shall telephone her. In the meantime, I need you to do a little digging about the state of drug abuse in Romania. Our perpetrator drugged at least two of the four dead men, and maybe some wives. He had to get the drugs from somewhere. Can you find out where? Who might have had access?"

"*Oui, patron!*"

***

"At first I didn't realise it could be money," says Gabriela. "The numbers didn't make any sense to me in that context. It was an awful lot; they were way too high. It was only when we were paying for our dinner that I remembered that the Romanian leu was changed to the new leu in 2007. There are 4.88 lei to the euro, but before the change, there was the equivalent of around ten thousand lei to the euro. It's not an accurate conversion, but it makes the numbers in the lists make sense!"

"*D'accord*," says Faye. "So, it was money being paid to our victims!"

"I think so. The thing is Bancorex. The timeline is important. Before the 1989 revolution, Bancorex, as a state concern, didn't really have to make any profit – it could be propped up by the government. Then, after, it was a gigantic monster with no institution to prop it up. So, it began to fail.

"It took Radu Vasile, the prime minister, about ten years to close it down. There were billions of US dollars in losses because of one thing: non-performing loans to ex-*Securitate* officers and politically corrupt businesspeople! Most of them were never repaid – and I don't think anybody truly knows how much all this cost the country in the end. There are still secrets about it, although we know how much was added to the national debt. It was around one and a half billion!

"I think these things we have found hidden are lists of those loans …"

"And that our murder victims are ex-*Securitate* officers!" says Faye, almost shouting.

"*Oui,*" says Gabriela. "And that's our connection!"

They get up from their chairs and spontaneously hug and dance around the small living room. Gabriela gets out a half-full bottle of *ţuică*, Romanian plum brandy, and they each drink a small glass in celebration. Faye's throat bursts into temporary flames.

"I can go back to Bărăbanţ now," says Faye when her breath returns. She realises that she is unlikely to see Gabriela again, and they both grimace at the thought. She is beginning to feel that her Romanian friend really is a friend who is trying desperately to help her. Her only real worry is why she is so desperate.

Gabriela pours another glass of *ţuică* for each of them.

***

Fleur has managed to obtain the secondment of four uniformed officers from other departments and posted a guard, looking for Nikolas Pellisier, on Tour Eiffel, Arc de Triomphe, Notre-Dame and Les Invalides. These are arbitrary; there is no way she can predict where *petit* Nikolas is likely to drop another piece of disposable clothing. She feels that she should probably change the sites from time to time. But knows that Robert will not allow her to persist in this surveillance for very long.

In cheerful defiance of Robert's order, Clémence Godard is, presently, in Place Jean-Paul II, on the Île de la Cité, close to the Notre-Dame. Fleur has come to visit her, to check if she needs coffee and snacks. In March, Paris is rarely warm enough to begin the spring season. They have chosen to station Clémence there because it is the closest site to the *Trente-Six* and, therefore, closer for Fleur to leave her desk to check on her colleague. It is also one monument which has not, previously, received any of *petit* Nikolas's clothing.

"*Ça va?*" asks Fleur. Clémence is huddled in her chair, under a lap rug, pretending to be older and more disabled than she is. She looks up at Fleur with a patient smile.

"Nothing yet," she says. "Perhaps it's too early?"

"I am thinking that there is probably a prime time of day for the perpetrator to take Nikolas for a walk. What do you think?"

Clémence twists her face in doubt. "*Je ne sais pas,*" says the young woman. "I think he'd vary it so as not to be seen …"

"*Oui, mais certainement.*" Fleur looks thoughtful and says a rude word about Monsieur Robert and his refusal to allow enough resources to rescue a poor little boy.

"Where do you want to go tomorrow?" asks Fleur. "Like a change?"

"Of course," says Clémence. "This is very boring. But maybe we shall have enough luck to see them today? Have any of the other pairs seen anything? Don't suppose they have, or we'd have known by now."

"I'm hoping for Les Invalides," says Fleur. "I hope whoever it is is taking the boy to see the sights of Paris—" She suddenly stops as she realises that the natural conclusion of that sentence is probably "before he kills him". She shakes her head as if to clear the thought and stares at Clémence, hoping she missed it.

She didn't.

***

"*Docteur* Boulet?" says Patrice when the telephone in her office in the American University is answered with "This is Petra".

"*Oui,*" says the forensic psychologist. "How can I help?" The telephonist has told her who is calling, and she stands ready to assist. That is what she is like.

"Er," says Patrice, "I'm calling from Romania. I have something I thought you might be able to help me with."

"If I can," says Petra, "I'd be delighted to help. What can I do?"

"It's your psychology side I'm interested in today," he says, "for now. This situation is getting me down and I only have one week left in which to solve the crime."

"And that doesn't fit your usual method and timeline. *D'accord,* what is the crime?"

"Four men have been murdered in three different places in Transylvania. No Dracula jokes, please."

"*M'en garderai bien,*[50]" says Boulet.

"The places are not many miles apart, but they are different villages. Two of the men were killed in one place – but at vastly different times. So, much separation. The one who was killed first was a couple of months ago and wasn't found until he was well decomposed. The others were killed a few hours before they were found, so not."

"The difference is because?"

"The three were married and living with their wives, who were in bed with them when they were killed."

"Drugged?"

"Likely fentanyl. Hard to tell whether apoxia caused by the drug killed them before hypovolemia, due to having their throats cut. The wives are likely to have been strongly

---

50   I wouldn't dream of it

sedated with something else – but we are too late to know what. More discussions with wives necessary."

"Ah. Hard to see yet why you want me."

"It's more fantastical than you can possibly imagine."

"Ah," again. "Throats cut. Or bitten? Are we back to Dracula?"

Patrice sighs deeply and says, "Of course we are. It's Romania, isn't it? I started by banning all references to vampires, but it finally caught up with me. I certainly hadn't realised that the Count is still undead and well in Transylvania!"

"Surely not! Didn't all that go out with the communists? There were still monsters, but they were real. Didn't that frighten the population enough?"

"Apparently not," says Patrice. "I want to talk to you about vampires. Well, no, I don't. I really don't. But I must. Because, apart from the fact that about half of the local officers still seem to believe in the disgusting things, and the other half are so entirely dismissive that they won't talk about it, I just don't seem to be able to put it down. It keeps coming back from the dead, so I have to deal with it. I do not want to!"

"*Alors*, what do you want to talk about, specifically? There are lots of ways to approach it, but you should know that my knowledge is only academic, not from experience."

"*Non*," says Patrice, "I didn't imagine you had much actual experience of the real thing ..." He laughs nervously. She is silent a moment to collect her thoughts.

"*D'accord*, tell me if any of this is not what you want, and I'll stop and take another path. *Alors*. The vampire myth is pretty universal. We find it throughout the world, from China to Europe to ... oh, I don't know, if there were people in Antarctica, it would be there too.

"I think most scholars think of it as a metaphor that came to life in pre-scientific times when the people didn't have explanations for very peculiar happenings. Like religion. How are you on coincidence, Patrice? One of those *flics* who don't believe in it?"

"Not at all," says Patrice. "No progress without chance; no evolution without variation. Intuition isn't everything, but it is something. There is no luck, and there are no vampires."

"*Bon.* You, I can work with. The certainty of death wasn't always a certainty, of course. People could rise from the dead if they weren't actually dead. Physicians weren't always either skilled or ethical.

"The Church had a problem too. How to deny resurrection? When your deity did it, why not others? Crawling out of a grave is hard but not impossible. As long as you're not really dead. Then we have to think about the whole 'This is the cup of my blood' thing.

"We agree that there are no vampires. The popularity of the myth is down, I think, to two things. One is superstition – which is not fixed, and is very long-lived – and the other is literature. Polidori, Le Fanu and Stoker all bear blame for that – not to mention the moderns, like Madame Rice, who have sucked in the young and distractible. Somehow, it's caught the imagination.

"None of it is great literature. But it is persuasive to some. There have been, are, what one might call 'real' vampires. People who are delusional and think they are vampires, Sanguinarians, who take microdoses of blood (some of it their own) as medicine, a few criminal gangs who commit 'vampire murders' – probably what you've got here."

"I have heard the term 'Renfield Syndrome'," says Patrice. "Is that a thing?" Petra laughs. Her laugh is low and musical. Attractive.

"*Non*," she says. "Not a thing, though it has been on telly! Funny thing. The psychologist Richard Noll started it by making a parody of DSM-speak in 1992. He thought the American Diagnostic and Statistical Manual of Mental Illness – you know what it is – was getting stupider and stupider (which it is). He's regretted it since because the public took it up, like it does.

"It was supposed – Renfield, that is – in the public mind, to be a new name for what had been known as 'clinical vampirism'. You can find the number of fifty thousand cases, between 1892 and now, in Krafft-Ebing – if you believe in Krafft-Ebing. That works out to almost four hundred cases each year – to save you doing the sum!"

"Thanks!" says Patrice, wondering where she is going.

"But really, there are very few cases of clinical vampirism which have ever been described. And Renfield, if you take it from Stoker's book, wasn't a vampire anyway. The difference is remarkable. Between an erotic obsession and an eating disorder!" She laughs again, and Patrice joins her. He likes her sense of humour.

"Really, clinical vampirism is part of a cluster of symptoms around extraordinarily violent crime. The Renfield thing has never appeared in any decent diagnostic reference."

"*D'accord.*"

"I'm assuming," she says, "that there was no forensic trace of saliva or anything you could get DNA from at the scenes?"

"Right," says Patrice, "and no bite marks either. Obviously. So, no one has tried exhaustively to make it like a bite. I realise that could have been done. Although I myself would not particularly like to install the bite marks ..."

"Nor me," says the psychologist. "But it's proving difficult for local police, and others, to admit that, even without evidence. Why do you think that is?"

"*Je n'ai aucune idée.*[51] That, really, is why I wanted to talk to you. What makes people cling to ideas which are ridiculous? Which are so terrifying? What is it all about?"

"Some would say that it's part of the idea that we all like to be frightened – especially when we are safe at home by the fire. But this is far from that. Others would say that it's tradition; it's been there so long that memories just haven't had enough time to shake it off. Some would say it's largely pretence, towards the maintenance of the culture."

"You wouldn't say any of those, though, would you?"

"*Non*, I would not. Although I do think that time has much to do with it. Culture, in Romania, is Latin and therefore emotional, romantic. A Slavic temperament would, I think, be less likely to lap this sort of thing up. I am asking myself whether Dracula is scarier than the late Monsieur Ceaușescu? You could think about that for a bit."

20

Colette has combed through her Romanian travel literature to find places she can visit during the second week of her stay. She accepts, by now, that Amélie is unavailable and she will have to go alone.

She decides on Sighișoara, where Vlad Țepeș was born, and the salt mines at Turdu, where ... whatever. There will be ample time, she thinks, for the further reading of the *Dracula*. But she will find a place to settle in Sighișoara and read it where Vlad III Dracula first saw the light. It's a longish bus ride, three hours and thirty-two minutes each

---

51   I have no idea

way, so an early day and a latish night back. Perhaps she'll give the salt mines a miss.

Colette has briefed Amélie that she will be away for the whole day so as not to worry her – as if. The girl-child says she'll be fine.

Colette views the lovely countryside through Transylvania. She has already established that there seems little evidence of much Dracula connection in Sighişoara – there's a café and a small museum, apparently, but only set up in modern times. Should it be true that Drac was born and lived until *4 ans* in Sighişoara, he really didn't spend very much time in Transylvania at all.

The bus takes its passengers straight to the citadel, avoiding the relatively short but uphill foot climb occasioned by the banning of traffic. The town is quaint and colourful, with painted houses, pink and red, yellow, and blue, green and lavender, with wooden accompaniments. It has a population of about thirty thousand and is a UNESCO World Heritage Site. She wanders for a while close to the monastery, up the Scholars' Stairs, with its wooden roof to shelter church and school goers from the rain. Romania is very green; it has a lot of rain. As well as lots of upland country. Abraham does not make that completely clear – the heights! He writes good mist though. The Clock Tower is lovely from outside, and from its tower has a wonderful view of the lower town.

The tourist stuff says that the citadel has been much like this since mediaeval times, but the modern part of Sighişoara is in the lower town. It bustles and has a large complement of restaurants. Colette, however, has made her decision to go back in search of Dracul. At least it will be *amusant*. The citadel looks brilliant from here, and there is a great view of the Venetian House from the Clock Tower.

The Casa Vlad Dracul is billed as a centuries-old building, although secretly (not so) it has been rebuilt recently. Colette is looking for lunch now. Although she can hardly resist the Romanian jam-and-cream doughnuts, she settles for a *ciorbă*, Romanian soup, which is lighter than the beef tripe soup (*ciorbă de Burta* – too heavy for lunch!). This is called *rădăuțeană* and is made with chicken breast, sour cream and plenty of garlic and vinegar, for a sour taste. She particularly enjoys the rough wholemeal bread as she wonders how vegetarians and, worse, vegans, avoid starvation in carnivorous Romania.

Perhaps the aubergine salad?

Lunch over, she visits Vlad's bedroom (won't be, will it?) and finds something of a horror rather than a sober museum. She feels something touch the back of her neck and supresses an unseemly scream. It is a huge artificial spider! There are also vampires asleep in coffins …

After this, Colette abandons Dracul's arachnid-infested lair for a small, horror-free café, which serves the aforementioned doughnuts and good coffee.

Today's Stoker reading-fest concerns the letters of Mina Murray and Lucy Westenra, Dr Seward (from the lunatic asylum), and The Hon Arthur Holmwood. Colette gets two separate funny looks from her fellow *gogosi* eaters. One, when she laughs loudly at Stoker's rendering of the letters of young women – incredibly hysterical and sweet, with Mina, the down-to-earth sensible one, pledged to be a helpmeet to the seemingly serious (but secretly hysterical) Jonathan Harker, and Lucy, the flirty one (is Stoker signalling promiscuous, or potentially so?), with three proposals of marriage on one day.

Colette's first laugh comes from the general creaky, wordy, complete ignorance of Abraham's knowledge of how young women speak to one another. The second comes from his rendering of the north-country dialogue (with smatterings of unexplained Scots) of the old seafarer whom Mina asks about the White Lady and other legends, at Whitby.

Colette is not very taken with Lucy's comment about Desdemona's having adventures poured into her ear "even by a black man", as if that were an inferior form of romance. Or with Lucy's vapid comment: "Why can't they let a girl marry three men, or as many as want her, and save all this trouble?" Just Stoker's wish list? Or his imagination about being a girl? Colette stops herself taking a break to consider Abraham's possibly tortured sexuality; she doesn't have time.

She doesn't laugh at any of this.

***

When René calls for him to answer an urgent telephone call from Paris, Patrice finds that Petra Boulet wishes to speak to him urgently:

"I had a thought which I wanted to share with you," says the psychologist. "When we spoke, I said my knowledge is only academic. That wasn't quite right. I didn't see that it was relevant to what you were asking. But I've been pondering ever since and I think my experience might help you, although I have no idea how."

"*D'accord,*" says Patrice, "please feel entirely free to contribute!"

"My wife and I travelled to Romania in the early nineties," she says, no humour showing now. "We were part of a voluntary organisation which wanted to do something about the dreadful state of the orphanages. You recall the news then – about terrible things, inhuman things, about that?"

"I do," says Patrice. Remembering it is hardly bearable even now.

"We adopted twins," she says. "A boy and a girl. Mihaela and Dorin are eighteen now. What few people know about all that is why it happened. And it's down to Ceaușescu's desire to be a great statesman and the saviour of the Romanian people."

She stops, taking a breath, fighting through the horror still in her head.

"His intention was to encourage the 'pure' Romanians to breed and simply crowd 'mixed race' people out of the country. Including the very many Hungarians in Transylvania and elsewhere. He directed all women of child-bearing age to have at least four children; later he changed it to five. There were financial allowances. He banned contraception and abortion" – she takes another breath – "but couldn't, of course, ban children being born with 'defects'. Where the children weren't seen to be perfect, or the parents were unable to manage, the babies were consigned to orphanages.

"There was little food, little of anything really. A lot starved. A lot died. We could only take two. They are beautiful and happy. And we couldn't love them more if we had given them birth."

When she has stopped, and Patrice has concluded his wondering about why Petra felt she needed to tell him all this so urgently, he says:

"Thank you for sharing all this with me."

"But you're wondering why?" she says.

"*Un peu.*"

"There is a reason," says Petra. "I wanted you to know, although I have no idea whether it is important, that when there was no food, the staff at the orphanages used to give the children micro-transfusions of blood. Of course, much of it was infected – they had no way of testing it. So, they had a terrible HIV/AIDS epidemic. Which Ceaușescu, obviously, denied was happening."

When the psychologist has hung up, Patrice says to himself that he was wrong. The idea of "pure" Romanians is Nazi-inspired after all.

***

Clémence puts down the telephone and turns to Fleur with a grimace.

"*D'accord. Quoi?*" says Fleur, hoping it isn't something especially nasty.

"Madame Barthélemy," says Clémence, "has an infection."

"Uh?"

"In her earlobe. Where RR ripped the earring from. The wound has turned black. She may have to have it amputated. The ear."

"Have these people never heard of antibiotics?" asks Fleur. "What the hell is she talking about?"

"Wasn't her," says the younger officer, "it was him. The little husband. She is quite ill, apparently, and he is going to sue Rannequin for assault. If she loses her ear, he will be asking for punitive damages. I think that's an American thing, *n'est-ce pas?*"

"Did you deal with it?" asks Fleur.

"Of course," says Clémence. "I said that we will be charging his wife with interfering with the course of justice by reporting that she had two earrings stolen instead of one."

"What did he say?"

"Nothing. He hung up."

"*Eh, bien.*"

***

"Monsieur d'Aroque." Patrice addresses his junior officer, asking him what his next move would be.

"*Alors, patron*," he says, "the task you gave me about the drugs hasn't produced very much. I have enquired about the situation in Romania and although they say that it is less of a problem here than in many countries, I am not sure I believe it. The figures I got were from the 2011 report …"

"So, seven years old, then?"

"*Oui*. There seems nothing newer. At least nothing accessible to foreigners. The report says that the premier drug is cannabis, which is predictable. Then the usual heroin, cocaine, the old 'legal highs', et cetera; not much about opioids. Although they must be there, obviously.

"I talked to an old timer, who happened to speak French, and he says there is loads of OxyContin and fentanyl around on the street and therefore in the evidence lockers. He says any police officer can get hold of it. No trouble. Others might have a problem – although they can get it from a known drug dealer. All in all, not difficult."

"Thought as much," says Patrice, "but one never knows."

"*Alors*. Given, then, that the murderer would have got the drugs for the men easily, we need to find out, from the wives, whether they, the wives, were drugged, or not really there at all, or anything else."

"*Oui*," agrees Patrice. "But also we need to analyse the words of the wives. Their experience is different from that of the police who responded, and of ourselves. There may well be gems concealed in what they said. What we require is the actual words the wives used, and then the words of the policepersons. Then we need to analyse which of these are essential and which we can disregard."

Benjamin calls up the transcripts of the questioning of the wives on his laptop.

Patrice says that he would like each separate word section to be compared throughout, and if there isn't a comparable one from one wife, then a space will indicate that.

"Let us begin with Madame Dobrescu," says Patrice, "when you yourself and Faye Benoît spoke to her. Please read the actual text to me."

"Madame Dobrescu, when we tracked her to Madame Dincă's house, says:

- What is it you want to know?
- I had been dreaming. Deeply asleep. I do not usually sleep so deeply. Sometimes I do not sleep at all. But that night I had. It was late for me not to awaken until almost seven. And I was surprised that Luca was still in bed too. He usually gets up at six and takes a walk. He had blood all over his chest. I put my fingers on his neck and there was no pulse. I put my hand to his mouth and there was no breath. He was dead. I had no way of knowing how he died.
- [*Police: What about all the blood?*] *Oui, mais certainement*. I meant that I had no idea who had done this thing. I had seen and heard nothing.
- [*Police: How long have you lived here, etc.?*] Is that important?
- We have been here five months since the end of September last year. We came from Bucharest when Luca retired from his office job. We have two children, Maria and Eugen, who have children of their own now and don't need us. There are no other relatives, so it was easy to come up here where Luca's family originally came from. I myself have not worked since we married, I have

supported my husband and children. I had three
miscarriages and could have no more children
after Eugen. My husband had a pension, and we
supplement it with our own vegetables and selling
goat's milk – we have a nanny goat around the
back. We did. Before.

- I was a secretary in a government office. Very
  junior, but that was a long time ago and can have
  nothing to do with what happened.

- [*Police: Had Luca any enemies?*] *Non*, not at all.
  Everyone likes Luca, he is a friendly man!

"That is all, *patron*," says Benjamin. "Do you want me
to go on with what was reported by Officer Mercard when
he talked to the Romanian officers?"

"Not yet," says Patrice. "Let's look at what Madame
Dobrescu actually said, and decide what is superfluous and
what is not."

"*Oui, patron!*"

"*D'accord.* We can rule out a few things immediately.
For the moment, at least, cross out the sentences where she
asks 'What is it you want to know?' and 'Is that important?'.
Those appear irrelevant. Although they are part of her
general attitude of efficiency and the perception that she
knew exactly what to do.

"Perhaps you can identify for me which are the most
important things she said?"

Benjamin looks nervous for a moment, then clears his
throat and points out the passage where Diana Dobrescu
says she had been dreaming, that her level of sleep was
unusual, that her husband was also still in bed and that he
was dead.

"She seemed as if she were quite calm," says Benjamin.
"Feeling his neck, which was very bloody and sliced – how

did she manage that anyway? And then not panicking when she realised he was not breathing."

"*D'accord*, what else?"

"The bit where she says that she didn't know how he'd been killed, when it was obvious."

"And?"

"Something in her biographical statement," he says, "but I'm not sure what …"

"Try and think," says Patrice.

"Um … the miscarriages? Why would she tell us about those? Don't women usually keep that sort of information quiet?"

"*Oui*," says Patrice, "usually. Because miscarriages have devastating effects on them, on partners, on marriages. She told us, perhaps, because it is important. Why would it be important?" He reminds the junior officer about the Ceauşescu policy of four or five children for each woman. They talked about this at the last general meeting.

"Ah," says Benjamin. "What happens to the woman if she can have no more children?"

"Good point," says Patrice, "I don't know. See if you can find out, please. And ask if they still have a goat."

21

Colette looks again at her Romanian travel brochures and the pamphlets she has picked up since she got here. There are still many things she needs to see to make a complete connection with the country. And only about three more days to do it. She hopes to take Patrice for a tour of

Dracula's (alleged) castle before they return home, although he is doubtful that he will have time.

Where should she go? What would be one of the must-see places? Her favourite place has been the Museikon, where she got involved in how an icon is constructed. It had been incredibly interesting. She has become more interested in Dracula by now – although not in any supernatural way. It is the metaphorical which interests her, and the management of monsters.

She ruffles through the papers and comes out with the idea of travelling to Snagov, to the north of Bucharest, where, in an island monastery, Vlad Țepeș is supposed to have been buried (after he properly died). Apparently, there is no body, the tomb is merely symbolic. Uh huh. The only thing that worries Colette is the prospect of another long journey; she is spending much of her sightseeing time travelling. Still, not to worry.

The receptionist at the desk in the hall tells her that the quickest way to get to Snagov is by plane. It only takes fifty minutes and is not expensive. Colette books there and then.

The monastery and the church provide her with many paintings and icons to admire, as well as the empty grave. The monks are supposed to have hidden Dracula's body from the Ottoman Turks, but his head may have been boiled in honey and displayed. This sounds disgusting. Vlad did, though, endow the monastery and fortify it, building the tower in the fifteenth century. The tower is still there. It is a fine, sunny day, and she finds a bench in the garden where she can sit and read her book.

This morning's section concerns Dr Seward's diary and is about his insane asylum patient Renfield. Is this here to revolt the reader? The zoophagy is being developed as the patient feeds his flies to his spiders. We know a lot more about eating disorders these days.

Bit slow off the mark, Seward gets to the idea that Renfield thinks he can absorb life from eating live animals. It has taken the doctor much intellectual effort to get there, and Colette applauds him for it. He has decided that Renfield is a homicidal maniac *(quoi?)* who intended, perhaps, to eat the cat to whom he intended to feed his sparrows. There is a rhyme, isn't there? thinks Colette. "There was an old lady who swallowed a fly, perhaps she'll die ...", which continues in increments of life?

She notes that Seward does not care if said maniac eats the sparrows, but draws the line at a kitten. He ponders that he, Seward, might have an exceptional brain – and might pursue some wonderful knowledge if only there was sufficient reason for the effort!

Colette thinks about Abraham's brain and how he clearly has some capacity and competence, although he didn't bother graduating from Dublin's Trinity College – and later bought his master's degree for money. He did, though, pass the London Bar – not easy – but never practised as a lawyer.

She puts down the book of fiction and gazes around at the garden, at the lake, at the monastery. She remembers, unusually for her, that Jesus advised looking at the sparrows.

***

Patrice's cell phone rings and Benjamin tells him that women who couldn't have the required number of children in Ceaușescu's Romania could, if they had enough money, buy their way out of trouble; otherwise they could be arrested, and the families fined.

He has also turned up some information, which he refers to as "unsavoury", concerning the existence of gynaecologists, who examined women every three months in order to prevent them from taking black-market abortion pills, imported from other countries, and what the people called "the menstrual police".

The Madame Dobrescu no longer has a goat.

***

Jean-Claude Fortin is very tall and towers, glowers, over the small figure of Clémence Godard in her wheelchair. They are positioned on the avenue, outside Les Invalides, in the hope of Nikolas Pellisier and his kidnapper deciding to pay a call on the remains of Napoleon I Bonaparte in the red porphyry casket. *L'Empereur* is, of course, buried here, guarded by a low lintel which prevents anyone from entering without bowing their head in respect.

Clémence is beginning to think that this whole thing is pointless. Perhaps they are wrong about the bits of clothing being messages from *le petit* Nikolas? Maybe it's something else entirely?

Fleur has turned up Fortin from somewhere to help her, and Clémence is finding him incredibly hard to talk to. She doesn't usually have this problem as she is quite gregarious, and once people have got over the wheelchair status, they can be forthcoming. Getting people to talk is one of her superpowers!

Her superior officer had thought she could herself be with Clémence as a team for this mission, but that has not worked. Fleur needs to be in the office, coordinating the many things which are going on. She cannot wait for next Monday when the rest of the team returns. The quiet period has been harder than she expected.

Fortin is not a young man, although Clémence is not sure of his age. He might be forty or fifty; his hair is thick but sprinkled with grey. He is good-looking, she supposes, but not at all her type. Just as well; he has a thick gold ring on his third finger. Firmly married. She has asked him where he comes from, who is his wife, does he have children? He has told her: Angoulême, Christine, and one, a boy, *15 ans*. With no extra information whatever. *D'accord.*

Clémence thinks they must look like a very odd couple if anyone is watching. Although she doubts anyone is. They look like they've had a row. Which they will, eventually. Clémence can feel it approaching.

Suddenly, into the stream of tourists risking the March sunshine, comes a woman with a young boy. She is elderly, maybe his grandmother, and is holding his hand – at arm's length. He is wearing a brightly patterned red *pull* but no topcoat. He has dark hair, looks smooth and cared for, although not styled in a modern way.

As the pair approach Clémence and Jean-Claude, the police take note of the expressions on their faces, the woman determined, the child excited. They are walking fast, not sightseeing. Walking for exercise? Now, they have passed by, and Clémence spins the chair around and gestures to Jean-Claude that she means to follow them. He jumps to take hold of her handles, even though she has told him not to. He can certainly make her go faster, and she is grateful for that in this instance.

The old woman and the young boy do not look around. They seem to have no idea that they are being followed. They enter the building and start down the stairs. Clémence can go no further but, as they proceed towards the great bronze door, forged from the cannons taken at the Battle of Austerlitz, Jean-Claude follows them.

This is the part which is hardest for Clémence: having to sit back while someone else does things. She sighs, even though she is excited because she really thinks that Nikolas Pellisier is the young boy who is with the woman. She passes the time by reciting the extract from Napoleon's will, which is inscribed on the lintel at the foot of the stairs:

> *"Je désire que mes cendres reposent sur les bords de la Seine, au milieu de ce peuple Français que j'ai tant aimé.*[52]*"*

It isn't long until Jean-Claude re-emerges, handcuffed to the woman, with the boy still holding her hand. They walk across to Clémence, and Jean-Claude says that the woman does not wish to be questioned. He has insisted and is about to take them back to *le Trente-Six* for interview.

Clémence, pretending to be senior officer (because she really doesn't know if she is), arranges transport, and all four go to *PJ* headquarters.

***

Patrice and René have not had time to look at the murder of Monsieur Bunea in a phenomenological manner. They are now about to consider Patrice's interviews of Mme Bunea and the officers, Lupu and Danti, to produce the essential items.

"Madame Bunea," says Patrice, "was another unexpected type of person. Well educated, the head teacher in the Oarda High School, fifties, well put-together, I think. Good English. Small but pleasant house. Living within their means. Nice taste, sandalwood polish.

- The couple lived in Oarda for fifteen years, after taking jobs in local schools. They were settled and did village events and issues but not politics. She said that politics isn't good for teachers
- They helped people who needed it and got on well with everyone

---

52   *"I wish my ashes to rest on the banks of the Seine among the people of France whom I so much loved."*

- She could not think of any enemies (of either of them)
- Both travelled when students. He spent some time studying English in UK
- Came from Bucharest – where had jobs in high schools
- He originally came from Constanța; she, from Moldavia
- Both at university in Bucharest and met there
- No children – didn't want any, "had enough at school"

Patrice stops speaking and waits for René to make a comment. René considers for a moment.

"We can, can't we, discount their travelling when students? And where they originally came from? My sense is that the coming from Bucharest may be essential? And the having no enemies could be a lie, *n'est-ce pas*? Are there really any teachers who haven't had differences of opinion with parents about children, or with other teachers who disagree with something they've done? I think, perhaps, that their avoidance of politics (and her telling you about it) and them not having or wanting children are the two most crucial items."

"I think you are correct," says Patrice. "Well done! I feel that the answer to the enemies' question is quite likely to be at least gliding over a truth she does not wish to face – but is it relevant in this case? It may not be.

"The declared avoidance of politics and the desire not to have children is a dyad, isn't it? They did not take part in politics since they came to Oarda. Does this mean they may have done when in Bucharest? They did not have children, although before the revolution, they were of child-bearing age, she twenty-nine years in 1989, he thirty-nine years. She said the thing about having enough at school in a throwaway manner, not serious ..."

"But it would have been serious," says René. "Very serious indeed in a land without contraception or abortion. They couldn't just decide not to have children; how would that work?"

"It wouldn't," says Patrice. "Unless they were very rich or very favoured by the Ceaușescus, or members of the *Securitate*. Also, who else, apart from teachers, strictly would avoid politics?"

"That's it, isn't it?" says René. "Anyone who is hiding would avoid politics. Our murder victims were all in the secret police!"

They are talking in the dining room belonging to the chief of police, and her husband, Nicu, who is much older than she, comes in to offer them coffee. He is concerned that he can offer no pastries; they ate all the doughnuts last night. They express their delight with good Turkish coffee, which they don't like.

"The report of the Romanian police officer Lupu, interpreted by the Assistant *Commissaire* Paduche. She doesn't have either French or English, is detailed but concise about what Madame Bunea said:

- Madame Bunea said she had been in the house all night
- Madame Bunea had heard nothing, she had not awoken
- There was no disturbance
- Madame Bunea said he did not have any enemies and they are 'part of the community and have been accepted there for many years'

"Three of those," says René, "are about her, Madame; that she was there all night, that she had not awoken, that there had been no disturbance. So, can we discount those, *patron*?"

"*Non*," replies Patrice. "But we can put them aside for a minute. The important one is likely to be the quote 'we are part of the community and have been accepted there for many years' – that, I think is quite significant."

"Do you think she was lying, *patron*?"

"*J'en doute,*[53]" says Patrice. "Is it significant, though, that she needed to say it? Why shouldn't they have been accepted?" He pauses, thoughtful, then says that he is interested in what Officer Lupu said too.

"I have written down what she said when I spoke to her, in addition to her written report:

- Nichita Bunea was lying in bed with his throat open
- There was a lot of blood
- Lupu wondered why the killer hadn't drunk all the blood if that was what he wanted. Wastage is not usual in other cases she has seen
- Lupu ordered Danti to telephone the coroner and to guard the bedroom door until the SOCO arrived
- Although stationed in Oarda, Officer Lupu did not know M *et* Mme Bunea to speak to, although she has seen them in the street."

"Did she think the killer was a vampire, then?" asks René.

"That was what I wondered," answers Patrice. "And when *Commissaire* Paduche was leaving, I asked her if many of her officers believe, still, in vampires. I tried to make light of it, but she took it seriously and said, 'Many people still believe in the old stories, this sort of thing doesn't easily go away.'

---

53   I doubt it

"I mentioned that I should have expected that the forty-two years of the communist regime would have taken care of that, wouldn't it? And she asked, 'In a country which traces its history back to the Romans?'

"It made me realise that we shall have to bracket our suppositions about other people's cultures. We can't assume everyone is French!"

***

Salle d'entrevue trois[54] is overwarm because the heating in *le Trente-Six* is yet again malfunctioning. The building is decrepit, and some departments will be moving soon. The new Complex Crimes Unit is expecting to stay exactly where it is. Once it moves back to the newly painted fourth floor.

Fleur is in the senior investigative officer seat, Clémence at her side but metaphorically gagged. Jean-Claude Fortin is standing propped against the door to the corridor. The older woman from Les Invalides is in the suspect's chair, bolted to the floor. The child has been separated from her and is being spoken to by the childrens' officer next door.

They are having trouble getting a name from the woman. She keeps generating obviously false ones, some French, some not. Fleur thinks she recognises Russian names, Italian names, some seem strangely like Klingon. Fleur stops herself from banging her fist on the table, although she would really like to do it.

"Come on, madame," she says, "just your real name. How can I talk sensibly to you if you won't give me a proper name?"

The woman screws up her mouth and spits generously at the detective.

"Ugh!" Fleur manages to get out of her proximity and

---

54 Interview Room Three

Clémence hands her a tissue, with which she wipes her cheek. "Please don't do that!" The woman smiles with her lips; it doesn't reach her eyes. She says nothing.

"I need to talk to you about the young boy you were with at Les Invalides," Fleur says, "and who he is, and who he is to you." She stares at the woman, who does not make a move. Does she not understand? Maybe not, but she appears to have access to lots of made-up names, and lots of transmissible spit, so she does understand something.

Fleur wonders whether Mlle Fleriot next door has found out whether the child is Nikolas Pellisier. Fleur would love to be able to call Mme *et* M Pellisier and tell them Nikolas is back.

They have been staring at one another for five minutes when there is a movement in the room and suddenly Jean-Claude has walked over from the door, pushed Clémence out of his way, and is facing the woman directly, bending over the table, getting in her face.

"Who the hell are you?" he shouts very loudly, their noses about an inch apart. Clémence is looking shocked and trying to reorient herself by the grubby window; Fleur has jerked away from the table, automatically giving the male officer the space he needs against her will. The woman murmurs:

"Catherine DeJoie." Her face is expressionless; it looks like the truth. Fleur retakes her previous position and asks:

"And who is the boy?"

"He is my grandson, Paul DeJoie. He is staying with me as his father is in Portugal on business for a month. His mother is dead." Clémence slides forward and asks her for her papers, which she produces, confirms her identity. She has no papers for her grandson.

"*D'accord*," says Fleur, "you may leave now." She finds

it difficult to conceal her disappointment. They leave the interview room, to find that Mlle Fleriot has already finished with young Paul, and they are standing in the corridor. As the pair leave *le Trente-Six,* Fleur turns Fortin around by pulling back his arm.

"If you ever do that again, you're going home with your balls in a paper bag."

22

René telephones Faye, in Bucharest, to call her to the next day's meeting.

"I think we found it!" she says as soon as she comes on the line.

"Found what?" asks René.

"The connection between our victims. Although not yet Monsieur Mitrea, because that was another time."

"*D'accord,*" says René. "And the connection is?"

"They must have been members of the *Securitate*. They were secret policemen!"

"And you can prove this?"

"Well, er, not quite. But we think so. Gabriela and I. We have discovered papers hidden in the secret archives which may say that they were given loans of money to retire, all part of the Bancorex collapse scandal – a lot of *Securitate* people and heads of newly private businesses were given money, virtually to disappear them, make them go away. When they became kind of too hot to handle."

"That is very interesting," says René. "The *patron* and I have come to a similar conclusion ourselves."

"*Merde!*" she says. "You sent me to the archives to get me out of the way. So that you could work it out yourselves!" She is tired, she has worked hard. She is emotional.

"Not at all!" says René. "It is additional information. What we have done is worked things out from what people said, the detail of what they said. You and, who is she? Gabriela, have found physical evidence which is strongly circumstantial and corroborative.

"We still have a long way to go – and little time left. Let's get you back here as soon as we can. We'll all be meeting tomorrow morning – the *PJ* team – to consider the information around Monsieur Dabija, and then a meeting with the Romanians in the afternoon, when we tell them what we know and tuck in all the loose ends."

"Will that be the end of it?" asks Faye. "*Peut-être,*" says René, "but I doubt it."

***

The main shopping street in Alba Iulia is very pleasant and has few vampire souvenir shops, *Dieu merci*! Colette is looking for a gift for Jean-Pascal and is not doing very well. She has found a squeaky for Sartre, whom she misses very much, and is confident that he will love it. But what to get Jean-Pascal? He is at an awkward age. He always has been. Maybe something connected with the driving?

She wants this to be her last opportunity to shop; there are only three days left before they go home. And she has booked a walking tour of Bran Castle for her and Patrice, as both a treat and a joke. She hopes Amélie will come too, although she doubts it. The girl is now looking forward, in dread, to going home and leaving her new friends.

Colette is beginning to doubt that she will finish her

comic reading of *Dracula* before she gets back to Paris and her normal routine. Perhaps she can find time? But close reading does take an extraordinary number of hours – which she doesn't have when she is working at her usual job. Never mind. She could probably read for a PhD in the thing.

This morning, she was with Mina Murray and Lucy Westenra in Whitby, Mina worrying about Lucy – even though she has put on weight (she writes "stouter" – this is Abraham's word, *n'est-ce pas*? A young woman – or any woman – does not call another "stout" unless wanting to insult). And Lucy has redder cheeks, always a sign of danger – she is showing more hysteria by the day ... and Mina is not smelling the rat at all.

The weather is used, and well, as a metaphor for the trouble which is coming. The Russian schooner *Demeter* is in trouble at sea, in a terrible, doom-laden storm. And when she arrives, an enormous dog jumps from her deck and disappears into the cliff, under the collapsing graveyard. Any feelings of doom yet, Mademoiselle Murray? *Non? D'accord.*

Mina has pasted a press cutting into her diary, and here Monsieur Stoker shows his talent and credentials as a journalist – even though his forte is theatre criticism. The writing is suitably colourful and action-laden in a fine *style ampoulé*[55] description of the storm and the ship beaching in Whitby Harbour, with a dead sailor two days tied to the wheel. How did he know it was two days?

All of it chosen to illustrate the psychic connection between the increasingly hysterical Lucy and the Count (whom we know is on the *Demeter*). Impressions of things to come!

***

---

55   literally "bombastic" – equivalent of "purple prose" in English

The French members of the homicide team, with Faye on Zoom, assemble in the dining room of Chief Gadianu and are served tea by Nicu, who appears to enjoy his servitude. They are to work intensively on the case of Monsieur Dabija, the butcher in Bărăbanţ.

Patrice explains that there is a space in their thinking which should be occupied by Monsieur Mitrea, but that, so far, they have made little progress – on account of the condition of his body and the fact that he has no obvious relatives.

"*Alors,* we shall put him aside for a while and discuss the situation surrounding Monsieur Dabija." He looks around the room, nodding slightly to each staff member. This may be an easier meeting for the four French detectives than this afternoon's meeting for the whole team. Possibly including Monsieur Melichian.

"*D'accord,*" says Patrice. "What did Madame Dabija actually say to you, René?"

"Not a great deal, *patron,*" says René. "I got much more at second-hand from Officers Theodorescu and Florescu. She did say these things, though:

- The story as told to the police is correct
- She doesn't think the competing butcher killed him
- Monsieur Dabija was not very good at business (they were going broke) whereas the other butcher was doing 'well enough'
- She is not especially sorry that her husband has died."

"*D'accord.* Faye, could you tell us which of these statements is most important and which can be dismissed?"

"*Oui, patron,*" says Faye. "It is important that it is unlikely that the other butcher, Monsieur Tabardici, killed him, and that he was not good at business. I think that the fact she is not sorry about his death is probably irrelevant to the group of cases. Even if she killed her husband, we are not thinking she killed all four, are we?"

"*Non*," says Patrice. "Let's go on to the testimony which the Romanian officers gathered, shall we?" René coughs and sips what is left of his cold coffee.

"*Patron*," he says, "the officers reported that the couple has lived at their shop and flat for six years, since Monsieur Dabija had *60 ans*, and that Madame Dabija made the following statements:

- Monsieur Dabija had had a previous job in administration in Bucharest but had, in his youth, trained as a butcher
- Mademoiselle Maria Dabija is married and lives with her husband and two children close by. She is the grown-up daughter of the Dabijas
- Madame Dabija was very distraught (although not upset by husband's death?)
- Her husband was a regular, aggressive drunk, and was drunk that night
- He was killed on the sofa, which was covered in blood
- Madame had first thought it might be animal blood
- She realised it was his blood and had come from his throat. He was dead and cold
- Her daughter and the baby had come around to comfort her. Her mother sent her away because the baby was crying
- She said that Dabija and Tabardici were in furious competition and hated each other

She said it wasn't Tabardici; it was a punishment from 'Them'!"

"*Bon Dieu!*" says Patrice. "That is a lot. Why that much, do you think? Benjamin?"

"Making a lot out of a little?" asks Benjamin, not at all sure.

"You are probably right," says *le patron*. "What about the rest of it, René?"

"It seemed odd to me," says René, "that both Romanian officers paled as the condition of the body was described, even though Monsieur Theodorescu wasn't supposed to understand French, or German – Florescu and I used a hybrid, and it worked reasonably well. And they both laughed uncomfortably together …

"I asked about whether the flat had been disturbed but they said it had not – it was clean and tidy, even though he was drunk. The Dabijas seem not rich but comfortable. I was wondering whether Madame had cleaned the house, even if her husband was lying dead. It's a bit like, maybe, Madame Dobrescu lighting the fire while her husband was lying dead, *n'est-ce pas?*"

"What else did you find peculiar?" Patrice is so practised at getting at things his officers hold back that few of them ever do it any more.

"I couldn't help but think what butchery and admin have in common. Does the admin involve some butchery of its own?"

The four officers stare at each other as this persuasive question stands before them.

***

Clémence and Fleur are depressed about the Pellisier case.

209

Both had solved it in their own minds before Jean-Claude and Clémence brought in Madame DeJoie and her grandson. They had been so sure it was Nikolas Pellisier and his kidnapper. The obvious next move is to go back to a landmark and *surveille*. Both find the prospect of this totally miserable. As so much of police work is.

"Do you think that it might be worth talking to the detective, Tony Serres, again?" asks Clémence. Fleur wrinkles her face even more than normal, and says she is not sure he can help any more.

"He might, I suppose. Maybe," she says. "What do you think he might know that we don't?"

"He has probably got a different perspective from the one we have about the parents," says Clémence. "They may have told him other things. I don't really mean a different story, just ... er ... well, maybe there are some tiny bits of difference that would help?"

"If the *patron* were here," says Fleur, "his head would be boiling. *D'accord*, let's get Tony in and give him a girly going-over. He'll like that!" She reaches for the half-smoked cigarette which isn't there, changes her mind, and drinks from a bottle of mineral water.

Tony Serres arrives an hour later and, after commenting on the fact that "the girls" are still on their own, settles with them and a pot of coffee to read out the Pellisier parents' statements from his various contacts with them.

There is absolutely nothing to see here.

***

The second sitting of the *PJ* enquiry, into the death of Monsieur Artur Mitrea, is sandwiched, tightly, into the end of the lunch hour, before the Romanian troops arrive. Patrice has been thinking that there would not really be much to say – especially as Faye has not found anything to attach the older man to the other victims.

Patrice is about to be proven wrong.

"Monsieur Artur Mitrea, *84 ans,* no relatives, no friends, it seems. Killed in his flat in Bărăbanţ," he says.

It is Benjamin who has interviewed Officer Maria Meleghi, whilst René had talked to Officer Florescu, on a different occasion.

"*Patron,*" says Benjamin, "we talked about this at our meeting with the Romanians, and Mademoiselle Meleghi spoke for herself then. Do you want me to repeat what she said?"

"*Non,*" says Patrice, "that won't be necessary. What I should like is for you to pick out anything which strikes you as odd, out of place, or especially intriguing."

"*D'accord,*" says Benjamin. "We spoke to ten other neighbours, as well as Madame Caranfil, who lives next door to Monsieur Mitrea, but none of them had anything different to say. They were uniform on these:

- No one knew him well, even though he has lived there at least fifteen years
- No one ever saw any visitors or family
- No one liked him
- He yelled at local kids
- He was self-contained and did his own shopping
- Madame Caranfil thought he was stingy, but he might just have been poor
- They think he came, originally, from Bucharest
- No one knew how old he was
- No one, including the gossipy Madame Caranfil, wanted to talk or speculate about the murder."

"*Alors*, which would you say is the most interesting statement?" Patrice knows that the younger man is already there. After all, M Melichian had mentioned it at their previous meeting. Suggested it's a cultural thing.

"The last thing," says Benjamin. "Monsieur *le Contrôleur Général* Melichian suggested that we are working on Paris attitudes – but I can't agree with that. There is something else. But, apart from that, I think it's significant that Monsieur Mitrea appeared to be especially poor. Maybe it's because he retired before the others? Maybe he'd spent all his money?"

"Ah," says Patrice, "that is interesting. Benjamin. Can you make a note of that and remind me of it later?" He says he can.

René had interviewed Officer Florescu, who had attended the Mitrea crime scene, along with Officer Meleghi, as well as having attended the death scene of M Dabija. Also in Bărăbanţ.

"One thing before we continue," says Patrice. "Does anyone think there is anything odd in the two murders happening in Bărăbanţ, whereas the others were one in Pâclişa and one in Oarda?" No one does, until Faye, on-screen, says that perhaps Monsieur Mitrea was the first and, maybe, a trial run?

"We don't think that the others were spontaneous and random, do we?" she asks. No one does.

"Florescu," says René, "made the following statements:

- Monsieur Mitrea had been dead some time and was well decomposed
- There was a smell of decomposed food but no 'death smell'
- There were copious dark stains, as of blood, on the pillow and blankets all around the head but especially on the level of the throat

- You could tell his throat had been torn. 'Perhaps he had his throat cut with a knife? Or maybe he was garrotted?'
- Florescu did not appear to believe either of these things."

"Are there things there which are suggestive of Faye's thought that Mitrea was a dry run, or a practice?" The other three look thoughtful; Faye is keen on her idea, but the others are not. They shelve it for now – but will not forget it.

"*D'accord*. We must remember, also," says *le patron*, "that we have a full post-mortem report on Monsieur Mitrea, some parts of which we may have to use instead of the detailed information we might have got from a wife or other family. *Alors,* now to the information which Madame Benoît has brought from Bucharest ..." He gives the floor to Zoom Faye, with a gracious gesture.

Faye describes a little of her own and Gabriela's despairing search in the national archives; knowing there must be items there which would help them, not knowing where to begin or, even, how to make a plan. She cuts to their recruitment of luck and their charge into the coloured folders – producing names and numbers. And, finally, Gabriela's intuitive leap to the changing of Romanian currency.

"So," she says, "we realised that the numbers against each name, if translated into old lei, made sense as suitable sums of money, the sort of amounts which were granted as sweetheart loans to the new 'elite', businesspeople becoming oligarchs, and secret policemen who needed to disappear. It seems plausible, *patron*."

"I am sure it does," says Patrice. "And, with our analysis of the language in witness statements, it is extremely persuasive. We shall present it to the full group when the rest arrive."

23

Another piece of clothing, a green American baseball cap, has been found in a litter bin near the Sacré-Coeur, on the Butte Montmartre, the highest point in Paris. The detectives have no way of knowing whether it is anything to do with Nikolas Pellisier or if it is just rubbish.

The child's father, Roland, has apparently been searching by himself ever since the original glove was found. Yvette, the mother, has stayed at home in case Nikolas comes back. Which doesn't seem at all likely.

Roland Pellisier arrives at the *Trente-Six* reception desk, yelling to see Detective Olivier immediately. This is the morning Clémence has asked Tony Serres to come in again, bringing all his documents so that they can examine them. They will probably be here together. *Alors*, maybe that will be for the best? Who knows?

Roland slaps the green cap on the desk in front of Fleur and says where he found it. Could it be his son's? It isn't something the boy has ever had but the kidnappers may have got it for him, *n'est-ce pas*? To disguise him, maybe? They could do that, couldn't they?" He runs out of breath as he comes to the end of his desperate plea.

"It isn't very likely," says Fleur as she lifts the hat with a gloved hand and extracts an evidence bag for it from her top drawer. "Kidnappers don't usually do things like that. Although it may be, of course." She looks sorrowfully at the man, who is worn down by worry and grief.

Clémence wheels closer and takes his hand in hers, saying how sorry she is. There is a knock on the door and Monsieur

Serres arrives, with a strong whiff of cologne. The smell of spaghetti sauce from Roland Pellisier has strong competition. The private detective greets M Pellisier and asks, tactlessly, how is he? The chef looks at him coldly, not trying to answer "How do you think?"

"Tony," says Fleur, "Monsieur Pellisier has just brought us this cap. He found it at the Sacré-Coeur, in a bin, like the other things. But we do not know that it is Nikolas's. It is very new, and his parents don't recognise it."

"It probably isn't his," says Serres. "It would be unusual for kidnappers to buy something for him." Clémence suddenly has a thought:

"We know this isn't a 'normal' kidnapping," she says. "We have never thought so. Maybe it is something else?"

"We have never received a ransom request," says the father. "It could be that they don't want to give him back."

"Is it," says Tony Serres, softly, as if to prevent the Fates hearing, "instead, child-stealing?" he says.

"And they are coming out now in order to test whether it is safe to do so?" Clémence is excited, pink, steepling her hands before her face.

"I take it that there is no name tape in the baseball cap?" asks Fleur.

"There isn't," says Roland, "and we would never have bought him one of those. It is too American. He is a nice French boy. He is our son!"

"*D'accord*," says Fleur, "if this is a child-stealing rather than a kidnap, what differences would that make to our next step?"

***

The full meeting of the homicide team is convened in the dining room of Nicu and Maria Gadianu. Nicu is a little

215

overwhelmed in his refreshment duties by sheer presence of numbers. There are fourteen of them, with the *chestor de poliţi* expected shortly.

They begin without him, in the hope that he will fail to turn up.

Patrice thanks them for all the work they have been doing, translated into Romanian by *Capitaine* Roşca, and explains that this will be their last group meeting. The French members of the team will be travelling back to Paris on Sunday. Chief Gadianu looks as if she might be thinking of thanking them for their work, but a look from Roşca persuades her otherwise.

"The case will not be over," states Patrice. "We cannot expect it to be, in the time we have had available. It will be necessary to hand it over to our colleagues in the Romanian police, here. But there are things which we need to discuss with you ahead of time and give you the opportunity to ask any questions you wish. Each of you will get a copy of our report on the investigation – when it is completed – and can read it in your own time."

"What was the point, then, of bringing you in?" asks Melichian, crashing through the door. He is very angry, white, strained, about to go off with a bang. The room goes silent and the participants around the table stare at him. Chief Gadianu stands up and makes a conciliatory gesture. The *contrôleur général* ignores her and begins a diatribe against the methods of the Paris *Police Judiciaire*.

Even Patrice, who had suspected, previously, that Melichian was the devil incarnate, was stunned by his outburst. Surely he had known that they would not be able to arrest anyone in the short time available. Without knowing how the country worked, how the culture functioned?

"Please calm down, Monsieur Melichian," says Patrice. "There is no advantage in having a stroke!" He laughs lightly. Melichian, a bit surprised, drops into a chair. *Le patron* begins to outline the case, going on to describe Faye's work in Bucharest and how it backs up what has been proposed by his own team's phenomenological analysis.

"We have several useful leads for you, as well as a few theories which you will need to explore, and although we have not yet identified the murderer, we believe we have clues to where you will find him or her.

"We also have a profile, somewhat like, but also different from, the type of profile usually provided by the FBI in America. We do not agree that their method is backed by good science, whereas we think ours is more useable. It is something which will have to be proven over time.

"*Alors,* the profile of the murderer" – he turns the top page of those he holds in his hand. "We feel that the murderer of three of the men – *Messieurs* Bunea, Dobrescu and Dabija – is most probably the same person, with the murder of Monsieur Mitrea only carried out by the same person if learning took place between Mitrea's killing and the next one. We think that the murderer is a man, although he does not have to be an especially strong man, but could have one or more accomplices, who might be women or girls.

"Two of the men, *Messieurs* Bunea and Dobrescu, were drugged with fentanyl or similar, whilst Monsieur Dabija may not have needed to be sedated as he was dead drunk. It could not be established whether Monsieur Mitrea was drugged because of the condition of his body. It became obvious that street drugs may be obtained easily, and there would be little problem in administering them in food or drink to the victims."

"We do not have a great drug problem in Romania," interrupts M Melichian. "There is very little drug trafficking, except in marijuana. There is only a little heroin and cocaine, and 'legal highs'. We have no figures for opioid abuse because we don't have any!"

"You don't have figures because no one has looked at the data," says René, "and the government policy is to play it down."

Monsieur Melichian becomes redder with fury but cannot challenge this truth. Patrice lets him boil whilst being ignored. He proceeds:

"There is, however, a difficulty in administering drugs to sedate the wives sufficiently for them not to be disturbed by the killing of their husbands, except for Madame Dabija, whose husband slept on the sofa in a different room.

"We have concluded that Monsieur Mitrea may have been a test case or practice murder. It is likely, from the post-mortem, that the gash in his throat was deeper and less professional, possibly someone trying his arm, or resuming something he'd done previously but needed to practise. *Alors*, it is highly possible that Monsieur Mitrea did not belong to the series of murders but was killed for this other purpose. This, also, may go some way to explaining why there were two murders in the same town.

"Madame Benoît and the archivist in Bucharest found no trace of Artur Mitrea's name in the national archives, but we have concluded that this is not necessarily relevant to this investigation as they may not have gone back sufficiently far.

"As to the connections between the victims, and this will also except Monsieur Mitrea, the findings in the national archives strongly suggest that the three men, Dobrescu, Dabija and Bunea, either worked together on a team, or had connections with a team, which opaid them to disappear, sometime after the revolution in 1989. There is circumstantial evidence, which was hidden in the files at the national archives – of which we have copies – that suggests that the numbers against the three names were amounts of money paid to them.

"In line with numbers of businesspeople, who became the new elite in Romania, many then-current members of the secret police were given large loans to remove them from the firing line of citizens who may have wanted revenge following their actions under the communist regime.

"As everyone here knows, the fact that these 'loans' were never repaid, or expected to be repaid, resulted in several crises and, finally, the collapse of Bancorex, the State-owned bank.

"We feel we can assume that *Messieurs* Dabija, Dobrescu and Bunea were not among the elite developing after the revolution, so it appears likely that they had been secret policemen, perhaps with records of extreme methods. This may be supported by all three families seeming to have been largely exempt from the provisions of the *'decretei'*[56] legislation, and there are questions in our minds about whether their wives, who all seem to be both younger and of a higher class than their husbands, may have been selected for them by the *Securitate*. This leads us to imagine that the wives may have been accessories to the murders, rather than having been drugged bystanders." Patrice takes a breath and M Melichian butts in:

"And what, lacking a murderer, do you suppose is the motivation?" he asks.

"I imagine," says Patrice, "that it will prove to be revenge. But we cannot yet be sure. The whole thing will turn on someone's confession."

"How in hell can you get a confession when you don't have a clue about a suspect?" Melichian shouts. He is losing

---

56 Literally "the sons of the decree" the Ceaușescu law which prevented abortion and contraception and resulted in children who could not be afforded by the population, hence orphanages

the plot, and everyone knows. The Romanian officers seem not to know whether to be embarrassed or angry, shamefaced or supportive. Apart from Madame Lupu, who remains her steadfast grey colour, they come in shades of pale to dark red.

"Obtaining that," says Patrice, "is part of our plan for tomorrow."

***

Pucelle's task, if not simplified, seems lighter – asking about Irina Alexandrovna, not having to overuse the name Elephant; although she still uses it somewhat because she is sure that it functioned as the large person's name for quite a time. It shows, Pucelle feels, more respect for the Russian woman.

Most people she asks shake their heads, one or two Russians engage her in spare conversations. They do not know Irina Alexandrovna but are interested in what support her organisation can give. A Kiswahili speaker asks the tall Black woman if she is Maasai; she says she is from Martinique.

A Russian speaker from Ukraine advises Pucelle to take her support and go to hell.

24

Colette is reading Abraham's version of the log of the *Demeter*, a Russian ship, largely in ballast from Varna, Bulgaria, just with some large boxes filled with what is described as "mould" but we know is the soil of Dracula's homeland. It is Friday in Alba Iulia and Colette is herself

220

preparing to return home.

Like some of the police officers with whom Patrice has been dealing, the ship's log details the strong feelings of the uncanny among the sailors on *Demeter* and their superstitiously crossing themselves. This is, for Stoker, part of the general idea of the inferiority of foreigners (and, consequently, the superiority of the British). British masters are sensible; foreign servants become hysterical at the drop of a top hat.

Then crew members on *Demeter* begin to disappear. One of those left thinks he has seen a man on deck, not a member of the crew. A search of the ship, meant to allay fear, does not do so. Eventually the mate, a Romanian, gets the idea that "It" is on board. With only him and the captain left, he goes after It with a knife – which goes through It as if It isn't there. He vows to search through all the boxes in the hold to find It. At last, Colette thinks, he's getting the idea.

But the captain blames the "madman", the mate who has now thrown himself into the sea. He has killed the crew one by one. Except, of course, he hasn't. The captain lashes himself to the helm, along with a crucifix and rosary beads to protect his immortal soul, and consigns his fate to the mercy of his God. *Bonne chance avec ça!*

Odd, isn't it, Colette thinks, that the cargo boxes are addressed to a solicitor in Whitby when the ship was not headed there? The huge dog has disappeared. Sad, as the pet-loving town of Whitby wanted to adopt it.

***

Yvette Pellisier arrives at *le Trente-Six* already in tears. She has come in answer to a summons from the detectives, following their examination of the papers brought in by

Tony Serres. They are reluctant because upsetting her again for nothing is against their feminist principles. Clémence offers to go and get coffee, but the woman refuses; she wants to get this done and return home to continue doing whatever she does to cope.

Fleur says that they have a couple of questions for Yvette after reading M Serres's various reports and records.

"I thought," says Yvette, "that he might be coming back when Roland found the baseball cap, but you said it wasn't likely to be his. I was sad."

"It didn't have any indication it was Nikolas's," says Fleur, "and Monsieur Pellisier said it wasn't anything you would have bought him."

"*Non,*" says Yvette, "Roland is very anti-American. He hates their manners and their money."

"So, he would not have given the boy a baseball cap?"

"He would not. But he said he found it, anyway, in the bin."

"I am sure he did," says Fleur. "But it must have been left there by someone not connected to Nikolas, mustn't it? You can see that."

"But why?" asks Mme Pellisier. "It is new, clean …"

"We need to focus away from the cap," says Clémence. "It is a distraction. It cannot belong to Nikolas. That it is found in a bin is a coincidence, *n'est-ce pas*?" She turns the wheelchair slightly so that she is facing Mme Pellisier but across the corner of Fleur's desk.

"Yvette," Fleur says, "I wonder if we can go back to your original statement to the *flics*, two years ago, and then what Monsieur Serres says you told him? There are a few things we should like to clear up. We apologise, again, about the original team neglecting you. You should have been interviewed again, at least once – and the *PJ* team should have known that Monsieur Serres was involved."

"*Désolée*," says Yvette, still tearful, "I should have insisted Roland informed you. But I didn't think of it."

"That is okay," says Fleur. "We could not have expected you to do this; you were too distressed. We do, though, wonder why your husband did not do it … *ne t'inquiète pas pour ça*, it will not be important. We shall be speaking again to Roland.

"For now, just go back to the day Nikolas was taken and tell us what happened in your own words. It was Tuesday, *n'est-ce pas?*"

"*Oui*, it was about 08.30 and we were going shopping. I had a big list because it was going to be Roland's birthday and I had decided to cook something special for him, his favourite. He is a chef and even cooks at home, so it is unusual for me to cook. I can, but I am not usually allowed to – oh, I didn't mean that it isn't 'allowed'; he doesn't forbid me or anything. I just don't usually do it!" She seems flustered as she says this, Clémence takes note, and of the three repeats around "usual".

"It was a cold day, so Nikolas was wearing his woolly hat and scarf, and his overcoat, and gloves. He was excited because we had agreed to bake a cake in the afternoon together. I was teaching him to bake a few things."

"I see," says Clémence. "Does he enjoy the baking?"

"*Oui*," says the child's mother. "He has been doing it since he was five. But he still enjoys it."

"*D'accord*," says Fleur. "What then?"

"I drove to the local supermarket and parked in the parent and child spaces. I was arranging my shopping list and putting my own gloves on when the passenger door was suddenly thrown open and a man in a ski mask pulled Nikolas out of the car and slammed it behind him!" She begins to cry anew and Clémence hands her a wad of tissues.

"The man doesn't say anything?" asks Fleur.

"*Non*," says Yvette, "nothing. And, no, I didn't recognise him at all. He was big, with enormous shoulders, and all dressed in black."

"What happened then?" encourages Clémence.

"How do you mean?" asks Yvette.

"Where did the man go? Where did he take Nikolas?"

"Ah, *oui*. He ran across the car park and got into a van."

"Did he drag Nikolas by the hand or what?"

The mother looks doubtful, thoughtful, and then says:

"By the arm, I think. I think he got hold of his shoulder, maybe. Oh, and the van was white. A Citroën of some sort. Dirty."

"And he drove away?" asks Fleur. "Immediately?"

"*Oui*," says Yvette. "Well he must have, *n'est-ce pas*?" She sits back as if finished. Fleur sits forward in her office chair.

"I don't know," says the older detective. "I wasn't there ..."

"It was a long time ago," says the mother mournfully. "I can't be sure I recall."

"Very well," says Fleur, "I think that's all for now, Madame Pellisier. We shall be back in touch with you very soon and will keep you informed about how everything is going. We shall not desert you again."

"Oh!" says the woman. "Will I have to come back again? I've told you everything I know."

"We shall have to leave that for now," says Clémence, running the chair to the door to let the other woman out. "*A bientôt!*"

***

"We appear to agree that the wives of these victims know more than they are saying. Who, then," asks Patrice, when the room is clear of Romanian policepersons, "is our best prospect for a confession of knowledge? We will talk to more than one – but it would certainly save time if we could guess correctly at the beginning ..."

"Madame Bunea," says René.

"Madame Dabija," says Faye.

"Madame Dobrescu," says Benjamin.

"*D'accord*," says Patrice. "René, why Madame Bunea?"

"Because, *patron*," says the detective, "she is the one who said that they had been accepted in the community, when we didn't know it was an issue. Because she presented her story as if it were a story, because she intimated they had a choice over having children."

"Plenty of reason there, then," says Patrice. "Madame Dabija, Faye?"

"*Patron*," says Faye, "Madame Dabija seems least upset about losing her husband. Also, she must have cleaned the flat, mustn't she? She says there was no disturbance, but her husband came home very drunk. He would have made a mess, *n'est-ce pas?*"

"*En effet*," says Patrice. "Excellent point. Benjamin?"

"Madame Dobrescu," says Benjamin. "Because of having lit the fire while her husband was lying dead in the bed. And because of all the icons. And, I think she's going to leave soon. She has sold the goat!"

Patrice's lips shift to a line of disapproval.

"The fire, yes, we can accept that as an anomaly," he says. "But the icons, no. Why not, René?"

"We have to bracket that as a personal prejudice," he says. "Just because you, Benjamin, and others of us, find the icons objectional, they are not a sign of guilt of anything – except, possibly, gullibility."

"You should have stopped after the word 'guilt', René!" says Patrice with a laugh, "There, you showed your own prejudice. *D'accord*, are we agreed that it would make all this much easier if the wives had each killed their husbands?"

Each member of the team nods her or his head a little but then decides that he or she has perhaps gone too far.

"That," says Faye, "would be a too easy assumption – and we could extend it to say that the killing of Monsieur Mitrea had been someone else teaching them how to do it …" She goes off, dreamily, thinking that through. "But then the killings wouldn't be clearly by the same hand … It would be easier, though, for the wives to drug the husbands and not need to be themselves drugged, of course."

"*Très intéressant*," says Patrice. "We should require a coordinator, though, should we not? Someone who knows the women – and the men, possibly? And what about the motive? Revenge? Perhaps, but definitely served cold. Not out of the question.

"I am thinking we shall get the wife we decide to target into a police station interview room and—"

"Interrogate her?" asks Benjamin.

"Question her," says René. "We have plenty of useful techniques and should be able to get a clearer impression of her when she's not at home."

"Faye," says Patrice, "will you kindly telephone the central police station at Pâclişa and ask them if we can have a room tomorrow? Benjamin, get someone to go and visit Madame Dobrescu and bring her in to the station. Faye, when she has returned and I will interview Diana Dobrescu, with Benjamin and René behind the glass – assuming they have it."

"*Oui, patron!*"

***

Whitby is not Paris, and the middle-of-the-night scene of the town, which Mina Murray finds as she pursues the sleepwalking Lucy Westenra, is not covered in the glow of the City of Lights. There is a bright, full moon. Spooky, *n'est-ce pas*? Colette, alone in her hotel room, with coffee, sandwiches and *Dracula*, carries on with her reading.

Lucy, of course, is sitting on the girls' favourite bench – with a dark "thing", man or beast, standing behind her reclining figure. Dear Mina rushes to get to her. Brave? Stupid? Sees a dark, long figure, with red eyes, bending over her friend. *Oh, pour l'amour de Dieu!*

When she gets there, her friend is alone, and Mina thinks she must have pricked the woman with the pin as she tried to fasten the shawl to keep her warm, for the "skin of her throat was pierced" in two tiny red points. A couple of nights later, they see a big bat out of the bedroom window, and then Lucy murmurs, oddly (or not), "His red eyes again, they are just the same." Then she sees Dracula on "their" bench in the rosy (red) glow of the sunset.

Mina sees the tiny wounds on Lucy's neck are larger and aren't healing. Lucy is weakening. If she isn't better soon, Mina will call the doctor. About time.

25

They settle Madame Pellisier in Interview Room Three, and Fleur and Clémence confer in their temporary squad room. Their "soon" has turned into the afternoon of the same day on which they have already interviewed her.

They had, somewhat reluctantly, done this in order to unsettle her. Their suspicions had become strong that there was more to this than anyone had previously thought. It cannot, so, wait.

"Thank you for coming in again so soon," says Fleur. "We have a few more things we need to check with you."

Mme Pellisier is not crying or, indeed, smiling ruefully now. She looks rather angry and says that she feels twice in one day is too much. She is terribly tired.

Fleur and Clémence join together in their apology; they do not mean to upset her more than is necessary, they just have a little thing or two to ask her. Clémence, trading on disability as being in some way equivalent to the trauma of losing a child, asks Madame Pellisier about her relationship with her husband. The woman says she does not understand what that has to do with anything.

"I don't know why you are asking that," she says. "We have a very ordinary marriage. We have been married for ten years. My husband works all the time, as usual with food service – it has anti-social hours and pays poorly. It is hard work, too, and very tiring." The expression on her face states that that is about all she has to say.

"How does Roland get on with colleagues at the restaurant?" asks Fleur.

"Well enough," says Yvette. "There is always conflict in kitchens. And the best chefs have generally very bad tempers – they shout and swear at the staff, sometimes humiliate them. It is *effroyable!*[57]"

"Does Roland ever lose his temper?" asks Fleur.

"*Non,*" says Yvette, "not at all. He wouldn't." Neither Clémence nor Fleur believes her. This is the time when they have to start hassling her over this point.

---

57   appalling, frightful

"It is very frequent," says Clémence, "that when men are upset and humiliated by the violent tempers of other men, especially men in leadership roles, that they bring their anger home, and take it out on their wives and children …" She leaves it like that in the hope that Mme Pellisier will pitch in. She does.

"Oh, no, that never happens!" she says. "It has never happened. Roland is not a violent man." She does not appear to be upset now; she is just lying smoothly, in order to conceal.

"You mean that Roland has never come home and told you that the chef has been pushing him to the edge of sanity again?" says Fleur.

"Oh, well, sometimes he is angry. He tells me about it. But he shouts, that is all. He has never, ever, punched me or Nikolas. Even when either of us has said something stupid! He is very good to us."

"What sort of thing would Roland think is stupid?" asks Clémence.

"Oh, I don't know," she says. "Just something crass that makes him think we don't understand. Something silly, stupid." She closes her mouth again as if that is all they're going to get.

"Does Nikolas say stupid things sometimes?" asks Fleur.

"*Non*, not so much," says his mother. "It is mostly me."

"And what happens then?" asks Clémence, leaning forward, confidentially, intimately.

"Oh, he just pushes me or something, just so I can remember not to do it again." She starts to weep silently, recognising she has given ground. She sniffs and accepts more tissues from Clémence.

"Has he ever used his fists on you?" asks Fleur. "When he is terribly, horribly, upset? Sometimes men can't help it, they have to react. Because he can't hit the chef, obviously … and you have said something *plus stupide*?"

The woman looks frightened and ashamed, as if she is afraid to admit the wrong, ashamed that it has happened to her.

"I should have come to the police," she says, the tears drying. "*Oui*, all right, he hits me when he is angry, he loses his temper easily when his job frustrates. And I do say stupid things; I'm not as clever as Roland. But he never hits Nikolas. He never has." She stops, waiting for something else to happen. All three of them wait in silence. The *flics* wait for something else to fill the gap they have purposely left.

Yvette Pellisier tries to speak and collapses into a stammer. Fleur, taking the lead, and the nasty part, is ready to pursue her.

"Madame, there is no point in lying to us. We know when you are telling the truth. And when you are not. You may as well tell us now and save time later. Then you can go home."

"I have told you the truth!" says Yvette. "I cannot do anything else." The tears are flowing copiously now, wetting the front of a pale-yellow lacy blouse. The *PJ* do not say anything. They wait.

"What more can I say?" she asks.

Nothing. Nothing. For ages. Then:

"He doesn't hurt Nikolas." From Clémence.

"*Non*, I did not say that." No response. Fleur rises from her chair and says she is going to the lavatory. Clémence stays where she is, saying nothing. Time goes by. Fleur does not return. Yvette begins to look more agitated, as if arguing with herself. Where is Fleur?

"I didn't say he doesn't hurt Nikolas. I said he doesn't hit him."

***

Faye, newly returned from Bucharest, and Patrice have set up their stall in the Pâclişa police station interview room that is the only one to have one-way glass, allowing observers to see and hear in an adjoining room.

Madame Diana Dobrescu occupies the interviewee chair and appears reasonably calm. Patrice explains to her that they need to ask her some further questions at this time, so that they may release her husband's remains for her to bury. She makes a solemn nod at this and waits for a question. She is surprised when Faye asks about religion:

"One of our colleagues noted that you have a large number of icons and holy pictures on your walls," says Faye. "I am wondering whether you are extremely religious, or if your late husband was?"

Mme Dobrescu takes a deep breath, and says that she herself is not religious and only goes to church for family weddings or funerals. M Dobrescu, though, had become more religious with the passing years.

"Luca's grandfather was an Orthodox priest. It's in the blood," she says. "But his father, he used to say, didn't have any faith. His grandfather used to try to beat the faith into his father, and that obviously killed any trace of it. Luca was brought up a rabid atheist. But after the revolution, he began to get interested in religion. Started going to church and talking with the local priest, Father Basil."

"Why do you think he did these things?" asks Patrice.

"How should I know?" she says curtly. "I don't know anything about it. All I had to do was put up with the bloody holy pictures littering up my walls. And, your colleague will have seen, some of them were bloody martyrs, horrible deaths! And then he ended up like that himself."

"Do you think there's any connection?" asks Faye, in wonderment at her comments.

"Had he become obsessed with blood?" asks Patrice.

"Why would he? Why would you ask that?" says Mme Dobrescu.

"There's a lot of blood in this case," replies Patrice. "But there are few bloody icons anywhere else. So we naturally wonder if they might be significant ... anyway, perhaps we shall talk to Father Basil. Do you think he will be able to give us any more information?"

"*Je ne devrais pas le penser,*[58]" says Mme Dobrescu. "How would he know anything?"

"*Se déplaçant le long,*" says Patrice, moving along, "I need to ask you about your marriage. Were you and Luca happy together?"

"*Occupez-vous de vos oignons!*[59]" says Madame. "That has nothing to do with you!" Colloquial, thinks Patrice. Very well educated ...

"On the contrary," says Patrice. "It has everything to do with whether you killed him. Did you?"

"No I did not!"

***

Patrice often goes for a walk in the streets of Paris, sometimes with Sartre, with whom he discusses dilemmas in the cases he has under investigation. Now and then, the canine philosopher reminds him of something, helps him to see more clearly. Today, he has no Paris street, nor a Bedlington terrier on a lead. But the urban limits of Bărăbanţ provide a substitute place, although he is increasingly conscious that time is ticking away.

There has to be, he thinks, someone to coordinate this series of crimes. They know, now, that the murders are not

---

58   I should not think so

59   Mind your own business!

only connected but part of the same thing, the same case. Carried out with one motivation – revenge on *Securitate* members – with opportunity constructed using the wives of the relevant victims. Means is provided by the possession of a suitable knife, the cooperation of the women, the temporary insensibility of the victims. Not to forget the possibly permanent insensibility of neighbours. Which may well be cultural.

Sartre, not actually present, and not actually speaking, asks, "What about Monsieur Mitrea?" Patrice repeats that and thinks, yes, something there, *n'est-ce pas*? A conspiracy of silence around the death of the oldest victim – maybe not connected to the others at all? But no, he cannot see that. Dr Apostol said that his throat was cut too, although less expertly. Patrice walks further.

Concentrate on that one. Is it possible that it could have been a lesson? But if it was, who was the teacher? There is no possibility of the neighbours coming up with anything. This has been tried by several people and there is nothing there. The only way forward is through the wives, or through one of the wives.

***

"Father Basil," says Patrice, after introducing himself to the Orthodox priest, whom he has asked to visit at the church instead of his house. Patrice feels that, perhaps, it may be easier to talk about religious pictures in church – there are certainly incredible amounts of them there too.

Patrice is keeping in mind what Colette said after her workshop at the Museikon, that icons represent a bridge between the faithful and the saint or other holy figure; they are not just a picture to remind the person. He knows very little about the Orthodox Church, and has not had sufficient time to give himself a little training course. Happily, the priest speaks English.

"I am enquiring, as I'm sure you know, into the death of Mr Luca Dobrescu." The priest ducks his head in acknowledgement. "And I received your name today from his widow, Diana. She said that he had spoken to you a lot recently. I am wondering what that was about, and hoping that you can tell me anything which was not told to you under the seal of confession."

The priest is relatively young, younger than Patrice had expected – which had been a grey beard, around ninety years old – a full beard, certainly, but a dark one, heavy, with matching bristly eyebrows, and a prominent silvery crucifix on his ample breast.

He is not a light man, well-developed shoulders hidden under his black cassock, and one of those tall hats on his head. He has a melodic voice, though. Patrice is somehow aware, perhaps Colette has mentioned it, that a good singing voice is a pre-selection requirement for Orthodox priests.

"Of course," says the priest, "I cannot break the seal of confession. It is held in the utmost sanctity by Orthodox Christians. The person confesses to Christ Jesus himself; the priest is simply the witness. But I am sure I am free to tell you much about Luca Dobrescu. I have known him only for little over a year, but have talked to him a great deal. Much of our talk was not confidential in any way.
""Thank you very much, Father," says Patrice. "I would not presume to ask you about Mr Dobrescu's spiritual life, just his life in the world. Can I ask when you last saw him, please?"

"The night before he died," says Father Basil. "He came to confession. But we can't talk about that. Previously, I saw him at the church for Divine Liturgy on Sunday, but I was speaking with a small group of worshippers outside afterwards and, although I saw Luca walk past, I did not have the opportunity to speak to him. Before that, it would have been in the middle of the week that he came for a chat.

"I think it would have been Wednesday, I can look it up. We talked for about an hour in my study. He was talking about forgiveness, whether God would forgive someone who had changed his life around. He explained that it was hypothetical, not personal; it was likely on behalf of someone else."

"A friend?"

"I expect so," says the priest. "He didn't tell me who it was."

"What other sorts of things did Luca consult you about?" asks Patrice.

"Religious things," says the priest. "But you shouldn't think of them as consultations. They were just conversations. He had been brought up Orthodox; his grandfather was a priest, but his father, an atheist. So he was trapped between memories of the dead and was finding his own way as he aged. He went to church as a child, with his mother, but from being a teenager, his father taught him religion was women's stuff and he had to be a man.

"So he was on the way back to the church. I think he might have been a holy man had he had the opportunity."

"What about his wife?" asks Patrice. "Does she come to church?"

"Diana? Lord, no," says the priest, and permits himself a deep laugh. "She's a good communist! Oh, I shouldn't say that, we are all materialists and capitalists now. Or so we are supposed to say." He abundantly chuckles into his abundant beard.

"Mrs Dobrescu is still a communist? Do you think so? Are a lot of people?"

"No, no, no," says Father Basil, "I misspoke. I should not have said that. Please excuse me. It is important that our American and European allies know that we have thrown off the communist yoke for good."

"But you are telling me that you haven't?" says Patrice.

"That isn't for me to say," says Basil. "I am only a humble priest in the service of God and the Orthodox Church. There is one thing, though, that I think I need to tell you, Mr Lanier. I believe that Luca Dobrescu was afraid of being killed. He was worried about his immortal soul. Because of the past. But I am not able to tell you anything about that."

***

"How did Roland hurt Nikolas?" asks Fleur, using her lowest, most soothing tone. She is willing to wait, until tomorrow if necessary, for the woman to confide. She can, of course, already guess what is about to show its filthy head. The three women sit together in silent contemplation of the ugliness of which family life is capable.

"He has abused Nikolas since his sixth birthday," says Yvette. "I had to get him away." She says this quickly, to get it out, to get it over. The *PJ* wait in silence, wait for her to say anything more.

Eventually, she does.

"I had to work out a plan. And I started as soon as I found out about it. It made me sick. Nikolas asked me if it was right that his ... father ... to come into his bedroom at night and ... do things he didn't like. Roland had told him that it was quite normal, that it would happen as he was getting older now. He said that he should not tell me, as I would be jealous of the time he spent with Nikolas rather than me. Mothers are like that."

Fleur has dealt with child abuse before, especially when she worked Vice. Children of the *poules* are frequently abused by boyfriends and pimps; she has often helped the women make plans to remove abused children from danger. She is competent, she has heard all the words, felt all the horror. The feeling of utter outrage has never gone away.

Clémence has never had to deal with a case before. She sits there, still, in the jaws of the abominable.

"What was your plan?" asks Fleur. Yvette looks at her in misery, not wanting to talk about it any more. Then she makes up her mind and lets it all come out in a rush.

"I called my stepmother in Blois. She is a nice person, she took good care of me and my father when my mother died, when I had *10 ans*. She said that she would take Nikolas to live with her and my father, until I could find a way to get away from Roland without him killing me."

"Did he threaten to kill you if you took Nikolas away?" asks Clémence, getting her voice back.

"*Non*," says Yvette. "He does not know that I know what he has been doing. I have never let him see that I knew, never talked to him about it. But I knew that he would become violent with me if he ever found out. I did not intend to stay with him, I intended to go to my son. But it became very difficult. Roland would know I had gone to my old home if I disappeared. He has telephoned there often, asking if Nikolas has turned up ..."

"*Alors*," says Fleur, "what was the rest of your plan?"

"I decided that the only thing to do was to go along with the idea that Nikolas had been kidnapped and taken away; not to go to visit him, not to telephone. Nothing. But then, two months ago, my father died and I had to go to Blois. My husband would not go; he did not like my father, so I went alone. And, of course, I saw Nikolas and he was crying, and I was upset, and my stepmother was inconsolable. So, we had to make a different plan."

26

Settled in their interview room at Pâclişa, Patrice and Benjamin, this time, have had Madame Dabija brought in to answer further questions. It is very clear that she does not greatly wish to discuss her late husband. She does, however, seem willing to answer any questions the *flics* might have.

She is calm and cooperative, and is well dressed, with a black skirt suit, and white blouse printed with tiny yellow roses. Her scarf, of silk, is yellow, and her shoes, black patent leather. Her fingernails are professionally manicured and finished with polish of the palest yellow imaginable. She looks as if she is attending an interview of another kind.

René and Faye are in the adjacent room, beyond the glass. It is René, of course, who first interviewed the widow of Gheorghe Dabija. He has said that Mme Dabija had almost nothing to say, except that their business had been poor and she did not think there would be any need for the other town butcher to kill her husband.

"I have been thinking a lot about the condition of your apartment, Madame," says Patrice. "The police officers who first arrived after the murder say that it was very tidy, with nothing out of place. It seemed to me that you would not have cleaned with your husband lying dead on the sofa, would you?"

"No, of course not," says Mme Dabija. "I keep the flat tidy at all times. It is not large and there have only been the two of us since Maria married. There is little to clear up."

"But," says Benjamin, "you say that your husband came home drunk that night, the night of the killing. Did he not disturb things? Throw things around? Bump into furniture?"

The woman looks coldly at the younger police officer and says that, no, Gheorghe did not usually do that. He just threw himself on the sofa and went to sleep.

"You did not speak to him much?" asks Patrice.

"No," she says. "It is impossible to make him understand when he is like that. He can't hear what I am saying, he isn't listening. If I tried to calm him or anything, he would just ignore me. He could be nasty when drunk but, like some other times, he was already past interacting with me by then. All he could do was sleep!"

"You said, though," says Benjamin, checking his notes, "to Officers Theodorescu and Florescu, that you thought, at first, it was animal blood and he had been cutting up meat. But you realised it was his blood. Did you think that he had been butchering between coming in and being killed?"

"I didn't think that much," says Dabija. "I just said what I thought at the time."

"You don't seem very upset at your husband's death," says Patrice. "I wonder. Was your marriage not a happy one?"

"No, it wasn't," she says, sullen now, wanting out of here. "I hated him. He was always a drunk and he was getting worse. I wanted rid of him. I am packing to move to Bucharest."

"And your daughter?" asks Patrice.

"No, she isn't coming. She has a husband and two young children. She is all right here, now her father has died. She doesn't really care either."

"I was curious," says Patrice, "at your having only one child, even though you were married during the Ceauşescu years. Were you unable to have more?"

"No," says Dabija, "I didn't want any more. Not with him, anyway! I got away with it. The requirements weren't always policed properly."

"Oh," says Patrice, "I rather thought they were …"

***

"I am going to stay in Romania," says Amélie. "I have many friends here, I can learn Romanian and get a job in a café or hotel. It's easy, they are always looking for French speakers."

Colette is so shocked that she cannot get her breath for a minute. This is almost the last thing she expected. She had asked Amélie to begin packing to go home and released a rush of – what? Awfulness, horror.

"You don't really expect me to say that that will be okay, do you?" she says.

The girl looks sullen and grunts that she is sixteen and can do as she likes. Her mother says that, at sixteen, she certainly cannot. Not that she will be sixteen for another two months. Colette feels that her legs are about to collapse under her; she sits in an armchair and faces the child.

"I knew you wouldn't let me!" shouts Amélie. "You always stop me doing what I want. Even at home!"

"*Alors,* you think that by staying in Romania you will not have to do as you are told?" she asks.

"*Non,*" says Amélie, suddenly becoming upstanding and middle-aged. "I will be married and my husband and I will have a good life together."

Colette feels the bedroom spin around her. That is the very last thing she had expected. She wonders, to the side, how much worse it can get. She already knows the answer to this. Her daughter picks up her *sac à main* and stamps out of the room before Colette can stop her. Possibly, she stamps out of the hotel too?

"The plan," says Yvette Pellisier, "is simple. We arranged that my stepmother and I would flee France altogether and take Nikolas to Belarus, where *Nana* originally came from. She is still a Belarusian citizen and we would not be extradited back to France. It is the only way to save my son!"

"Then there was no abduction, no taking of Nikolas from your car?" says Fleur.

"*Non*," says Yvette. "I took my son, when his father was working at the restaurant, to his grandmother's house. While my father was alive, they could hide him – and they did for nearly two years. Then *Papa* died. And we had to think of something permanent. My stepmother had to leave the house.

"The landlord did not like foreigners and she did not have the right of residence, and not being a French citizen, there was no way to fight it. So they had to return, temporarily, to Paris. They have been staying in a little *pension* for nearly a month now,

while I've been getting train tickets and the things we shall need for the journey."

"And what was the point of Nikolas dropping his glove, and other things, in the bins near city landmarks?" asks Clémence.

"I did not know of this," says his mother. "When I managed to arrange to meet my stepmother and Nikolas, secretly, he said that he was lonely and wanted to see me. *Nana* had taken him out for a walk each day because he was not very well being indoors all the time. She is not allergic to fresh air like French people, she does not think that colds may be caught in that way. She has cut Niki's hair short and dressed him in different clothes. Few people would recognise him, but his father would, of course.

"She took him out during the mornings. We timed it so that Roland was working, doing preparation in the restaurant. The afternoons would have risked him seeing Niki, so she avoided them. The police weren't interested. *Nana* told him that he would have to be patient, that he couldn't risk seeing me. So he decided, his own plan, to leave messages where he could without *Nana* seeing him. So that I would find them."

"Did he really think," asks Fleur, "that you regularly go through waste bins? That doesn't seem likely …"

"Oh, but I do!" says the woman. "I am committed to recycling textiles for the *Médecins Sans Frontières*! It is amazing what tourists throw away! New things which can be sold or recycled as fibres. Nikolas has been with me when I have done it in the past … sometimes they throw away perfectly good cardigans because they are too hot.

They are *gacheur*![60]"

Both Fleur and Clémence think that this plot by Nikolas is clever; the child had just not thought that the police would find out and talk to his father. Shame. Fleur decides on their next strategy.

"We shall have to take your stepmother and Nikolas into custody," she says reluctantly, "because it is necessary to sort all this out – we have to check what you have said. I shall need the name and address of the *pension*. And the name of your stepmother."

"Of course," says Yvette Pellisier, a tear of relief escaping down her cheek. "*Elle s'appelle* Madame Catherine DeJoie."

One could have heard a pin drop.

***

----

60 wasteful

René and Faye are interviewing Madame Bunea, the final one of the wives. She has her blonde hair in a loose chignon and is wearing charcoal slacks over black boots, and a dark-grey and scarlet print shirt. Her nails are long and match the scarlet in the blouse. She has spectacles, with dark frames, on a gold chain around her neck. Both *PJ* accept her presentation as a headmistress. She looks as if she would be a good one, though severe.

When they have explained that they have a few questions to ask, the widow sits in the chair and waits for them, making no effort to answer what they have not asked. She knows, anyway, that she has already been interviewed by the Head Man. This cannot be much.

"Madame," says René, "we have access to the report *Commissaire* Lanier made of what you told him, and it has made us want to ask for a bit more information. It turns out that Monsieur Bunea's name is on one of several lists of names and amounts of money, which were concealed in lists of people who were given loans from Bancorex, after the revolution. These loans, as you may recall, were never intended to be paid back; what the Americans call 'sweetheart loans'. This was, of course, why the bank went broke and was closed down in 1999, when the government couldn't save it."

"We understand," says Faye, "that people who qualified for these loans fell into two categories. One was those who would become oligarchs, in the Russian sense, big businesses, and men, who would transform Romania into a capitalist country, suitable to attract American investment and be developed at the heart of a new 'Romania in Europe' – and the others, who were loaned, virtually given, money to lose themselves in the countryside and, perhaps, set up some kind of business or other way of keeping themselves alive.

"These seem to have been members of the *Securitate*. And your husband is one of those on the list. We do not think he has been living like an oligarch, so ..."

Madame Bunea looks at Faye with distaste and says no – that cannot possibly be right.

"My husband was a teacher of English and a good man—" She has just got the words out when there is a sharp knock on the door. Because Faye is directly engaging with Mme Bunea's denial, René goes to check. Benjamin says that there is an urgent telephone call for Faye – it won't wait. Faye, hearing him, excuses herself and leaves to take the call. The Pâclişa desk officer tells her, in Romanian, that it is Gabriela Balauru, calling from Bucharest.

"Faye?" says Gabriela. "I have urgent news. I have been searching a little more through the files and I felt that we might have missed something in our delight at finding the names we wanted. So I looked at them again. And I made a mistake. One of the names was wrong! Well, a bit wrong. It wasn't Nichita Bunea, it was 'Niculina'. So it wasn't him!"

"His wife's name is Daciana," says Faye, "so that kind of spoils things."

"It may not," says Gabriela. "It could be her second name, *n'est-ce pas?*"

"I suppose, although she seems to go by Daciana," says Faye.

"I thought you said she was from Moldavia?" asks Gabriela.

"Yes, that's what she says."

"Unlikely, then, that she is really called Daciana. Daciana is a name you rarely find outside Transylvania."

Positive evidence, then, that Gabriela is using her cultural knowledge to be of help. The only question still being: why? Faye decides to come straight out with it.

"That is really helpful, Gabriela. You have helped me

so much – even though I did think at first you might be a spy for the government!" Silence from the other end of the phone for several beats. Then the other woman speaks in a strangled tone:

"There is a good reason for that," she says, "because I was. Until I resigned from my position at the library."

"Quoi?" Faye nearly shouts. "You did what?"

"I am not on vacation," says Gabriela, "I resigned. They told me I could not continue unless I reported on what you were doing. Apparently we are not as far away from the old days as I hoped. I helped you because they told me to – I had reported your visit to the library, as I was expected to do, and was given the surveillance. When I said I would no longer do it, they tried to force me. I will not be forced; the country I want to build will never do that!"

"But why," asks Faye, "did you not want to do it?"

"Because you are my friend," says Gabriela, "and I do not think all foreigners mean us harm."

Faye is thinking this through, wondering how her friend was able to carry on working with her at the old archive after she had resigned. She asks this and Gabriela laughs heartily.

"Oh, easy," she says. "They took my library keys from me, including even the ladies' room. But they did not realise I had the big key to the old archives!" There is a strange noise, and she tells Faye that she is tapping the "Dracula" key against the telephone receiver.

"Their inefficiency still knows no bounds. It is how we shall defeat them!"

***

In the interview room, Faye passes René a note with the new information written on it. The senior detective reads it quickly and then focuses his gaze on Madame Bunea.

245

"Why did you not tell us your first name is Niculina?" he asks fiercely. She takes a step back, even though she is sitting down.

"It is not," she says. "It is Daciana."

"No, it is not!" says René. "And it is you who was a secret police officer, isn't it?"

"No," she says, "it is not. It is my husband."

27

"Now that the Pellisier case is solved," says Fleur, "you know we shall have to return to the baby food, *n'est-ce pas?*"

It has been difficult over the past few days, bringing in Madame DeJoie and her grandson again and requiring the woman to prove her identity. The whole thing had been unsavoury and both women were upset. It might have been even more difficult if the detectives had not been female.

They managed, in the event, to do everything gently. They had had to arrest Yvette Pellisier for abducting her own child and for perverting the course of justice. It was necessary to present her to *Juge* Zabi for his decision about prosecution.

In the event, the *juge d'instruction* dismissed the case against her, and felt that there was no case to answer in the case of Madame DeJoie. Both of them had moved heaven to rescue the child.

Roland Pellisier, though, had to be arrested and prosecuted for child sexual abuse. He is likely to serve a long sentence, much of it in solitary confinement. Most

"ordinary" criminals do not appreciate child molesters –
who do not last long in prison.

"I know," says Clémence. "And I still have no clue how
the glass got into the baby-food jars. I just don't see how
it could have been done. There must be something we are
not taking into account. What could it be, do you think?"

"*Je n'ai pas la moindre idée,*[61]" says Fleur. "Unless we
are looking at it from entirely the wrong angle and there
never was any glass in the baby food?"

***

In the book, Renfield is in psychic communication with
Dracula – his Master, although we don't know how this
was arranged; Abraham hasn't explained – and the patient
escapes the asylum, only to be caught by Dr Seward and
the anonymous "attendant" and chained to the wall of the
rubber room. *Ce pauvre bougre!*[62]

It amazes Colette how much class discrimination is in
the novel, perhaps all novels from this era; it is full of
privilege, due to rank, and entitledness (as the Americans
call it). She is horrified, as a daughter of *l'égalité*, to read
that Van Helsing is singled out for speaking to Renfield "as
if he were an equal". She is freshly concerned about Mr
Renfield, whose zoophagy, flies and spiders, seems altogether
more revolting than Dracula's blood-drinking – that can't
be right, can it?

She has decided that the main themes of the novel are
the rampant class consciousness and misogyny of Victorian
Britain. Although she has read a couple of instances of
racism, it is not so prominent. Not that it wasn't there in
those days – it is just not so visible in the space and time

---

61   I haven't got the slightest idea
62   Poor sod!

of the novel. It was part of the "normal" air they breathed in those times.

The form of misogyny prominently displayed separates women into whores and madonnas, as usual. But it is interesting that vampirism is illustrated as conferring voluptuousness – the sweet and virtuous Lucy (despite her wishing she could marry three men!) turning into a whorish vampire bride, with the ingestion of Dracula's blood.

The case of Mina Murray Harker is, of course, worse. Madam Mina, as Van Helsing calls her, is the smartest person in the book but is sidelined for her own safety – although she does not stay sidelined for long. She is beautiful and sweet and possibly more virtuous than Lucy; she is totally devoted to her husband and subordinates her life to his and to helping him as a (totally useless) solicitor.

Colette reads further into the novel: the wasting death of Lucy Westenra, and Professor Van Helsing's being brought from Amsterdam, wreathing her with garlic flowers (were garlic flowers used against vampires before *Dracula*? Colette resolves to look it up), defending her with a crucifix and communion wafers. One wonders what kind of doctor Van Helsing is, and why he speaks German (*Gott in Himmel, Mein Gott*) rather than Dutch. Colette's own stereotypical Dutch person is invariably a polyglot. She has this from long experience.

Colette tries not to be offended by Van Helsing's broken English, of which rendering Abraham should be ashamed, as well as the doctor's slimy way of talking to the females. Of course, Lucy and, in her turn, Mina, are to be defended by the men, who are "noble". They even decide, on Mina's behalf, that she is to have nothing to do with the "men's work" in battling the vampire. No woman could possibly stand it. They are, naturally, too delicate, weak and sweet. Colette is furious about this. How dare they? Not only are they keeping Mina from harm, they are making her decisions for her. Well, that didn't work, did it? Ha!

Then she comes across the best-written scene in the book, reading the description of Dracula arriving as a white mist to visit Mina (in bed with the regularly insensible Jonathan), feeding from her delicate neck, then throwing open his shirt, creating a wound in his own chest, forcing her to suck from him.

Colette realises that this bit, above all other bits she has read before, is realistic (within the conceit of the novel), erotic and stunning. It is the closest thing to an actual rape in the whole work. She sees that Abraham can write. He just doesn't much choose to.

***

The revelation of Madame Bunea, that her husband had been in the *Securitate,* quickly turns into a confession that there had been a conspiracy to kill him and his colleagues, seven retired secret police officers. She will say nothing about the remaining three, nor about Monsieur Mitrea.

At first, when Patrice comes in to question her personally, she insists that she is innocent, although she is willing to admit that she knew of the plot, and that she was waiting at the house of a friend for the killing to be over. She was not part of it. Her friend will give her an alibi. When Patrice asks her about her name being in the file located by Faye and Gabriela, she reluctantly says that she was a secretary at the Ministry of the Interior, which was responsible for the *Securitate,* and that she did get some money. Not much.

Patrice is not convinced that she herself was not in the secret police. She does not present as a secretary of any sort. It does not fit with her efficient executive persona, at any rate. He continues to question her about the funds still in her personal bank account, as well as in the account held jointly with the late Nichita.

She will only say that these are amounts they earned as teachers and the Bancorex funds had been spent long ago. There is really no way of knowing.

***

Since he received, after much wrangling, the bank statements of the murder victims and their wives, Patrice has been aware that there are great differences between the amount of money in them, as well as the huge differences in lifestyle – if you could call it that for people like the Dobrescus, whose poverty was abject.

There are more funds in the Dobrescus' accounts, one for him and one for both. When questioned, Diana says that her husband refused to spend the money, preferring to live on what vegetables and goat milk they could sell. This is borne out by the condition of their home and surroundings. The amounts of money in the accounts, originally in old lei, adds up to almost exactly the amounts detailed in Faye's photocopies of the National Archive material. Luca Dobrescu has spent nothing.

Madame Dabija doesn't care any more. She has had enough. The account of the butchery business is seriously overdrawn and there are many other debts to which she will readily admit. She says that they have spent everything they had in trying to support the business. There is nothing left.

The *PJ* know that there is no relevant money trail suggesting the Dabijas are guilty of anything other than being bad at business, and there is no obvious way of pushing Irina Dabija to confess to anything. She does not mention that Gheorghe has also drunk quite a lot of their cash.

250

***

"Who is this boy?" Colette asks her daughter. "And do you think you have known him long enough to be thinking about spending the rest of your life with him?"

Amélie looks at her mother with distaste and says that she isn't necessarily thinking of spending the rest of her life with Stefan. He is one of the boys in the group she has been having fun with since they came to Romania.

Colette, who has been under the impression that she herself is a broad-minded, liberated Frenchwoman, is shocked that she is shocked.

"You think marriage is that easy?" she asks. "You can just take it on and throw it off when you like? It's more than that, Am. People get hurt!"

"How would you know?" she says. "You can't remember when you were young, it's so long ago!"

Colette drops down onto the chair in front of the dressing table, the pain of her own growing up still fresh in her mind. Patrice had taken all that away, *Dieu merci!*

"On the contrary," she says, "that sort of thing, that pain, never goes away. Anyhow, what possessed you to accept when he asked you to marry him?"

Amélie smiles, still derisively.

"He didn't ask me," she spits. "I asked him. And he said yes!"

***

"But what," asks Clémence, "can have been the purpose of the Della *supermarché* reporting that there were glass shards in the baby food if there were not?" She is looking *abasourdie.*[63]

---

63   dumbfounded

"*Je ne sais pas*," says Fleur, "but I'm sure we can find at least one reason." She gets up from her desk and walks to a whiteboard on the wall. Writes "Della" at the top.

"Just have a think," she says to the younger officer. "There could be lots of reasons. They may, for example, be looking for an excuse to do something. To go bankrupt. To close the store. To make all the staff redundant. To get rid of all the parents who shop there and are *un fléau?*[64]"

"Seems a bit far-fetched," says Clémence. "It makes customers, especially parents, frightened that their kids might be hurt."

"But there is no danger of that, in reality," says Fleur. "There is no glass! If we are correct."

"I need," says Clémence, "to go back to Monsieur David Maurice and talk to him about his business."

***

René arrives in Oarda, looking for the house of Madame Bunea's friend who will give her an alibi. She lives a few doors away from the teachers and will say she was with her while Nichita was being killed.

Patrice has asked Mme Bunea who told her that her husband was to be murdered, but she refuses, so far, to answer. In time, perhaps?

Madame Marta Eder opens the front door as soon as René knocks. He thinks she may have been standing behind the door – but since when? She lets him in when he says who he is and that Madame Bunea has sent him. The suspect has resorted to a friend who speaks good French, of course. To her best advantage. In the time-honoured Romanian fashion, the woman offers coffee and perhaps a pastry, both refused politely by the Frenchman.

---

64   a scourge, a plague, a nuisance

"I am to ask what you were doing on the night of the twentieth of February, Madame," he says. "Do you have, by any chance, any note of it?"

"That was the night that my friend Daciana Bunea stayed overnight with me," she says calmly. "I was unwell. I had a fever, or something like that, and I needed someone to take care of me. Daciana had visited during the day, and she offered to come back and stay for the night. She is a good friend."

"Were you aware that that was the night her husband, Nichita, was murdered, while she would have been away?"

The woman's eyes shift to the side as if looking for assistance. She licks her lips nervously, brings the eyes back to René.

"Uh, well, uh, I didn't know until afterwards," she says. Her voice sounds dry, as though it is difficult to enunciate. "She telephoned to ask if she could come around. Then she told me. It must have been terrible!"

"But she was definitely here all through the night?" asks René.

"*Oui, oui, certainement*, of course she was. She was here all the time. It cannot have been anything to do with her!"

"What time did Madame Bunea telephone you in the morning?" he asks.

"Oh," she says, "I don't know. About, maybe, nine o'clock?"

"And what time had she left your house?"

"About eight o'clock," she says.

"So, she did not ring you straight away?"

"*Non.* She would be waiting for the police, I suppose. Wouldn't she?" She licks her lips again, eyes shifting in all directions.

"Are you sure she was here?" asks René.

"*Oui.* She was here. I was ill. She looked after me."

"And that was the eighteenth of February?"

She looks confused, before agreeing.

"*Oui*. It was definitely the eighteenth of February. I remember the date because it is my son's birthday." She develops a satisfied look on her face.

"*Non*," says René, "*ce n'était pas*. It was the nineteenth of February."

***

The call comes in the middle of the afternoon, just as Fleur arrives back from her daily journey upstairs to the fourth floor of *le Trente-Six*. She is preparing to tell Clémence that their old *salle squad* is almost finished, with new paint (although a touch blue for Fleur's taste), and waiting for new, clean desks to be delivered tomorrow. The windows have been cleaned and fresh white vertical blinds installed. The phone rings.

Fleur, passing by, picks up and says, "*Allô!*"

The low but precise voice of an officer on the scene tells her that detectives are required, immediately. There has been a homicide in the nineteenth *arrondissement*. A man has been stabbed to death by his wife. It is a mess. The wife is still present, admits it, has been arrested.

"You have called the *médecin légiste* and Scene of Crime?" asks Fleur. "Why do you need us then?"

"The suspect has asked us to call you," says the officer. "Apparently, you are familiar with her?"

"*Ah bon?*"

"*Elle s'appelle* Madame Yvette Pellisier."

***

Amélie comes in to their bedroom as Colette is getting ready to go downstairs to read for a while in the lounge.

The girl-child's face is folded into wet wrinkles; she is weeping bitterly and cannot speak.

Colette, who immediately knows what has happened, does not attempt to persuade her to tell all about it. She just takes her daughter in her arms and holds her as she sobs as if her heart is breaking. Because it is.

When Amélie has dropped off to sleep, Colette returns to her place in the hotel lounge and orders coffee from another waiter, not Lidia. She settles into a solid read; she will leave her daughter to sleep and wail in whatever order she likes, before returning to give her a big hug and let her know it is all right. Even though it isn't.

Lucy Westenra is coming and going, sometimes better, sometimes worse, surrounded by garlic flowers. Colette has asked Google whether garlic was known as anti-vamp before Stoker and discovered the answer is yes. It seems that garlic has been used from pre-Christian times as a remedy for evil spirits and disease. This especially holds in Romania, where inhabitants eat a lot of it. Colette has noticed that this is true throughout her culinary experiences in the country.

Garlic has also been used as a pre-antibiotic antibiotic, for disease. Sufferers from rabies, common in dogs, wolves and bats, as well as human beings, are seriously bothered by the allicin enzyme in it – as they would be by any very strong flavour which overwhelms their taste and smell receptors. *Alors* ...

Everybody's dying, thinks Colette. Well, it's around the middle of the book, *n'est-ce pas*? Lucy's mother is first, Arthur Holmwood's father (so we'll have to call Arthur Lord Godalming!), Mr Hawkins in Exeter, then Lucy herself. One is tempted to cheer at her eventually setting her shoulder to the wheel and dying! Now is time for the funeral and funeral rites and, as the reader knows (or at least suspects), her rising again as vampyre.

Lucy walks as "the bloofer lady" and feeds from children. Nice. It is Arthur who assumes, after encouragement from his brave cohort, to stake the woman he loved, and Seward and Van Helsing remove the vampire's head and fill the mouth with garlic. Colette cannot find a mention of what they do with it … Lucy's papers, and everyone's diaries, are read and felt to prove the unbelievable theories of Van Helsing.

Another example, thinks Colette, of the "rights of men" – it is the right of Arthur to kill-slash-free Lucy's soul because he "loved her best". Read "owned her".

***

"Madame Bunea's alibi is *bof*!" says René when he telephones the *patron* from Oarda. "It was easily done. Madame Eder does not have the date straight in her head. She thinks it was the eighteenth. *Alors* …"

"*Eh, bien,*" replies Patrice. "The others don't have an alibi; they admit they were there in both cases. *D'accord.*"

"Unless they too are lying?" asks René.

"*Merci de ne pas compliquer les choses,*[65]" says Patrice. "It's bad enough as it is!"

"Can I come back from Oarda now?" asks René. "I think I've finished here."

"*Oui,*" says Patrice. "My next thought is around Madame Elena Dincă, and I want to speak to her soon."

"Dincă?" asks René. "Who, the neighbour? Of the Dobrescus?"

"Mm. There's something off about her, don't you think?"

"Oh," says René, who hadn't thought of it. "Do you want me with you?"

"*S'il te plaît.* Get back to Pâclişa. Meet me at the station house, though, and we'll arrive at the cottages together."

---

65 Please don't try to make it more complicated

✳✳✳

The ultimate insult, for Colette, is when Van Helsing presses part of a communion wafer to Mina's forehead in order to deny her to the Count, and it burns, leaving a red scar – which everyone takes as a sign of her "uncleanness". Wow, thinks Colette. Blaming the victim again!

The scar disappears at the end when the "noble, brave men" (Mina says, "No wonder weak women love them so") stake and behead Dracula, when he is weak and in his box. Not with a bang; with a whimper. Brave of them, do admit. Oh, and Quincey Morris, the random American, who is more or less pointless to the story except as in forming part of the cohort of "crusaders" after truth, is killed. Colette closes the book for now.

28

"Yvette!" cries Clémence as she enters the apartment in her wheelchair. The other woman is sitting on a sofa under the window, blood on the front of her blouse and skirt, on her stockings, stockinged feet. Her face is still and set, with no expression, her long dark hair loose, curtaining part of it.

The body has not been moved, and Dr Rousseau is kneeling on the floor next to it. He has no need to biopsy the liver for time of death; had he been twenty minutes earlier, the corpse might have been revived. There are two scene-of-crime technicians in the room already, taking pointless photographs. There is little point in taking fingerprints.

The officer who had telephoned Fleur simply points to Madame Pellisier without a word. Both *PJ* go over, and Fleur sits down next to her. Fleur wants to touch but avoids doing so – the SOCO will want to sample her husband's blood from her hands, even with a confession, in case she changes her mind later. Neither Clémence nor Fleur think she will.

Fleur asks her how she is. Stupid question. How do you think? Yvette Pellisier doesn't say any of that. Instead, she mutters, "Thank you for coming."

"Do you want to tell me what happened?" asks Fleur. "Or you can wait until we get to the station …"

Yvette moves her head from side to side slowly. She seems to be indicating later, as if she just wants to sit with them now. Clémence looks over to the *médecin légiste*, to see where he is up to. He is examining Monsieur Pellisier's abdomen, having already gone over his chest. The man's body is a mass of blood, with little between wounds. He must have been stabbed many times. Clémence cannot see a knife or other instrument; the police must have removed it – possibly so that it cannot be used again.

Rousseau asks one of the scene-of-crime officers to help him turn the body over. They find just bloodstains, trickled from the front. There is no knife wound in the back. All the damage has been done straight on, in sight of the deceased, while he remained conscious. Punishment.

Clémence's short forensics course advised her to consider that type of killing a revenge crime. She goes, without asking, to get Yvette a glass of water from the kitchen. The woman drinks it all without a word.

Dr Rousseau straightens up and looks around at all the others in the room before saying:

"*D'accord,* I have finished for now. Madame Olivier, I expect you will arrest Madame Pellisier and take her to the

Trente-Six? Eh, bien. And you, Monsieur Scene-of-Crime, will carry on here? The mortuary van will be here in a few minutes. *Bon.*" He fastens his bag and takes it with him, saying *à bientôt.*

Fleur goes into the hall to fetch Yvette's coat, and they escort her to the police station.

***

Colette is delighted that Amélie is sleeping; she has been awake all night, sobbing. She's said little to Colette, who can't possibly understand. Colette, who understands very well, knows there is little to say, at this moment. The words will come later, when her child begins to feel a touch better. Colette's girlish romantic troubles are long in the past, but she recalls them in exquisite, screaming detail. *Pauvre petite fille!*

She goes downstairs to read; she will not have much time left for the novel.

John Seward, doctor and keeper of lunatics, is summoned to visit Renfield, who is very agitated and who will have one of his violent fits if Seward does not attend. Van Helsing asks to go with him – possibly a valid request; he may be able to help – but Arthur, Quincey Morris and Jonathan Harker all ask to go as well. For the purposes of voyeurism.

Renfield wants them to certify that he is sane. He really, really wants to get out now.

Why? we ask ourselves.

He is found, lying on the floor of his cell with a broken neck and a fractured skull. They think he has done it himself. Dracula has appeared to him outside the window – the whole purpose of the Renfield character is to be able to invite the Count into the asylum, *n'est-ce pas?* He shows the poor lunatic flies and moths and cats and dogs, and red-eyed rats. And says, without words, "All these lives I

259

will give you, ay, and many more and greater, through countless ages, if you will fall down and worship me!"

And Renfield opens the sash window and says: "Come in, Lord and Master!"

Colette finds her capacity for shock still in place. The parody of Jesus's Temptation stuns her. She closes the book for the last time.

***

After thirty years as a police officer, Fleur Olivier holds her tongue when something as awful as this goes wrong. She was quite settled that Yvette and her mother would be able to get the boy Nikolas away from his abusive father. They had a good plan, at least the second time. He might have found them in Blois, but he would be unlikely to have found them in Belarus. They were not even going to Minsk.

And then Yvette goes back to the apartment and stabs Roland thirty-eight times, in the chest and abdomen.

Both Clémence and Fleur are stunned; they thought the case was over, and the boy and his mother safe. They are presently shuffling their papers in the interview room, with Yvette sitting opposite. She is wearing handcuffs, and her fastened hands are resting on the table. Her eyes are looking without seeing and her face has still the look of a sculpture of a face. Not real.

"Yvette," says Fleur – she cannot yet make up her mind to refer to her as "Madame Pellisier" – "can you tell me what happened? Were you in the house when your husband came home? Or was he in when you arrived?"

Yvette tries to move her wrists to her knees so she can straighten her skirt. They had her change her clothes at the apartment so that the forensic scientists could have the ones she was wearing. She cannot move her hands properly; she gives up. She waits for a few moments so she can get her breath, takes a drink of water:

"Roland came home, and I was waiting."

"Where is Nikolas?" asks Clémence.

"Gone away. I was packing. Roland saw me putting things in our bags. He was angry. He started shouting, asking where is Nikolas. I said hadn't the police picked him up yet? And he said what for? He didn't know! I told him they would be doing – I didn't tell him why, I just looked at him. And he knew then. At that moment.

"He started yelling, what had I told them? He said I was a liar. He loves his son. Then he started asking me where is he, again. I must give him to Roland immediately. Then he hit me!" She sweeps her curtain of hair aside and displays cuts and bruises on her cheek. "I fell, and he kicked me hard in the ribs. So, I got up and ran into the kitchen." She stopped and began to weep a bit.

"There was a kitchen knife, one of his best ones, in the block. It's perfectly balanced. I don't know why it is there, it's usually at the restaurant. I picked it up and he stopped in the middle of the floor and just looked at me with his furious red eyes."

"And what happened then?" asks Fleur.

"I sliced his shoulder with it. The blood started to come up. He slapped his hand onto it, trying to stop it bleeding, but it was already bleeding a lot. Down his arm. He pulled his hand away to check the damage and said, "*Regarde ce que tu as fait, salope.*[66]"

She takes on a more dreamy look, maybe seeing what she has done again.

"So I stabbed him in the chest. I don't know how many times; I could not stop it. Then I went on to his stomach.

---

66   Look what you've done, you bitch!

I just kept on stabbing and stabbing. He hurt my baby. He tortured my baby with terrible things. He had to pay the account with blood. I could not let him do it again. How could I do anything else? I had no choice!" As she pronounces the last four words, she turns her head slightly and catches the eye of both Fleur and Clémence. She repeats:

"I had no choice."

***

"Madame Dincă?" says René, when they have entered her small house and looked around to see no sign of Madame Dobrescu.

"Your friend has gone home?" asks Patrice, "Is she feeling better?"

"*Non*," says Dincă, appearing to have learned French in the interim. She looks somewhat different too; she is no longer as old as she seemed, and she is wearing a dark-coloured dress and jacket. She is also clearly packing to leave. "She has left to return to Bucharest," she says.

"The Romanian police told her not to leave the area until they had finished questioning her," says René. "Did she not understand?"

"I have no idea," says Dincă. "It is nothing to do with me! I hardly know her."

"I was under the impression," says Patrice, "that you have been the Dobrescus' neighbour for some time. Wasn't it all the time they have lived here? Something like five months?"

"*Oui*. But I have only been here a year. And they arrived last September. From Bucharest. I am originally from the Black Sea, and I am returning there very soon. It is too wet here."

"I must ask you a few more questions," says Patrice, "before I can let you go."

She says a sharp word that neither of the policemen understands, and allows them to see her irritation. She does, however, respond on a completely different basis from when she was interviewed previously.

"Please tell me exactly what happened that morning, the eighteenth of February, when you awakened?"

"It was early," says the woman, "but I had made the fire. It was cold. Diana came to the door. She banged heavily and shouted. She said to come quick, something had happened. I let her in the house, and she was angry and upset."

"Angry?" asks René. "Why do you say that?"

"*Non*," says Madame Dincă, "I did not mean that. Perhaps, er, distressed. Very distressed?"

"You said 'angry'," says Patrice. "Why do you think you said that?"

She looks at him with disgust, as if he has caught her doing something wrong. She shrugs her shoulders and does not answer.

"*Se déplaçant le long*," says Patrice. "Was it you who made the fire in the Dobrescus' house?"

"*Non*," she says. "Diana must have made it afterwards."

"With her husband lying dead in the bed?" asks René. Dincă shrugs again. Then says:

"Perhaps she needed something to do. Perhaps it was just her morning job. Maybe it was automatic?"

"Do you think she was upset at her husband's death?" asks Patrice. "Or was she, as you said, angry? Was she furious at him?" He stops for a moment. "Madame, did Diana Dobrescu kill her husband?" He leaves her considering that, then repeats, "Did she?"

"How would I know?" asks the woman. "She could have, for all I know. I told you. I don't know her well. *Écoutez,* I have a train to catch. I need to get away from here."

"I'm afraid not!" says René. "Elena Dincă, I am arresting you for being an accessory after the fact of homicide." He uses the usual French caution to people accused of crimes; he does not know the Romanian version – not that he has the right of arrest, he just hopes she doesn't know that. Patrice telephones *Capitaine* Roșca and asks for back-up, whilst René handcuffs the rejuvenated Madame Dincă.

"You are making a terrible mistake!" shouts Dincă. "There will be hell to pay!"

Patrice asks Iulia Roșca, on the telephone, to call Bucharest headquarters and have Madame Dobrescu picked up.

29

There is, however, Patrice speculates, a piece missing. Maybe more. He is now sure that Diana Dobrescu killed her husband, but did Madame Bunea kill hers, and Madame Dabija hers? Who, then, killed Monsieur Mitrea? Or did Madame Dobrescu kill all of them? If so, why?

There must be someone who coordinated it all, must there not? But who?

***

"It happens sometimes," says Fleur as she and Clémence get lunch, which neither can eat, at a nearby café. "There is nothing we can do."

"*Je le sais,*[67]" replies Clémence softly. "But it seems so hard on her. After all she has suffered."

---

67 I know that

"*Oui.* I truly thought she would get away with Nikolas and her mother to Belarus. I don't think he would have found them there."

"It depends, I suppose," says Clémence, "how much it damaged his ego. I can see how it might have meant everything to him to get his revenge …"

"I expect that is the conclusion Yvette came to," says Fleur. "Although I'm also sure there was something of the opportunity in it. I know she said he'd never really beaten her but I don't believe it. She was frightened of him, *n'est-ce pas?*

"Oh, I think so. But it is hard to separate what was fear for herself, and what was fear for her child. Probably much of each?"

"I was thinking about if it had been me," says Fleur. "Even though I cannot possibly imagine that Edgar would hurt me or either of our children in any way whatever. I think I would have seriously considered killing him, and somehow getting rid of the body."

"You would?" says Clémence shrilly. "Even if it wasn't just opportunistic? You'd plan it out?"

"*Oui,*" says Fleur. "I should plan it carefully so that I would get away with it. I would not think that there was anything else I could do."

"*Bon Dieu*! Would you really do that?" asks Clémence. Fleur looks serious, starts to smile as if telling a joke, goes back to serious. The truth is that she would. To defend her kids.

"Do you want coffee?" she asks her junior officer. Clémence says she does, and asks what sentence Yvette Pellisier is likely to receive.

"There is likely to be a chance that her *avocat* will say that her mind was disturbed at the time she killed him. The multiple stabbings speak to that, although there's no scope for accidental killing. I'm sure her mind was disturbed. But where does that leave us? Can it be treated? Is she in her right mind now? Did she long intend to kill him? Or would she have been content to run away to Belarus?"

"It doesn't seem like she planned it," says Clémence. "But she did take the presented opportunity."

"And she definitely killed him," says Fleur. "There can be no doubt about that!"

***

Their last day in Romania, Saturday, is overcast and resolutely rainy. It is as well that Colette has selected a mostly indoor excursion, Bran Castle, aka Dracula's Place, to take Patrice and Amélie and reclaim her family. As expected, Amélie won't go. She is not going out with her friends, she is staying in the hotel, crying for Stefan and her first betrayal. Colette and Patrice sympathise but cannot help.

Chapter Two, May 5, of *Dracula,* describes the Count's castle as

> *"... on the very edge of a terrific precipice ... with occasionally a deep rift where there is a chasm [with] silver threads where the rivers wind in deep gorges through the forests."*

It is compatible with what they see as they approach Bran.

The castle is quite interesting, although Patrice wonders aloud why they haven't gone to Vlad Țepeș's birthplace.

"Because it's a fake," says Colette with a shudder, "*avec* artificial spiders."

"Ah," says Patrice, not aware that his wife is an artificial arachnaphobe. She isn't, of course.

"At least this is a genuine castle, although not Dracula's. It is said, although I am not sure by whom, that Vlad Țepeș was imprisoned here for two months after being captured by the king of Hungary."

"Ah, well then," says Patrice noncommittally. They walk around the gardens, after paying their entrance fee, and take note of the precipitous height of the walls rising from the rock. It is very destabilising, and they hurry to sit down to regain their balance. The garden has lots of water, not just that falling from the heavens, wet grass, and leafless trees. It is probably pretty in spring, with flowers and such.

The entrance has a formidable oak door with iron furnishings, intimidating, ancient. The castle was reputedly built between 1377 and 1388 and sits on the old border between Transylvania and Wallachia.

The rooms are white-walled and have solid oak furniture and oriental rugs, and fireplaces, including the one in the lovely music room (with incongruous upright piano) which looks so white and modern, and halfway up the wall, that it could be Scandinavian, although obviously not.

The inner courtyard is refreshing, with a view of the black-and-white pattern of outside walls, a little reminiscent of Elizabethan England. There is, unfortunately, a wishing well. The round tower roof is covered in beautiful rosemary tiles, shaped as scales, and Patrice feels that this Romanian castle could, on a good day, give some of the Rhineland ones a run for their money.

The Laniers pass through Queen Marie's room and the main bedroom, in which the extraordinarily carved canopy bed is so short as to be unable to sleep a medium-height man lying down. Colette feels a little light-headed from observing the drop from one of the upper terraces, and takes Patrice for lunch in the restaurant before they go to explore the dungeon.

When she was here alone, Colette did not go into the dungeon; she was afraid of being accidentally locked in. With Patrice along, she wants to go. Perhaps this is the dungeon where Vlad the Impaler was imprisoned? It would be super to have something authentic at last.

They go inside, through the narrow door, into a narrow room with a narrow window, giving a dull winter light. There are cobwebs which look contrived, as if from one of those machines you can rent for Halloween. It is creepy, though, especially when they are lightly pushed through a concealed doorway into a dark room and all light is immediately extinguished.

***

How in the hell did we get here? Patrice asks himself. What was I thinking?

The cellar room is running with damp and is pitch-dark, except for the narrow ray of jaundiced light from a cheap torch, bought in the village and desperation. Was there no clue in the name "dungeon"?

Colette tries to focus the inadequate beam on something, anything, which would give them a chance at orientation. It is too dark even to find the door through which they entered a few minutes ago.

Happily, neither of them is afraid of small spaces nor of the dark, but they would have preferred that the guide had not slammed the door after them with such a final-sounding crash. Although there are four other people in the group, it seems that just they have been selected to be subjected to the frightening process. They have already banged on the door, to no avail. But have now lost the direction of it.

"Be calm," says Patrice, "he'll open it in a minute." He sounds calm, although he recognises a slight lurch in his stomach that something is wrong. How can it be? *C'est stupide!*

"I thought," says Colette, "that I'd be able to hear something through the door. But there is nothing, it's too thick."

"A very old door," says Patrice. "Direct the torch beam onto my watch. How long have we been in here, do you think?"

"A couple of minutes only," she says. "And they won't leave us for more than, what … five minutes?" She fumbles for his arm. He takes her hand and directs the torch to his wristwatch. It says, dimly, that it is 14.36. They stand, arm in arm, patiently waiting for the light to be restored. Before the light from the torch goes out, the wristwatch tells them it is 14.52.

They are calmly trying to decide what they can do, if anything, when the noises begin. Ah, that is *bof*! But who do they think they're fooling? The sounds are not loud, but they are regular, bump, bump, bump. They begin to speed up, and Colette says that that is to make them panic. Patrice says:

"Take no account of it. Someone is trying to frighten us."

"They are succeeding," says Colette breathlessly. "The guide must have forgotten about us and walked away. He'll come back when the group gets to the exit …"

"He can't really have miscounted," says Patrice. "There were only six of us." Colette doesn't say she knows that, even though he is sure she does. "I believe that the door is to my left. Hang on to my arm and we'll move that way. If we feel around the walls, we may be able to find another door. Which may not be locked, *quoi*?"

Patrice imagines it will be locked but does not say so. When you investigate murders for a living, which he does, you sometimes elicit vengeance. Perhaps this is it.

They shuffle around the walls as if their ankles are tied together, feeling with fingertips, trying to miss nothing. It seems to be taking hours, although it can't be. Noises stop eventually but begin again as soon as they start to be thankful. They hear a scream, a long way away. Colette waits for Patrice to acknowledge this before saying she heard it too. They agree, again, that it is *rien*, nothing, and continue feeling the walls for any prospect of a way out.

They have counted off two corners before Patrice says that there is something here:

"It could be a door frame," he says quickly. "Keep your hands where they are, though, in case it doesn't work out." She does exactly as she is told, although that is not her usual practice when dealing with him. It is a door frame, but the doorway is bricked up; he can feel the mortar between the bricks. He groans.

"*Qu'est-ce que c'est?*" she asks.

"An old, sealed door," he says with a sigh. "*T'inquiète,*[68] there may be more." He wonders if Colette can tell he's a bit worried, although not frightened. It would take more than a dark dungeon, and noises off, to upset him. Snakes, probably.

He finds another similar door, and another after that, mumbles a couple of *petit* obsenities into the void, and discovers something else – something he had not expected.

"There's a sort of handle," he says, "on the wall. It must open something, *quoi?*"

"No point without," she says. She sounds desperate, trying to maintain hope.

There is a scrape of metal on wood, a squeak.

"*Oui!*" he shouts. "It is a window!"

---

68 Don't worry – in Verlan, via *Ne t'inquiète pas*

***

Colette wonders why there is no light coming in through
a window, but as Patrice levers it open, halfway up the
wall, she realises that there is no light because it is not a
window onto the outside. On the other side of it, there is
more pitch-dark; it is a narrow passageway, going they
know not how far.

They have no choice. They start down it, downhill,
further down than dungeon level. Somewhere close to
Hell.

***

It's still dark. No relief in sight. No sight. Not even a spark.
Patrice can feel that Colette is shivering. He does not know
whether it is the cold, which is considerable. Or the fear. He
has thought about fear, often, and thinks anyone without
fear when they are in a difficult situation is not brave but
idiot.

He recognises courage; that which feels the fear and
goes ahead anyway. Because it's necessary. He does not feel
that this, in a castle dungeon in Romania, is necessary.

Colette's hand is still in the crook of his arm. He cannot
feel the temperature of it because it is encased in her glove,
one of the suede pairs she wears in winter. Irrelevantly,
he tries to think what outfit she is wearing that the glove
must match or contrast. Then dismisses it from his mind.

"*D'accord, mon amour?*" he says. She says, "*Oui,*" in
a loud voice, trying to convince them both. There is another
scream, stripping the silence, and she says:

"Do you know why hearing a scream makes us more
afraid, *cherie?*"

"*Non,*" he says.

"It's the rough edge of the sound," she says in her best scientific tone. "It gives a signal to the amygdala, deep in the brain."

"And what happens then?" asks Patrice, in the hope that this will distract her and curb the fear.

"The amygdala, which is part of the limbic system, where 'primitive' *émotions* are generated, sends impulses upwards to the cognitive parts of the brain, which are then perceived as fear."

"Ah," says Patrice, not having anything more germane to say.

There are some more bangs as they begin to move off down the dark corridor. The torch has given up; there is no light to confirm even that it is still a corridor. They cannot see the walls. A space without limits is an infinite space. An abyss.

"But," says Patrice, "the cerebrum sends impulses down to the amygdala, doesn't it? Telling it that there is nothing to be frightened of – we are on a tourist trip in Romania."

"*Oui, mais* the limbic system, instinctive since early times, sends more. There are a lot more nerve fibres running upwards than there are running downwards. The amygdala is in charge."

They seem to be getting closer to the place of the screaming, and to the banging and thumping, as they proceed down what they still believe to be the corridor. They can feel the slightly sloping floor, which is probably made of concrete; hard enough, anyway. They move slowly, cautious about any holes which may trip them. Onward and onward. When will it end? It is as deep as Alice's rabbit burrow.

If it is coming to an end, won't there be fresh air? Only if it comes out outside of the castle. If it is a secret passage, it could come out in a room, or another passageway. Patrice pushes down on the digestive disturbance this thought causes.

"Have we been locked in on purpose, do you think?" asks Colette. "I don't see why the guide would do it, but …"

"Surely not," says Patrice. "I can't imagine why anyone would want to do that. It's crazy. Someone has made a mistake."

"What kind of mistake?" asks Colette.

"Miscounting or something. Maybe we moved off before they could open the door again and check on us. Maybe our sense of time was off. We thought it took longer than it did. Maybe it was only two minutes, not five or ten. They are probably wondering where we got to. And if the door to the passageway is expected to be barred … they won't know where we have gone!"

This theory does not make sense; they had a look at Patrice's watch with the last of the torchlight. And someone could easily have maliciously locked the door into the corridor. Why not?

Colette's shudders take over her whole body. Both of them stop dead. They have been standing still for Patrice's count of eighteen seconds, when a door opens directly in front of them, and fresh air comes in with a light "whoosh".

The door does not open onto light; the room beyond is dark too, but not quite so dark as the passageway. A lighter shade of black. A pleasant voice which Patrice can identify says:

"Ah, there you are," in French. "No, don't move. You aren't going anywhere."

***

Jean-Pascal is rattled. Very rattled. He has just had his first car accident and is sitting on a sofa in the salon, with Sartre draped over his knees in comfort. The little dog does not know what has happened but is aware, on some level, that his third-best friend is in some distress. The young man does not know how on earth he is going to tell his *maman*.

He has been prevented from driving practice during the two weeks his parents and Amélie have been away in Romania and, as he is almost ready to qualify, he is a little anxious for his practice to continue.

His friend Remy Lachapelle, a reckless boy according to those in authority, suggests there is an opportunity J-P has not seen. It is such a pity, he says, that Jean-Pascal's practice has been interrupted by his parents taking themselves off in such a selfish way to Eastern Europe. They should have arranged for him to drive with someone else, should they not? There is a car, isn't there, in the garage in Versailles, which J-P is perfectly capable of driving? It is a nice car. And there are country roads outside Paris just asking to be driven on. Remy is already qualified, isn't he? And J-P almost so? And his mother's keys are sitting on the hall table ... she will never know anything about it – they will have the Goddess back in her garage days before Colette returns from the Drac-land.

This suggestion is so far outside J-P's comfort zone that he is confused. But he is eighteen years old and ready to go to university, to go to America to study. Ready to go out into the world. He is starting to grow a moustache, *n'est-ce pas?*

"Let's go," he says. "It'll be fine."

They take the *métro* to Versailles, walk to the garage and, having checked the oil and tyres like responsible drivers, they take the beautiful turquoise DS 21 out on the roads of a quiet, early spring Thursday. Driving the wonderful car, with its advanced hydraulic suspension, is ecstasy to one who has practised in crappy Peugeots. Jean-Pascal has travelled as a passenger in the DS many times but has never, of course, driven it.

The young men are having a brilliant day, this really is the life. Their life in the future. Their life as men.

When time comes to turn the car, in a house access lane, to reverse their journey to the garage, it is simple. J-P has performed the manoeuvre perfectly many times before. He reverses into the lane, slowly, until he crunches into a huge boulder, below his sightline, and hears the rear number plate crash to the ground. He quickly changes gear and moves forward, unhooking the back of the car from the rock. Stops in horror, wringing his hands. His mother's favourite thing (after her family) has just been injured. He assembles all the swear words he knows and finds none will serve.

Remy Lachapelle says "Oops".

*****

Pucelle examines the notes she has made over the last few days. They are sparse and she appears to have only the one piece of new information. That the Elephant is Irina Alexandrovna. Although this information has not helped, yet, to find her, it has somehow made her feel more comfortable. Perhaps because it appears the woman has another personality than that of a drug dealer and possible gangster.

The idea of the Elephant as mother is not hard to accept. During the time she was kept in the *apartment*, Pucelle felt *L'Éléphant* as the closest she, a foundling who had never known, nor had any idea of her parents, had experienced.

The fact that she stayed close to her child, Paon, the Peacock, since they left Russia, also testifies to her motherhood. Pucelle reflects long on these things.

Had she had the *PJ* behind her, Pucelle would have brought in the man to whom she had been directed, who gave her the name, and had him questioned. Patrice Lanier would have been able, she thinks, to extract more information from him. Looking at her pathetic paperwork, she contemplates what questions Patrice might have asked.

***

"What are you doing here?" says Patrice as what light there is in the nether parts of the castle resolves around Melichian's well-formed features and focuses their minds on the gun in his right hand.

"I really don't want to be," he says. "I had hoped that you would neutralise yourselves without me having to do anything. But, of course, you couldn't do that, French *nemernici!*[69] Why didn't you just go home?"

"You are the one, then?" says Patrice.

"I'm telling you nothing," says Melichian. "What do you think I am, a James Bond villain? Going to tell you all the details before I kill you, so you can escape and bring me to justice? *Ne me fais pas rire!*[70]

"What is going to happen now is that we are going to go out of the secret door, to my car, and then we are going for a ride. You will have taken an early flight back to Paris."

"You are going to kill us?" asks Colette.

"I?" says Melichian. "Of course not. You are going to have a bit of an accident. But I need to take your cell phones, now, and your documents, passports, anything you have to identify you."

"The telephones don't work here," says Patrice, feeling foolish because that isn't why Melichian wants them.

Melichian says several words which neither of the Laniers knows, and holds out his hand to Colette first. She produces

---

69   bastards
70   Don't make me laugh!

276

her phone, her passport and her European Driving Licence. Patrice does similar, with the addition of his *Police Judiciaire* ID and the document permitting him to supervise Jean-Pascal's driving practice. Melichian puts all of them in a leather holdall, which he hitches over his left shoulder.

"Was it your idea to set up a ring of vampire murders, so they wouldn't be investigated properly?" asks Patrice.

"*Fermez votre gueule!*[71]" responds Melichian. He begins to usher them towards the heavy oak door set in the far wall of the small, damp room.

"What was it all about?" There is no answer.

"Revenge, *n'est-ce pas*? They were *Securitate*, and had been especially brutal? They had to be killed because they could never be brought to justice?" Still no answer.

"But tell me, was it you who arranged to have their wives kill them?"

Melichian pushes Colette through the door, keeping his gun on her, to control both of them. Patrice follows and they emerge on a grassy promontory, with a short flight of stone steps going down to a terrace at the back of the castle. There is a black Mercedes drawn up to the slope, and a figure sitting in the driver's seat.

"And why now?" asks Patrice. "They were all retired and, presumably, out of sight?" Melichian pushes Colette towards the back door of the car, opening it and, from police habit, pressing his right hand on her head as she slides in. Both Laniers see that the person in the driver's seat has turned around and has a gun trained on Colette as Melichian transfers his aim to Patrice. They both see that the driver is a woman.

"Why did you decide to bring my team into this?" asks Patrice. He makes his voice as sincere as he can. He needs

---

71 Shut the (fuck) up!

to impress and distract. If he joins Colette in the car, they are finished. Melichian straightens up to his full height with a theatrical sigh, and says:

"*Êtes-vous un idiot complet?* You must have anti-corruption clean-ups when someone thinks of it, even in *la France*. Politicians and that? We have one now. The European Union is getting tougher – and I am retiring soon. I shall stand for election. I have a good hope of becoming an anti-corruption head of state, or a deputy who will rise in a little time. I have a fine and spotless record. But there needs to be some cleaning done." He jams his mouth shut with an audible snap. He has said too much. He could not resist the final self-promotion.

He has also inadvertently moved slightly too close to Patrice.

He is almost preening as Patrice's iron fist hits his jaw, then his nose, in two lightning jabs. The nose breaks with a loud snap, and the Romanian policeman staggers. Patrice, who has always been quicker than he looks, swipes the gun from his hand before he hits the ground. He places his foot on the man's chest and, aiming the gun at the woman in the front seat, tells both her and Colette to get out of the car, on this side.

Colette gets out easily, having taken the gun from the shocked young woman. The woman herself struggles over the central console and opens the passenger door. As she comes out, Patrice recognises Sofia Iordache, the officer from Pâclişa.

"Colette," says Patrice, "can you get a cell phone from Monsieur Melichian's bag there, and ask René to bring some officers to take in the *contrôleur général* and *Officier* Iordache and charge them with murder? And can you check that Monsieur Melichian is not actually dead, if you please? *Merci, dulcinée!*"

Chief Gadianu and *Capitaine* Roşca are surprised and not surprised by the arrest of *chestor de poliţie* Melichian. But they are surprised by that of *Officier* Iordache. Sofia has been an exemplary officer, hardworking and disciplined throughout her few years in the force. It is only during her interrogation that she admits she is Melichian's stepdaughter. It is unclear, yet, as to what she has done to help him.

Colette and Amélie return to Paris on the flight upon which they are booked, but Patrice, René, Faye and Benjamin all stay another two days. They spend Sunday in Alba Iulia, assisting with the interrogation of M Melichian and Mlle Iordache; the Monday in Bucharest, at the Ministry of the Interior, and interrogating Mme Dobrescu, Mme Dabija, Mme Bunea and Mme Dincă.

All except Mme Dincă, it seems, were *Securitate* officers who had been married to other officers to keep them quiet. It seems that it was always highly likely that the women would have to kill the men in the end.

Mme Dincă, a high-ranking, current *Securitate* officer, is their controller, who moves around Transylvania controlling an unspecified number of ex-agents with seriously bad reputations. There seems to be no way of identifying the other three potential victims who had been mentioned.

In his latest interview, Monsieur Melichian has calmly and logically explained that the three men, Dobrescu, Dabija and Bunea, had to be retired permanently. They were very bad men, who had done many appalling things. He vividly described a few of them, with the names of the victims, as well as the locations of documents detailing them.

"So, you see," he says cheerfully, "this matter has a happy outcome. There are three fewer psychopaths out there. The people are protected. And I can go on to be elected president next year! It will all be for the best."

Neither the French nor Romanian police can believe that the man still thinks that he is going to get away with it. He has no regrets, no guilt, no feelings of any kind. When Patrice telephones Île-St-Louis to check that Colette and Amélie are home all right, he tells her this and she says just one word: sociopath.

"And how is my sweetheart child?" he asks.

"In pieces," says Colette. "But she will recover. It takes time, is all. It's her first time, *cher*, but not her last. We all get used to it in time, *n'est-ce pas*? She's starting to talk about it a bit now. We shall talk; it will be fine."

"She had put too much into it?"

"*Un petit*. There's always one who loves and one who allows himself to be loved ..."

"Welcome to the land of cliché!"

"*Désolée*! This sort of thing lends itself ... You will all be home Monday night?"

"We shall," says Patrice. "Don't come to Beauvais, Colette. We'll take the shuttle back. Probably go straight to bed, I should think. We are called to a meeting with the *commissaire divisionnel* Tuesday morning at 08.30, so will need to sleep."

***

There are always more of what Pucelle is learning to call "clients" in the backstreets of Paris. They are not all part of the drug culture; some, many, are just destitute, with no way out of their poverty. As her past-broken leg develops into a permanent limp, she walks the streets collecting contacts. She is conscious that this is necessary work and takes some satisfaction from that, even though she cannot say it is enjoyable.

When she has completed several long days talking to Africans, Russians, Ukrainians, Belarusians, Syrians, Turks, and Arabs from a variety of countries, she gives herself a morning off and revisits the Russian man who had given her the name of Irina Alexandrovna.

This time, he lets her in and gives her tea on a tiny table which has appeared in the interim. He even tells her that his name is Oleg Mikhailovich. He asks her, in Russian, if she is still looking for Irina Alexandrovna.

"I am," she replies, in the same language. "It is important that I know she is safe and well."

"It is important to who?" he asks.

"Important to me," she says.

"Not to the police? To the authorities?"

"No."

"If that is true, I may be able to help." He stares at her as if assessing whether she is telling the truth. Then clearly decides she is.

"I believe you." He is silent then, as he selects what to tell her. This takes a while.

"I know where Irina Alexandrovna took her son when he died." He says just that, in a tone which indicates that he is truly sad, although not exactly grieving. Pucelle feels any information he has is to be delivered in *petites pièces*. She is comfortable to wait all day if necessary.

"She buried him," he says, "in the country, in a meadow. Where it was not cold."

"Do you know where?" asks Pucelle, not sure why she wants to know. What would she do? Dig him up and give him a Christian burial? Hardly.

"I do," he says. "But she has sworn me to keep it to myself. And I shall."

Pucelle, though, has suddenly thought that Irina Alexandrovna might have made a home of some kind close to her son's grave; to tend it, to keep him safe. This may be the key to finding her. How can she persuade Oleg Mikhailovich to give her an approximation of location? She puts that aside for the moment.

"I do not wish to disturb the grave," she says. "I only want to see that Irina Alexandrovna is safe. I do not wish to persuade her of anything, even to accept any help I might be able to give. I need to see her and thank her for what she did for me."

The tone of her voices rises at the end of the sentence, and breaks, because of the damage to her throat sustained during her captivity. The Russian man stares at her, as if surprised at hearing what almost approached a scream. He pours them another glass of tea and sips his own.

Eventually, he speaks.

"If you promise not to look for the Peacock's grave," he says, "I will take you to Irina Alexandrovna. It is a few kilometres."

"*Spasibo* – thank you."

***

It is a tumbledown cottage, a little way out of Paris, to the north-west. Obviously an abandoned farm, with wild weeds and rushes seeding the swampy land. There is a pond, overgrown, and with water birds easily disturbed. The two travellers, who have tramped the whole distance, in wind and rain, almost in silence, arrive at an entrance door, reinforced with uneven boards brought from another derelict building.

Oleg Mikhailovich knocks gently on the door. His rapping does not disturb the quiet air. The rain has stopped. He does not wait to be admitted; he opens the unlocked door and walks in.

L'Éléphant is on the sofa, propped by non-too-clean cushions, dressed, still, in old trousers and several sweaters. Her hair, though, has grown out from the rough street cut and is tied back in a band. Her face has a slightly softer, female look. Pucelle, looking at her for the first time since she declared herself to be Paon's mother, feels a rush of love.

They held her in the *appartement* for only a few weeks, but the love is permanent. It is all Pucelle has.

The Elephant, Irina Alexandrovna, is safe.

***

Their session with Mademoiselle Iordache looks, at first, as if it will produce nothing. She sits, in handcuffs, with her wrists in her lap like the convent schoolgirl she used to be. Her blonde hair is uncombed and needs a wash, and she wears prison overalls. Hers is the Nuremburg defence; she was only following orders. She is a steelier person than the young woman who threw up against the wall of the Dobrescus' house.

Capitaine Roşca, sitting with René, proves herself a ruthless questioner. Switching from Romanian to Iordache's preferred English, she notices René's bafflement and switches, again, to French, and explains to him what she is doing.

The idea, she says, is to persuade the girl to give them her stepfather; evidence, otherwise, is thin on the ground, even though he has confessed – many might believe that he really did do the right thing. Or that he was out of his mind when he did what he did ...

René, who considers this would be a perversion of justice, sits quietly to see what will happen.

"How did Mr Melichian persuade you that it was right to conspire to kill these three men? And what about Mr Mitrea? Four men died. Someone arranged for this."

"There was no persuading. None of that was anything to do with me," says Sofia. "He just told me what I had to do. I had to be involved in the investigation as my superiors ordered me. I had to ask the right questions. I had to be nice to the French policemen and make them realise that Romania is a very beautiful and civilised country. But there are still people who are afraid of vampires here … and that can make some things awkward."

"What else?" asks Roşca sharply.

"To pick up anything which the killers had missed when they cleaned up," says Sofia. "Silviu says that they always leave something. He said my young eyes would be able to see it, although I didn't find anything. And then, later, he asked me to bring his car around to the back of Bran Castle, where we would collect two of the French people" – she looks at René – "the boss and his wife, who were having a trip out to Dracul. He said I should take my sidearm as they might refuse to get into the car."

"Why did they have to get into the car?" says Roşca. "What did Melichian tell you he was going to do with them?"

"I thought we were going to take them to the airport," says Sofia. "They had been making trouble, and my stepfather wanted them out of the way. When they were on a flight back to Paris, everything would be all right."

"He did not tell you that he was going to kill them?" asks Roşca.

"No! Not at all!" says Sofia, looking horrified. "Of course he wasn't going to kill them. He just wanted them gone." Roşca, who has kept all refreshment away from the young woman, suddenly offers water, and as she gratefully drinks it, Iordache says that she really can't cope with dead bodies; there is no way she would be involved with any more.

René sees the light flash in Roşca's eyes as she spots something.

"What was it like when you had to be in Bărăbanţ, at that terrible flat when Artur Mitrea was dying?"

"That was ages ago," she shouts. "I wasn't there anyway!"

"It was when they found him, the end of the first week in January. The pathologist thinks he may have been killed around the New Year. You were on leave over New Year and staying in the town with your mother and Mr Melichian. I have sworn statements from your superiors."

Sofia has gone very pale and starts to say something, changes her mind, starts again. Her words are very uncertain; she is unsure of what she can say for the best.

"He made me go with him," she says. "He insisted. My mother said he shouldn't, but he said I must toughen up, this is part of being a proper police officer. So, we went, and I didn't like seeing it. It was horrible. Silviu said he deserved to die. He told me he had liked torturing women and children. He deserved to die much more horribly."

"Did you agree that he deserved to die?" asks René, when Roşca has translated.

"Yes," she says, "he really did. No one can do that and get away with it."

"So, what do you think happened to Mr Mitrea?" asks Roşca.

"Er, he was already dead," she says hesitantly. She shakes her head from side to side rapidly, as if she realises she has said something out of place. "Er, I didn't, er ..."

"He was already dead when you got there?" asks René, through Roşca. The young police officer tries deep breathing to clear her confusion. She isn't good at this.

"Yes," she says. "And then the others came in, and my stepfather told them that they needed to learn something.

And he showed them how to cut the throat so that the person would bleed out. If he was still alive. But he wasn't. It wasn't murder! He didn't kill him. He had already died!"

"What had he died of?" asks Roşca.

"I don't know. Heart attack or old age or something …"

"But Mr Melichian showed you all how to kill someone by cutting their throat?"

"I thought he was just showing us. It was a lesson."

"With what purpose?" asks René. "What use could that be to police officers?"

The young woman looks at him as if he should know that without asking. "So that we would know when it has been done in future crimes!" she sneers. Of course it was.

Capitaine Roşca asks Iordache who was present in Mitrea's flat when this happened.

"Oh, two or three other people," she says, surer of her ground now. "Women, older than me. I don't know who they were. I suppose they were officers from other places, who came over for the demonstration. Mr Melichian must have got permission to use the body for teaching purposes." She closes her mouth like a steel trap after this. She has said enough.

"Have we got any photos we can show to Officer Iordache?" asks René. "To see whether she can tell us who these people might have been?" Roşca says that they have and goes out of the room to fetch them.

Sofia Iordache identifies that Diana Dobrescu, Irina Dabija and Daciana (Nikulina) Bunea all watched Silviu Melichian slit the throat of the already deceased Artur Mitrea.

No one mentions that Mitrea must have been alive, at the time, or where did the blood come from?

It is 07.00 when Fleur Olivier arrives at reception and is told that she can move her team into their old *salle squad* because everything is now in order. She does a little dance of delight and rushes upstairs. Even the *classeurs*[72] have been moved in and, as she looks in the drawers of her own new desk, she recognises her personal things: her unused electronic cigarette, her worry beads from Greece, her multiple pens and pencils. Her grandmother's St Christopher medal. She is thrilled. Even the blue has been toned down a little.

She sits at the desk, soaking up the cleanliness. *C'est fabuleuse!*

The rest of the team will be back today – the meeting is set for 09.00, although Patrice will arrive two minutes late as always. Fleur wonders whether she should have bought pastries to welcome them back, but it is likely that Patrice will bring them, or have asked one of the others.

The door opens and René Mercard is first home. Fleur jumps up and envelopes him in a motherly hug. He is looking good after being away, less tense, pleased to be back. They exchange greetings and discover they are fine. The younger detective asks whether he should go for coffee? Fleur says no, she has asked Clémence to do it – for multiple cups, she has a more convenient method.

It is a few minutes later that Benjamin and Faye arrive together and exclaim at the state of the room. It is super! They each find a desk and ask if they are to go for coffee. Fleur repeats what she has said to René. Then Clémence rolls in with coffee on her knees. She has ascended in the

---

72   filing cabinets

refurbished lift, which is behaving beautifully. She asks René about Romania, about the cases, about the other members of the team – whom she doesn't really know yet. She stops babbling when she realises.

"It's industrial espionage!" carols Clémence to Fleur. Everyone else looks as if they have missed something – which they have.

"*D'accord*," says Fleur, "we can talk about that later. We are waiting for *le patron* so that we can talk about Romania."

Patrice arrives, adjusting his watch to Paris time, and beams at each of them. He is holding a *pâtisserie* box, which he places on the nearest desk. Fleur, senior officer, opens it and distributes cakes.

It takes them almost all morning to describe their trip to Romania, even leaving out the vampire stuff. They have, of course, to mention Monsieur Melichian's mayhem in the dungeon, and the efforts made to promote ancient superstition.

Patrice makes the joke that Colette could probably write a new thesis about the infernal Count – "but I hope she won't!" The whole team is glad that they managed to solve the case, even in the tiny amount of time they had.

They speak a little about what has been going on in Paris while they have been away. Fleur describes the apprehension, at last, of Roger Rannequin, and says that it may be helpful for René to interview the senator's son regarding any information he may have about the multiple car thefts.

Clémence speaks about the Pellisier case, in a quiet voice. It is clear this has upset her hugely and she will need support. The baby-food case brings the team back to life, with the new idea that there isn't any glass but there might be considerable industrial espionage.

As the team is considering this, the telephone rings and Benjamin hands the receiver to *le patron*, saying someone called Audry wishes to speak to him from Romania.

"*Allô!*" says Patrice. "*Ça va?*"

The French-speaking mortuary technician tells him that Dr Apostol has asked her to ring to say that the blood soaked into the pillow of Monsieur Mitrea was his own blood. Whatever happened later, the perpetrator did not have to obtain pigs' blood or anything else.

"*Vous rigolez, ou quoi?*[73]" he says, surprised.

"*Oui*," says Audry, "Dr Apostol has given the details to the new *contrôleur* and suggested Monsieur Melichian be charged with his murder."

"Does she think, Dr Apostol, that there will be enough evidence to convict him?" asks Patrice.

"She does," says Audry. "There are some useful fingermarks too."

***

It is 13.00 when the door opens again, and Amélie Lanier comes in. She has come to take her *papa* to lunch, by way of getting herself away from her mother (she does not mention this). Colette noticed, immediately they got back to the apartment, that her exquisite sky-blue flower vase had been replaced by one of inferior quality. It is that which Jean-Pascal's friends smashed when they had the party. Incredibly, he thought his mother wouldn't notice. He is much more deeply concerned with the fact that he has also damaged the Goddess. He can think of no good way to tell Colette.

Amélie, good sister, has thought of a way to get her father to do the hard work. She looks around sweetly at the others.

---

73 You're kidding me, right?

"I am going to call Jean-Pascal 'Dracula' in the future," says Amélie, as if she has been considering this for a long time.

"*Pourquoi?*" asks her father, unable to take a guess at the joke he is expecting.

"Because, when he looks into the rear-view mirror, he can't see anything either!"

Patrice looks mystified but Clémence, younger and quicker in some ways, gets there immediately:

"Bon Dieu!" she says. "He's wrecked the patron's car!"

"He hasn't!" shouts Amélie. "It's *Maman*'s car, and it was only a little crash. A number plate fell off, and he has already had it repaired ..."

Patrice, fresh from investigating foul murders in Romania, feels this is a very little problem. But will Colette think so? Not likely, *n'est-ce pas?*

FIN

A note from Elizabeth

Thank you for reading The Heights of Abraham. I hope you enjoyed it!

'Which Wolf Do You Feed?' is a short story connected to this bookand is about Romanian Police Officer, Roxana Lupu. To find out what she does when her superstitious neighbours think she's a werewolf, join my mailing list at: <u>Sign-up form – Elizabeth Mostyn Writes</u> ... for exclusive (free) content, release news, and other good things!

Please consider giving this book a review on Amazon, Kobo, Barnes and Noble, Apple, and/or Google Play. These are very important for authors! Thank you so much!

Look for Book 3 of The Phenomenological Detective – The Arc of Blood – Coming Soon!

* 9 7 8 1 7 3 9 4 0 5 2 1 2 *